The Strange Man

The Strange Man

Amu Djoleto

Black Star Books and Head of Zeus would like to thank the following organisations: The Miles Morland Foundation, The Ford Foundation, and Africa No Filter. This publication was made possible through their support.

First published in the Heinemann African Writers Series in 1967
by Heinemann Educational Publishers

This edition published in 2024 by Black Star Books and Head of Zeus,
part of Bloomsbury Publishing Plc.

9 7 5 3 1 2 4 6 8

A catalogue record for this book is available from the British Library.

ISBN (PB): 9781803289021

Typeset by Siliconchips Services Ltd UK

Printed and bound in Great Britain by
CPI Group (UK) Ltd, Croydon CRO 4YY

Head of Zeus Ltd
First Floor East
5–8 Hardwick Street
London EC1R 4RG

WWW.HEADOFZEUS.COM

To the Memory of NEE AMPONSAH

Chapter One

The house belonged to Old Mensa. It was usually a quiet place guarded by a vigilant, aggressive dog called Hope. It was an impressive building in its own right, put up in the early forties, and had been, when new, easily the best-looking building in the area and certainly raised the architectural tone of one of the suburbs of Accra, near the sea. The compound of the house—fairly big by local standards—was largely cemented and the house was roofed with asbestos sheets. There were the usual cement block walls, intended as a fortification against burglars, but which only made the compound rather airless.

The uncemented areas were intended as flower-beds, but after several unsuccessful attempts, including the use of all known types of good manure, to make them nourish European flowers, they were put to the use for which they were probably better suited. Various fruit trees were planted in them. The trees grew well, and when they started bearing, their fruit was attractive to all and irresistibly tempting to children; especially the mangoes and guavas.

It was this house which Old Mensa's enemies in particular thought he did not deserve. These people, whose chief preoccupation was to assess other people's achievement in relation to their own, thought he could only have owned such a fine house through the perennial mistake of God or Chance or Providence or Society. What Old Mensa had gone through during the fifty-eight years of his existence did not matter to them. The house, comfortable as it was, was a material manifestation. The human story was another aspect of the struggle a man might have to make if he was to be true to his own nature. Old Mensa happened to try to lead his own life.

'I don't think Old Mensa should be told his brother is dead,' said the sad-looking Protestant minister to Tete's wife at the funeral at Adabraka, an Accra suburb, the following day.

'No,' said the wife, sobbing, 'it's been decided he shouldn't be told right now. It could cause a relapse and Old Mensa too would be pushed over. Oh! Oh! Oh!' she cried, 'I can't understand this! It's cruel!'

The minister, a tall, stout man of about sixty who looked younger than his age, to the casual observer would seem very grave indeed, but if his face were seriously scrutinized, it would betray a curious mixture of cynicism, stubbornness, arrogance, sensuality and a distrust of anything new or mysterious, profound or radical. He had consciously learnt to look grave on all such occasions, and everybody had taken his gravity for granted because he was expected to be grave. He had, for a long time, often been unable to support this gravity by the correct emotion. People were always dying and he had very wisely composed certain stock phrases which he delivered mechanically, but in a very consoling voice, to suit the kind of person freshly bereaved. Now he said:

'Don't cry, woman. The happiness we all desire is in heaven, not here. The Lord has willed it so. Here on earth we cannot but expect disappointments, frustrations, worries, sadness and death. Your husband's soul should find a place in heaven. Jesus has opened his arms wide to receive him. Therefore, don't cry, woman. Your husband has done his work well on earth. He was our organist, he paid his church dues regularly and never missed the Holy Communion. What else can a man do? The knowledge that he is welcome to our Lord should be a source of comfort to you and give you the inspiration to live and serve the Lord with all your heart and with all your might till you too are called to Him in grace.'

'Whatever you say is true, sir,' she sobbed, 'but life is very cruel all the same! I've no complaints against God, life is so terribly cruel!'

'That's why I've asked you to put your trust in God. Be steadfast in your faith. Be devoted to your church and God, and you shall have as peaceful an end as your husband now enjoys. It is my duty to let these things be known to you at a time like this.'

When he had said these words, he inched slowly away from Mrs Tete, whom he had tried to touch but was not sure where, and joined a batch of elderly men at the funeral who were in charge of the funeral arrangements. Here he lost his gravity, smiled condescendingly and became completely business-like. There were a few things he would like to know. For example, he wanted to know when the body of Mr Tete would be brought to the chapel for the funeral service, whether the city council hearse had been laid on and whether a car had been provided to take him to the cemetery which was two miles or so away from the chapel, near the industrial area of Accra.

He was visibly vexed when he learnt no car had been arranged for him. He had, over a long time now, impressed upon his church elders that a minister living and doing his work in that part of Accra needed a car not for prestige or comfort but for the work alone. The church elders knew their minister was right and yet they were not anxious to provide him with a car—at least not yet. They were more interested in the minister as a person than in the efficiency of his work. They had secretly discussed the subject in the house of the chief elder, and had noted that the minister could buy a car with his own money if he had a mind to. After all, he owned a house which he had let out; he was earning a government pension, received a salary from the church and occasional gifts from church members, particularly middle-aged widows. What use did he make of all this? They had concluded therefore that if they could not ask him openly to use his own money and buy a car for himself (a move which, if tried, could split the local church in two, men versus women, since the women were more passionately devoted to their minister), at least they could stall his getting one; but if the pressure from the women proved too great for them, they would in the long run buy him the transport. In the meantime, they would like him to realize that he was not going to get it easily. There were two of the elders who as a rule took delight in thwarting the minister in any way possible. They had somehow discovered that the man of God was too powerful and influential and so made it their duty to make life difficult for him. Their ambition was to be great men if not in the secular world then in the church, and there was no place for the minister to be greater than themselves. Deep down they were jealous and inimical.

Some of the young men at the funeral, whom the minister had warned harshly whenever they tried to flirt with the choir girls, dropped their heads behind the backs of those who sat in front of them and laughed quietly but gleefully because the minister was not only annoyed in public but was also going to suffer some disappointment. They had always wondered whether the minister really understood life or them. How could they marry those girls if they had no chance of meeting them separately? Some of the young girls were happy for another reason. The minister had banned the wearing of lipstick and tight frocks to church. Any girl who did so was considered immoral or indecent. But to the girls' chagrin and lingering frustration, the minister dyed his grey hair black, pencilled his eyebrows and used women's face powder. Why should he want to look younger and more attractive than his years? And at the same time stop others from doing the same in their own way? Certainly he was more attentive and accommodating to them than to the young men of the church. They discussed these things over and over again at choir practice but had never been able to answer them to their satisfaction. One thing they were sure of: for them the minister was inadequate and they could never like him.

In a corner, away from the mass of formal mourners, a group of middle-aged men were conversing. One of them, Akoto, said: 'I think Tete drank too much. This is the result!'

Obeng disagreed: 'I don't think it was the drinking really. I think he ate too much good food.'

Tawia added rather blandly: 'On top of the two, he was a little too fond of women. He spent too much of his body on them. I've a theory that when you combine the three in excess, you're fast digging your grave.'

Ofori then chimed in: 'I don't believe such theories. I enjoy all three to the maximum and I am fit, very fit indeed. I'll quit at eighty-five, no sooner, no later. Of course, I watch my health, though; a dose of Andrews Liver Salts, once a week, is my longevity prescription. Anyhow, I'm not surprised Tete is gone. He was an unscrupulous, impossible storekeeper. I wonder if people do sell in heaven, but if he has his way, he's probably trying to sell trumpets to the angels by now at a smart profit. Do you know that, when he ordered an organ for our chapel, he had a clear profit of twenty pounds? He got it through a discount he arranged and yet every church member, particularly the women, thought he was simply marvellous because of his enthusiasm; but he was a determined schemer, particularly in this kind of cheating, and got away with it. I'm sorry he's dead, but strictly I don't think he should be allowed in heaven. I'm not so sure I'll get there myself, anyway.'

'Don't be ridiculous, Ofori,' Okai said, 'I just don't understand these silly ideas. Tete may have been a sharp businessman but that's a different matter altogether. As far as the church goes, he's done what he ought to have done and, if my understanding is right, through grace, his own faith, and pardon, the way to heaven must be open to him. That's why the church is there, I think.'

'Come,' Akoto said, almost roughly, 'do you wish to suggest that the church is like a travel agency? You obey its rules and regulations, give out the money to keep it going, hold fast to its doctrines and, sinner or not, you automatically get a ticket to heaven?'

Tawia laughed aloud and said: 'That's a bogus analogy and crooked thinking. Nothing is easier in this world than religious blasphemy!'

The others now laughed aloud, having forgotten they were at a funeral. People turned their heads to look at them with disapproval, but the middle-aged men were neither ashamed nor cowed. They merely lowered their voices and continued with the conversation.

Okai said, half-seriously: 'I think we'd better keep the church out of this,' and then added, looking really serious, 'The way Tete got sick and then died stemmed directly from his over-ambitiousness.'

'But who isn't ambitious?' Akoto asked, more interested in creating more laughter than in what had been said.

Okai ignored his question and went on: 'He made sure all his children got a first-class education, and it has always been a mystery to me how he managed to get all his six children into Achimota College. I tried to have just one of mine—and a clever one too—there, but failed. He later decided one of his children must go to the United Kingdom to read medicine. He didn't even seek a scholarship for the boy. He was too proud and confident to ask for state help. Now while this boy was in the United Kingdom he sent another son to the United States to study refrigeration engineering at the Massachusetts Institute of Technology. He didn't stop there. As soon as one of his daughters had finished at Achimota College, he sent her over to a hospital in Oxford to do midwifery. I hope you're getting the picture. He was trying to outshine his only brother, Old Mensa. It wasn't really a case of doing your best for your children so long as you have the means and the chances. No. He wanted to be great through his children, and thought he was engaged in a desperate race which to my mind didn't even exist.'

'Let's be honest,' Akoto intervened again, 'as nongraduate civil servants, we are all engaged in a desperate race to give our children higher education, aren't we, Ofori?'

'You're probably right,' Ofori said absentmindedly. His mind had been captured by Okai's story.

Okai did not take up Akoto's question and went on: 'Tete sent his second son to Britain to read law and—'

'Damn it, how did he get the money to do all that?' Akoto asked, incredulous.

'That's what I'm leading to,' Okai said patiently. 'In the first place, you can't estimate how much a man in Tete's job can make in a day. I mean a secured storekeeper handling hardware lines. It all depends on the sort of customers that come along. There are no price-tags on the goods, and a carpenter I know believes only in German-made tools. Many such people can't read, and Tete could make them pay anything simply by telling them the tools were made in Germany. Once, when drunk, he boasted to us he had made two hundred pounds in a day. That was in a buying season, but he could make at least five to ten pounds a day in the poor season.'

'I don't believe it,' Akoto said flatly.

'Akoto, there's a lot that goes on in this country that you

may not know. Can you tell me how everyone who owns a big beautiful building in Adabraka got the money? There's no doubt, however, that Tete made a lot of money and could be described as well-off.'

'We all know that,' Akoto could not help interrupting. 'He kept our church going with the money. Do you remember the harvest auction when he bought one useless glass of drinking water at a hundred guineas? He was—'

'Akoto, shut up, will you!' Ofori said impatiently, but Akoto was shaking with suppressed guffaws.

Okai took up the story again: 'There was a slump some time after the war; I forget when; but people weren't buying and Tete decided to get a twenty-thousand-pound mansion. It would be three-storey and could be used either as a medical clinic or as the residence of a rich consulate. The building was started, it progressed piecemeal and then he discovered it was going to cost far more than he had hoped. Now there were his children overseas; he had no bank account because he distrusted the banks; they could be dangerous in time of trouble, revealing evidence of your financial secrets and that sort of thing. Therefore he couldn't ask for an overdraft or take out a loan. Bad business, an expensive building taking years to finish and his children's letters demanding more money, took the money he had hoarded from him and his pride was hurt. What would he do? He started playing tricks with the daily sales cash. Stock was taken one day, and he was found short by six thousand pounds. That was big money, you know.'

'He should have been jailed,' Akoto said, without compassion.

'Well!' Okai said, heaving a sigh. 'That's not how things

work with some of these foreign firms. What they fear most is the police, not to mention the newspapers, and their public image. They hate prolonged court action too. In other words, the police probe too much, the press are thought to be too nosy, the courts time-wasting and humiliating, and the people too interested in such matters. You see, they usually underpay their storekeepers because they know they can enrich themselves. After all, before a storekeeper can enrich himself, he must have a good turnover and a good turnover enriches the firm. It's a kind of unwritten mutual benefit enterprise. The storekeeper keeps quiet, the firm keeps quiet, and the money is raked in. What Tete's firm does in this kind of situation is to ask the storekeeper to refund the missing amount; he must have the money locked up somewhere, they reckon. If he refunds in time, he may not be sacked, but put on another job, maybe a clerical one. If he pays back with difficulty he may be eased out on the hush-hush.'

'I want to know what was done to Tete,' Akoto demanded.

'Well,' Okai replied, 'he wasn't dismissed outright as one would expect; but a curious thing happened. Mr Budu Baiden-Danielson, that cultivated, gentlemanly-looking man from Cape Coast or Elmina, I don't know which, who was not only his boon companion and drinking friend, but also a fellow Lodge member, went to the general manager of the firm, uninvited, at dead of night, and told him that Tete had a huge mansion under construction. Tete should be told to sell the unfinished building and use some of the money realized in paying the debt. He advised the general manager to tell Tete that if he didn't do as suggested, the police would be informed.'

'But I thought they were good friends?' Ofori asked.

'Yes! Very good friends. But perhaps Tete trusted him too much and told him his secrets when he was drunk. Mr Baiden-Danielson was there when he said he had pocketed two hundred pounds in a day through overpricing.'

'Yes. But why did he undermine him in that way?' Ofori asked, a little shaken.

'For two reasons, I think,' Okai said. 'First, he wanted Tete's job as the hardware storekeeper; he'd been on the clerical side in the firm. And then he certainly envied Tete. He always thought he was better than Tete: in breeding, education and in the way he spoke English—see what I mean? After that night, he suddenly wouldn't talk to Tete any more.'

'Why do these people do that? They think they are better than everybody, and yet the only way they can get on is by ruining the very people they despise. Superior men should get on on their own,' Akoto said, very angry.

'What *are* you talking about, Akoto?' Ofori asked, somewhat puzzled.

'I say,' Akoto said with emphasis, 'superior men must get on on their own without destroying others in the process!'

'I don't understand,' Ofori said, not really listening to him.

Just then, a busy-looking elder of the church came up to the group and said: 'You people must behave like grown-ups. You've come to a funeral and instead of looking solemn and helping with the singing, you stand around chatting and laughing.'

'You go away,' Ofori snapped, indignant.

'It will be too bad if people get to know you are happy that Tete is dead,' the elder said with a grin.

'By the way, whoever made you an elder of the church? You've been carrying on with a choir girl, haven't you?' Akoto asked aggressively.

'Good heavens! I can sue you for this!' the elder said in a voice of feigned anger, though he was upset by the unexpected revelation, at this time.

'Oh, no,' Akoto said defiantly, 'you can't sue me. Your wife would get to know; you'd drag the name of our church in the mud and the minister would ask for the case to be settled out of court! Now if you're a man, try!'

'The trouble with our church nowadays is people of your type. Once a man is an official of the church, isn't he ever allowed to relax?'

'Do you mean relax with a young choir girl, who is about to be confirmed?' Akoto asked. The others burst out laughing and the elder quickly left, not wanting to be identified with these irresponsible men.

When he was out of earshot, Akoto remarked: 'That man is an idiot.'

'Forget about him,' Okai said, and went on: 'Let me finish telling you about Tete, before the cortège moves. The manager of the firm told him that the case would neither be made public nor handed over to the C.I.D., provided he was prepared to sell his uncompleted building to enable him to refund the six thousand pounds. I happen to know this manager; he's a very considerate man. But Tete got a pretty bad shock. He couldn't see there and then how the general manager had known he had property. Besides, if he sold his building he would be completely ruined, because he would have no cash to throw around and would

be forced to borrow money to look after his children overseas. An easy way out was to ask his children to apply for
state help, but the mere thought was like committing sui-
cide. What about his financial boasts, his rich-man swagger
and his disgraceful, insulting behaviour to his own people
at Botoi when his mother died? What really shattered him
was what his brother, Old Mensa, would think or say if
he heard about it. He became progressively depressed and
alcoholic before the paralysis.'

'Ah, Old Mensa, he is quite different,' Akoto said.

'Yes, true, true indeed; but he has a sharp tongue. I
wouldn't like to get involved with him,' Ofori said.

'You're quite right, Akoto,' Okai agreed. 'The two are different. Here you have Tete: tall, handsome, paunchy, jovial,
proud and boastful—a man who likes his food and wants
to be recognized at any cost. There you have Old Mensa:
medium height, a head like nutmeg but attractive on his
shoulders, a lined face, but always neat, ascetic, reserved
with a kind of glow about him. He fascinates me. He's so
unhurried and composed. You never see him often but
you're aware of his presence. I hear he keeps a daily record
of what happens to him and to others.'

'That's true, but I understand there are a lot of people
who *don't* like him,' Akoto said.

'Yes, indeed. But I've always thought most of his so-called
enemies are wrong, you know,' Okai replied. 'He was retired
prematurely from the civil service because of his outspoken-
ness and his campaign for better pay. Yet surprisingly he
has shown more charity to his neighbours than the priests,
ministers and moral politicians would have us believe.'

'Really?' Akoto would have liked more gossip, but at this moment the cortège moved for the church and they had to fall in line.

Old Mensa's house looked neat, beautiful and very quiet. Even the dog Hope, usually noisy when people called, was so quiet that one would have thought it had lost the zest for life. Those in the neighbourhood who had heard the news were so stunned with amazement that the pattern of life had once again become too bizarre for them to unravel. The doctor did what he could, but the medicine Odole took had done the wrong job. It did not only get rid of an incipient life but also the life which nurtured it. Odole's life should have been spared but the priests and theologians know best how to answer with certainty this wishful assertion.

Her father was still struggling to live but his survival was only a matter of hope. His wife was not weeping. She was dazed, bewildered and shaken with fright. As she gazed at her daughter, who lay majestic and vital as if she breathed, her own features seemed to take on a look of Odole in her serious moments.

Despite the onslaught of the tragedies, the ironical nobility of her physical presence shone all round her: she had acquired a spiritual and physical beauty at the age of fifty-four which only someone capable of genuine sorrow could, perhaps, for a while at any rate, appreciate.

Chapter Two

Old Mensa's father, Anang, belonged to one of the paramount divisions of Accra. His mother was an Ewe, whose parents had been forced to migrate to Accra after the Ashantis had dislodged them from their kith and kin during their expansionist wars. After Old Mensa's father had married her, the couple left Accra and settled in the village of Botoi below the Akwapim hills in Southern Ghana.

In those far-off days many inhabitants of the coastal areas of Accra had two main occupations. There were the fishermen who caught fish which their wives smoked and sent inland to the farming settlements to sell; there were the farmers who had moved northwards, some ten or so miles from the sea, where the scrubland began to be bush, and farther on became forest. Thus, almost all the farming villages below the Akwapim ridge in the district were Gaspeaking. It was these villages which provided the fishing people with their carbohydrate food requirements, such as cassava, yam, cocoyam, plantain, sweet-potato and so on. The relationship between the two groups was therefore symbiotic as far as their food requirements and professions were involved, but they were Gas who spoke Ga.

Religious influence at Botoi was blind and powerful because of early, grass-root missionary activity. The homes were arranged in rows and, though there was no local government sanitary organization, the entire village was scrupulously neat. Little Mensa and his family lived in a mud-house which had corrugated-iron roofing.

He was a happy little boy, carefree and handsomely built, and precociously articulate. Nothing impressed him so much as the towering Akwapimian hills, especially in the mornings when the mists rolled over their summit. He loved to hear the birds sing and would have loved to have them in his control. He was the eldest of three children. Tete came after him, and then their sister. Little Mensa's parents were fond of him. Even as a boy of seven, he could have his way in most things. He could organize his boy friends in the village for any mischief and was prepared to speak the plain truth often to anybody when they were caught.

It was usual in those days for a family to have two different farms, one close to the village which served as a subsistence farm, and the other about one or two miles away on a fertile spot. This was carefully tended as it was meant to produce cash crops. Animal husbandry was not particularly well organized in those days and so the goats, sheep, pigs and fowls would frequently visit the farms near the village. To stop this, wire fences were erected round such farms; but somehow the goats would break through them.

The village boys, for their own very good reasons, did not like the goats at all and considered them both a threat to themselves and a nuisance. They particularly and bitterly hated the he-goat which they treated with the greatest amount of disrespect, and, when unseen, with savage cruelty. What disturbed them about the he-goat may be summed up under four categories. First, it worried too much the nanny-goat both during the day and in the night and gave her no rest. This they considered unreasonable. Second, the he-goat would spend all feeding time asking the nanny-goat to oblige; then, when it was dark and the boys went round to drive in the goats, it would be far away in the bush searching for a bite before turning in. If the boys came home without it, then they would be in for trouble. They would be whacked on the backside for leaving the he-goat behind. Third, the he-goat smelt too much. Whenever the boys were in the church, worshipping God, it would not only foul the air they breathed but also make unpleasant noises at the nanny-goat and divert their attention from the Almighty. If they were caught looking its way, they would be told that God did not like children who would not listen to the sermon. Fourth, the he-goat always led the gang of marauding goats to the farms near the village. If those goats ruined the crops, it was the boys who were held responsible.

Since the boys trusted the saying that prevention is better than cure, they treated the he-goat in any awkward manner possible just to make it realize that it was making life difficult for them; that it was too often the source of their afflictions. It must be said, however, that the he-goat by instinct and experience knew that the boys hated it and that whenever it saw the boys approach and there was time enough on hand, it had to scram even if a nanny-goat had relented and was going to be nice. If it did not bolt away and allowed its lust to overcome other considerations, it would get a bad kick in the hindquarters from one of the boys. Any boy who succeeded in timing it and gave it a kick that got it bleating painfully away was the hero of the day.

'You know,' said little Mensa to his friends one evening when they were sitting on a log in front of Old Anang's house, 'I got Old Oko's he-goat this afternoon and I kicked it hard.'

'I want to kill that goat,' interrupted little Okle. 'It upset my father's soup this evening and I was beaten for not driving it away in time.'

But little Mensa thought he had a story which was more interesting than anybody else's, so he took over quickly from little Okle and said: 'I had been given some boiled plantain and stew. It was very good so I didn't want to eat quickly otherwise it would get finished in no time. My sister asked me for some of my stew but I refused her. She was sorry, so I teased her and stuck my tongue out. She didn't like it. Suddenly all the plantain dropped from the table onto the ground. Old Oko's he-goat had come for a slice and spilled the rest. I wanted to cry but my sister would laugh at me. Even my mother laughed and said I had been punished for not being kind. To show I wasn't upset, I also laughed. I took the stew without the plantain. Afterwards I heard the wicked goat making those silly noises, so I went out and hid in a corner. The nanny-goat came along. It stopped. The he-goat stood on its hind legs. I kicked it hard. It jumped into the air like a football, then it fell on its back, all four legs kicking in the air. It was also bleating, all the time. I was scared by the fierce bleating so I ran away.'

'That's very good,' Klu congratulated little Mensa, pleased that the he-goat had suffered at the hands of one of his friends.

'I'll give you a stick of sugar-cane tomorrow,' Okle promised little Mensa.

But little Mensa had a more sinister idea. Said he to his friends: 'I've a plan which we can carry out tomorrow. We can stop Old Oko's goat from worrying us and eating our food by doing one thing to it. I'll tell you what it is tomorrow provided you'll come to my father's farm near the village in the morning. Don't tell anybody where you'll be going. If you do, we'll all be in trouble. Don't tell anybody, will you?'

The boys agreed not to, and asked Mensa what it was about, but Mensa was, for his age, strong-willed and could keep an idea to himself for as long as he had decided to. For some reason or other, the boys trusted his leadership though they did not always like him.

Mensa was the first to go to his father's farm. It was a good farm. The soil was dark, moist and rich. The corn was tall, green, strong and beautiful. There were several fruit trees on the farm: tangerines, grapefruit, local oranges, bananas, pineapples, guavas, mangoes and other wild edible fruit. The other boys knew they would get a good treat whatever else they did on the farm; they arrived when Mensa had waited for about half an hour for them.

Before they arrived, Mensa had managed to rip a hole in the wire fence to lure in the goats. The goats, ignorant of why the easy hole was there, had squeezed through one after the other. Once on the farm, they trotted about with glee and started nibbling at anything in sight.

Mensa now started to deploy his gang. He spoke like a blood-thirsty general who was sure of a carnage: 'There we have Old Oko's goat! Okle, you go and stand at where I've made the opening in the fence. When we start driving away the goats, the he-goat will be the first to seek the opening. It will be fast and slippery but make sure you catch it. The rest of you will form a semi-circle which will later close up into a full circle when we've got all the goats in. A lot of them will escape, but never let Old Oko's goat slip through. We've got to capture it.'

The semi-circle moved and then started closing in on the goats. The animals, as expected, made for the opening. Okle stood his ground ready to grab one of the hind legs of the he-goat. The goat raced towards him, then got near and was finally very close to him. But as Okle was going to catch it, his body bent double to facilitate a quick and firm grab, the virile and powerful goat which was on the stampede, blindly rammed into him. The goat's horns hit Okle on the head. Okle screamed while the goat bleated. He was bowled over completely. The shock of the unexpected collision plus the sudden physical pain so paralysed him that he lay prostrate on the ground, his eyes firmly closed, as if he were taking a good rest after a good day's work. The other boys as a matter of course ignored the mishap. They had all suffered it before, but not to the same extent. So they closed in on the he-goat as fast as possible because it too had lost its bearings after the collision. They caught it and it bleated sadly because it knew the boys would definitely do some mischief to it.

Mensa started giving orders: 'Okle! Okle! Get up and hold one of the hind legs. Klu, hold the other. Odoi, you hold down the head. Darku and Otto, hold fast the forelegs. Now Klu and Okle, you keep the hind legs as wide apart as you can!'

'But why should we do all that?' Darku asked.

'You do as I tell you. There's no time to waste!' Mensa cried at him.

The boys did as they had been instructed.

Then Mensa took from his pocket a sharp pocket-knife. He quickly prised open the scrotum of the he-goat and removed one of the testes. The operation was short, swift but inexpert so the blood squirted fast and straight from the cut. The boys were totally taken aback and without being aware of what they did next, let go the he-goat. Unrestrained, the he-goat had to leave the farm but this time slowly because it was now no more what it used to be.

'Mensa, why did you do that?' Odoi asked in utter disgust.

'My father says if a goat hasn't got them, it doesn't smell and keeps out of mischief.'

'But this is not how it is done!' Otto protested. 'Whenever Uncle Okwei did it, he took out two soft balls, not one! I asked him one day why he took out the two balls but he told me to shut up otherwise he would remove my own. I had to run away.'

'Mensa!' said Darku, looking concerned. 'I think this goat will die. It can't walk properly and it has lost too much blood!'

'Mensa, what shall we do? We'll be caught!' Odoi said with fright and regret. He added: 'As for my father, he'll take me to the man who rings the church bell. That man is cruel. He'll get hold of my arms and twist them. I'll cry then but he'll tell me to stop crying otherwise he'll take me away to the cemetery and I'll never see my father and mother again. That man is wicked.'

'As for me,' Okle said, having recovered sufficiently both from the pain and the shock at bloodshed, 'I'll tell Old Oko that Mensa did it. Nobody will then worry me. I don't like the way the goat hit me.'

'You're a cowardly fool!' said Mensa, guilty and angered.

'Me a fool?' asked Okle angrily. 'Your head is like an Ashanti man's head!'

There should have been no offence, but it happened that that was a meaningless insult which had been made meaningful because it was meted out to Mensa alone whenever he did something infuriating. For the very reason that it was restricted to him, Mensa had cause not to like it very much. He thought it was meant to achieve only one result, no matter the relevance of its simile implications: to hurt his feelings.

'Okle,' said Mensa, piqued, 'this is the third time you've told me this. I won't forgive you this time. Come on!'

Mensa suddenly threw a punch. Okle threw another. The other boys quickly took sides. Darku and Otto backed Mensa and Odoi and Klu were seconds to Okle.

'Give him an American punch!' Odoi instructed Okle.

'Mensa, wrestle and trip him down like the way the Ijaws do it!' Darku directed.

The two fighting boys embraced, rocked, rolled and then heaved to the ground, Mensa atop of Okle. Darku and Otto shouted delightedly, encouraging Mensa to pommel the hapless and helpless Okle who lay flat on his back under him. He was about to do it when they heard:

'What the hell are you boys doing there?' It was a thundering voice from the bush.

The boys vanished.

And it was the voice of the man who rang the village church bell. He happened to be going along the common path near the farm of Mensa's father when he heard the noise being made by the boys. He was a man who had made it an article of faith to suspect those boys always. He therefore went straight and fast to find out for himself what the boys were up to. He saw the hole in the wire fence and then the blood on the ground. He did not know it was the blood of the he-goat; so, thoroughly shocked, he sped back to the village to report that something really tragic had happened. It was the kind of business he enjoyed executing; for whenever there was any news to be spread in the village, it was his greatest desire that he should know about it first; then he would trot from house to house, ask whether the news had already been heard and, if people said no, he would broadcast it in detail and with a flourish that should impress and satisfy the audience he was dealing with. Indeed, experience had taught him what every household loved to hear. There was one household which would want to learn about somebody's misfortune. There was another which would listen carefully, patiently and secretly happily to a bloody detail and then burst out in synthetic chants of pity and sympathy. There was yet another which believed in peace at all costs, so a story must be so presented as to make them sincerely sympathize with whatever was said. Moreover, whenever he was the source of a particular piece of news, he considered himself the most important personage in the village. He would look grave to begin with as he posed before his audience; then his face would crack into a broad grin, the muscle lines showing like the lines on a map. Then he would not stand still but shift from one leg to the other, a shift being accompanied by a particular and stylized swing of the hand.

Now he had made a scoop and so he set forth for the village half-walking, half-running. His feet were thin and nimble, his head big and close-cropped. He went first to Old Anang's house because he felt Mensa would by all means be connected with the bloodshed. He had two very good reasons for his suspicion. First, he was quite convinced that Mensa was an incorrigibly bad boy. Second, the bloody affair had taken place on his father's farm. Unfortunately Mensa's parents were not in and the house was almost empty except a dog which barked at him for looking unusual that morning. He was for that moment a disappointed man as he realized that he would not have any good audience at that time of the day as most of the villagers had then gone to their farms. He would have to wait until the evening, the time for peak listening, especially after people had had their dinner.

'I wish the next minute is evening time,' he regretfully muttered to himself.

But the boys were watching him. When they were routed, they did not run away to take the common path. That was always the wrong strategy. They had been trapping birds now and then, so they knew the forest well. They had their special hideouts where they hid whenever they either wanted to skulk or avoid being noticed when they had trapped a bird. Theirs was a Christian village where bird trapping was frowned upon, and so they had to do it in secrecy.

When they heard the ominous voice, they ran fast and hid in one of their hideouts to watch who it was. Then they saw the man who rang the village church bell. That was just too bad. Odoi in particular broke down so completely that he said in a hushed voice: 'If I had a shilling, I'd catch a lorry to Accra and go and stay with Aunt Oboshi. This man will kill me today. He'll twist and squeeze my hands and take me to the cemetery.' His body shook in fits of fear and he wept copiously. The others were also numb with cold and fear and grief and wondered what would happen next.

Mensa's lips were tightly compressed; for he always made it clear that he was not afraid of the man who rang the church bell. Naturally, it was this open defiance which led the man to think that Mensa was a bad boy. When the man left the farm shaking his head and muttering things to himself, Mensa rallied the boys' flagging morale and asked them to come along to the village to see what the man could do. They would have to take a short cut to ensure that they reached the village before the man. Odoi at first balked at the suggestion, but when Mensa told him that there was a boa-constrictor in the cemetery which the man who rang the church bell feared, and so it was clear he would never dare to take him there, Odoi with some hesitation took courage and agreed to accompany the gang to the village.

After they had covered a few yards, Odoi said to Mensa: 'Mensa, suppose that man takes me to the cemetery while the boa-constrictor is there, what will you do?'

'I'll go and take my father's big gun and shoot it!'

'But suppose you shoot and miss? There'll be both the man and the snake!'

'I'm sure when you're being taken there and I shoot, I won't miss.'

Odoi was clearly not impressed by Mensa's gallantry and was going to tell him so when Klu spoke. He said: 'Odoi, you know what? If there is a boa-constrictor in the cemetery and it is hungry, as I'm sure it is otherwise it won't be there, then if that man takes you there I'm sure it will swallow both of you and …'

'I'm going back to Accra!' Odoi cried. He refused to budge.

'No, no, no. You don't understand me, Odoi. What I mean is this. The snake wants somebody to eat. The man who rings the church bell has small legs so the big snake will want to swallow him first since it likes thin legs. Now, when it starts swallowing him, which will be very good, you can either run away or take a pocket-knife and stick it into one of the eyes of the big snake. When you've finished one, you do the same to the other. The snake will then become blind and it will never swallow anybody again.'

'But while I'm sticking in the knife, are you sure it will stop swallowing the man?' Odoi asked, his confidence somewhat restored.

'I think it will,' Klu assured him.

'Then I think it's better to run away altogether!' Odoi said, having made up his mind how to get rid of the man for good.

They were now fairly near the first house of the village, so Mensa said: 'We've got to make sure the man doesn't see us.'

'No, it's better he sees us. He'll think we haven't been anywhere,' Darku advised.

'I think we can go and hide behind Old Oko's house and listen to what kind of story he'll tell. Come on, then,' Mensa ordered. 'Let's go and hide there.'

'No, if we go there, we'll see the he-goat. It will also see us and run away and people will think we hurt it,' Klu warned.

'All right,' Mensa said. 'Let's go to my father's house and see what he can do!'

And so it was that just when they were about to enter the house, they saw the man but they lost courage so they quickly withdrew and hid in a corner. They were quite happy that there was no-one around to whom the man could tell his story. Indeed, they were as happy as the man who rang the village church bell was disappointed. And since what he had seen on the farm was such a heinous crime, he decided not to go to his farm that day. He would stay at home until the boys' parents returned from their farms. He also wished very much not to see the boys; for he might be tempted to ask questions and the boys might in turn be tempted to tell him lies. If that happened it could possibly wreck the effect of his story as he had intended to tell it. The boys too did not want to see him because they feared it was possible he would ask them awkward questions.

It then occurred to Mensa that if they wanted to make the man appear a liar to their parents, they should do two things. They would have to go back to his father's farm and hoe the area where they had spilled blood. They should then move to the farm of Odoi's father which was near to that of his father. There they would do some really good hoeing so that when they were asked where they were at the time the crime was committed, they could establish an effective alibi that they were on the farm of Odoi's father and were surprised to hear that such a bad thing had been done.

He told his friends his plan. They unanimously accepted

it. Their faith in Mensa was once more restored. Odoi in his jubilation suggested that they should bring home, when returning, a headload of cassava. This practicable suggestion was also favoured by all. Odoi was very satisfied because it was the kind of service his father liked and once his father was happy, all should be well with him. Consequently, he started boasting freely how he could hoe an acre a day if he had a mind to do it. He was so happy that he started insulting his bogy friend, the man who rang the church bell. He said his body resembled a hoe because his legs were thin and his head was so big. He found it difficult to keep his head erect on his neck so it always drooped. It was therefore obvious that like the hoe, if held by the legs (that is, the handle of the hoe), and then up-ended and pushed forwards and backwards, he would be just the most wonderful kind of hoe ever invented by man.

'And why haven't you done that yet,' asked Otto, wanting to tease Odoi, having forgotten meanwhile that Odoi was easier with words than deeds.

'No, I haven't done that yet because I'm not a big man now. When I'm huge and tall and have a big voice, I'll grab the fool by the legs and use him like a hoe on our farm!'

Klu was so impressed by Odoi's dream that he added: 'And I'll come along and make sure that when you're tired, I'll take over from you and hoe with him! The coward will beg for his release, but I'll scratch his cropped head with my fingers and ask him to keep quiet.'

Okle was not pleased with the idea so he asked: 'Suppose you used him that way and he died, what would you do? God doesn't like that.'

'No. He won't die,' Odoi assured Okle. 'He'll be a little tired and slightly hurt. That will be about all. But the most important thing is that he'll be so scared that he'll never report boys or frighten them.'

'I won't wait until I grow up before I teach this man some lesson,' Otto disclosed to his friends. 'I have a plan which can work well. I'll try it next Sunday. When we're at the Sunday School, I'll hide a stone in my coat-pocket. I'll go and sit behind him. The singing-master will be teaching us a song and the man will be there to sing his loud, bad bass. I'm sure he'll be in cloth. I'll ask permission to go to the toilet then I'll return by the back door. I'll crawl under the pews, then I'll tie a stone to the corner tip of his cloth. When the singing is over and he gets up to adjust his cloth, I'm sure he'll swing the corner tip on to his shoulder; but because of the stone, the corner tip will miss his shoulder and hit him, bang, on his mouth. I'll then pray to God that I shouldn't be discovered so that I can laugh well later!'

Odoi laughed contentedly and said: 'I'm sure if the stone hurts his mouth he'll cry!'

'Oh no!' said Darku. 'I've never seen an elderly man cry before. It's the women who do that.'

'I have,' Mensa said. 'When that man's mother died, he behaved like one of those old women. He cried and cried and shouted to God to bring his mother back to life. But God probably didn't hear him because the corpse lay on the bed stiff in beautiful clothes. I don't think it would like to come back to life and then would not have to wear those fine clothes any longer.'

'Are you sure, Mensa, that he wept and cried?' Otto asked, doubting the truth of what Mensa said.

'He did!' Mensa replied confidently. 'In fact some of the women were laughing at his ugly bass voice, and when he turned round to see what those women were laughing at, they quickly stopped laughing and began crying again. The fool, thinking that the women were really crying also started croaking, not crying. Indeed, that woman who sells rotten oranges that nobody buys … er … what's her name?'

'Aunt Rotten Oranges!' Odoi suggested.

'Nonsense,' said Klu, 'she's my aunt and you can't give her nasty names. Her name is Aunt Toshi.'

'Yes, I remember now,' said Mensa, suppressing a laugh. 'Her name is Aunt Toshi. Klu, your aunt, though she had tears running down her cheeks, was in fact imitating the way the man who rings the church bell cried. Many people were amused and happy but the clown couldn't notice anything!'

They had now reached the farm which belonged to Odoi's father, but instead of remembering the pledge to hoe first the bloody portion on the farm of Mensa's father and then do a vast acreage of Odoi's father's farm, they went and fed on some wild fruit and completely forgot about the morning's incident now that their stomachs were full. They went and cleared the dry leaves under a mango tree and slept soundly.

A sleep of that nature was invariably a deep one, for the morning of that day had quite tasked the boys mentally and physically, and, as always, sleep was the tonic they needed most.

Chapter Three

It was not until about three in the afternoon that they woke up having had some four hours' siesta. They did not like the idea that they had slept so much because they now had to work extra hard to have something to show that they had spent the whole day working on that farm. Nevertheless, they assaulted the undergrowth under the cassava plants with zest and hoed expertly like experienced farmers. That indeed was not how they did the job normally, especially when forced to.

They had done a little area, not an acre, when Odoi's father came to the farm to inspect the crops. He was very pleased that so many of the village boys had come to help his son clear the farm. He congratulated them and promised them a penny each for the following Sunday's children service collection. Odoi was proud of his father for making the promise. It then occurred to his father to ask them how long they had spent on the farm. Mensa was quick to say that they had spent the whole day there.

'And is this all you can do for such a long time? How many of you are here? Let me see; one, two, three, four, five and six. Ah, six of you; and this is all you can do for a day? Not much, I think; but still, it's all right. It's all right. 'I'm glad it occurred to you to come along!'

The boys were speechless and Odoi's father went on: 'Stop work now, good boys, and let's uproot some cassava to take home.'

The boys helped with the uprooting and, accompanied by Odoi's father, began the short trip back to the village.

It was when they were once more near the first building of the village that they were again worried. They just could not guess what was in store for them. They were wondering whether everybody had returned from their farms, whether their enemy had told the whole village the story, whether Old Oko had seen his half-castrated goat, whether if they were found to be the culprits they would be thrashed and, if so, what sort of thrashing. Those were depressing thoughts. But one thing they were sure of: they would have to lie. Yet the two other things they could not get rid of, which were simply too much for them, were fear and guilt.

Because of Odoi's father, they had no means of coordinating points that could help them build up finally a credible story which each and every one of them could tell.

As a rule, whenever they returned from their farms, the first thing they had to do was to wash. But on that day they forgot completely about a wash. Each one of them went home directly to help with the preparation of the evening meal. Each one was prepared to tackle any chores without complaint. They were all well disposed to work if only that could placate humanity so that they would be absolved from their sin. They were all such good boys that evening.

Mensa was in the house roasting a cob of corn when Old Oko entered the house. He jumped with fright and dashed off; but he was not a fool; he realized in a few seconds that

that was the wrong thing to do. He checked the speed he had already gathered, his heart pounding fast, and returned at ordinary walking pace to the coal-pot. He continued roasting the corn while his own nerves were being roasted. His father was relaxing in a deck-chair, pipe in mouth, quite contented with himself after a good day's work.

When Old Oko entered the house, Mensa's father was not pleased with his distraught look. He felt that something must have gone wrong somewhere.

'Anything the trouble, Oko?' he asked.

'The Lord have mercy upon us! The Lord have mercy upon us!' he wailed, almost bent double with grief.

'What's the trouble?'

'And they say this is a Christian village?'

'Anything wrong?'

'That man should be so cruel to man in his own village, in his own country?'

Mensa's father sat erect in the deck-chair. He hoped nothing really serious had happened. 'Any bad news from Accra?' he asked.

'It's unheard of! It's unheard of! That someone in this village should castrate a fully-grown he-goat! The deed was not directed at the he-goat. It was aimed at me! Whoever wants to maim me can do so now. I'm prepared to die!'

Just then, the man who rang the village church bell bounced into the house. He was breathless. For two minutes he could not utter a coherent sentence. He wanted his story to be as well-organized as possible but was so overwhelmed that he got stuck. He did not know where to start. Moreover, the presence of Old Oko and Mensa in the house so delighted him that he interspersed his fits of inarticulateness with broad disgusting grins. He tried to speak but could not frame one tolerably good sentence.

Mensa's father rose and asked the two gentlemen to keep calm. Their immediate requirement was chairs, he said. When they had seated themselves, they could take their time and tell him what stories they had. He asked his other son Tete, who had on that day accompanied him to his farm and was resting, to fetch two chairs. The obliging boy brought the chairs. Old Oko sat on one and the church bell man perched on the other. He was, to his delight, asked to open the proceedings. He grinned from ear to ear, eyed Mensa meaningfully, cleared his throat with a flourish and began his statement.

'Well,' he said, almost choking, 'my story is straightforward. This morning, I had a little stomach upset. It was therefore not possible for me to go to my farm under the hill. I decided to go and inspect my farm near the village. While I was going, the voice of God kept telling me that something was going to be wrong. As you know, it's in my make-up for His voice to warn me about future happenings, and I thank Him. He has blessed me with this since my childhood. Yes, I get to know of evil deeds before they're done.'

Old Anang smiled for he had heard about that special gift before. Old Oko, on the other hand, was not amused. He was listening intently to make sure whether it was going to involve his castrated he-goat. Mensa had been so frightened that he started making slowly for the gate. His father called him back and asked him to fetch him a box of matches. His pipe had burnt out. He had to return. He felt he could go to the toilet but he was not sure.

'As I was saying,' the man who rang the village church bell continued, 'the voice had assured me of something ominous that would happen. I was wondering what it was going to be when I heard the voice of your son asking Okle to murder Klu!'

'This is incredible!' exclaimed Old Anang, not sure whether his own disbelief was right.

'It's very true!' said the man who rang the village church bell. 'And I can swear on the Bible that it is. In fact, the idea of Okle being murdered by your son, Mensa, is so fantastic, indeed so serious, that I decided to act quickly. So I rushed to the spot, but the boys saw me so they scurried away. I looked round, searched the whole farm but they were nowhere to be found. Luckily, and I use the word in a special sense, at the spot where Okle would have been killed, I saw this pocket-knife, all very bloody, so I took it. I should have gone on to my farm, but the safety of the boys was more precious to me than my own welfare. I had to return to the village to see if I could find them and if possible give Okle some first aid which he would naturally need!'

He would have continued but Old Oko interrupted him.

'I know now who castrated my goat. May I know who put this matter of murder into your head? You're old enough to know that these little boys would never dream of murder. It has never happened and will never happen!'

'By the way, this pocket-knife is mine. It's bloody, true! Mensa must have done something wrong, anyway. We must in any case have to make sure whether Okle has been hurt in any way,' Old Anang said calmly.

'I saw him while coming here. He is all right. As I see it, it was the boys who maimed my he-goat. I've intended it for the Christmas. Now I have to slaughter it when the appetite is not there! But why did they do it? Why? They're quite young too.'

The man who rang the village church bell was clearly not happy. It appeared the offence he had attributed to the boys was either being altered or distorted or toned down without reasonable investigation.

'Oko, are you suggesting my story is untrue?' he asked.

'I didn't say so,' Old Oko answered him firmly. 'What I'm saying is that it is absolutely lunatic to suggest that the boys were cutting throats. Think of it, and you'll find that they must have used the pocket-knife in castrating my goat. Of course, for their age it is something very strange indeed. I had never thought they could do it. But that's all there is to it. Anang, call your son and ask him to confess!'

'All right,' said the man who rang the village church bell, 'you can say my story is untrue, but I too have the right to protest. I'm a man born to be fair. Anang, call the brat and let him tell us exactly what happened!'

He tried to adopt a conciliatory tone because he realized his lying would not work. He was also not very happy that he had not yet managed to have in his full possession the true facts. He needed them very much. Whatever they were, they should be interesting. He was quite clear on one thing: he would not try to defend the truth of his story in the circumstance. It belonged to the past and was no more relevant. He could use it in future but now he would patiently listen to what the boy had to say, then he would be armed with at least incontrovertible basic facts, then he would start the evening broadcast. If any senile character like Old Oko off-handedly tried to give another interpretation to his story again, he would insult him outright because he had a reliable source either for quotation or for reference.

Mensa was called by his father. He was sorry and worried, but he was not prepared to give in readily and confess. He was even more determined not to speak the truth when he saw that the man who rang the village church bell was very anxious to hear him. He did not like the way the man looked pleased with himself. He did not like his grin.

'What did you do with this pocket-knife?' his father asked him, holding up the knife. For four full minutes Mensa stood stiff without saying a word. And those were agonizing minutes for the bell man because he was in a terrible hurry to get all the facts; there were so many houses to be served with them. He was also bothered for another reason. Mensa's father was too liberal and soft. In those days of uninhibited physical violence against children, it should not have been difficult for him to ferret the truth out of the boy. First, he would threaten him in a shrill voice that his ear would be boxed, then after a minute, he would issue an ultimatum that it would be done forthwith and in a twinkle of an eye the actual execution followed. Finally, there would be no self-control and there was tragedy let loose for either the victim ran away, which many boys inevitably did, or he would be boxed, knocked down, kicked over, spanked anyhow and anywhere, and, in brief, generally fought and tortured without his fighting back.

'Don't you hear me? What did you do with this pocket-knife this morning?' Old Anang pressed on showing no visible sign of anger. This clearly annoyed the church bell man. It was foolish to extract a confession that way. He was restless so he called the boy's mother to come and listen to the questioning. He knew, in matters of that nature, women could come in useful, because they had their own method of making a child talk. They would shout and rail, complain and lament, cajole and threaten, smile and caress and the truth poured forth.

Mensa's mother, who was cooking but was listening to everything that was being said, was so appalled at the man's flamboyant display of malice that she decided to intervene in her own way. Mensa was her son. She could handle him and she would later on.

'Don't you worry,' she said casually and cheerfully, 'the boy will speak the truth at bedtime tonight or at dawn tomorrow morning. Whatever it is, we'll get to know sooner or later!'

'Do you want to suggest,' said the bell man, 'that when a boy attempts to murder, the hearing of the case should be postponed to bedtime or dawn?'

'I have suggested nothing!' cried Mensa's mother. 'Why are you so anxious to listen to what the boy has to say?' she asked.

'Because it was I who caught him!' the church bell man shouted at her.

'Where did you catch him? On your farm? I want to know!' Mensa's mother demanded, her hands on her hips.

'If it had been on my own farm I would have handed him over at once to the police,' said the bell man.

'Were you handed over to the police when you deserted the army when you were going to see real war in East Africa?' Mensa's mother asked, very satisfied with the force and accuracy of her high-powered missile.

Mensa was enjoying himself now for two reasons. First, he felt his mother had asked a very pertinent question; second, he could not help rejoicing at the expression of pain and discomfiture that clearly showed on the bell man's face. It made him old beyond his years. The bell man realized that if he did not take his time, the boy's mother would humiliate him to the amusement of those around. He was more interested in amusing people than in being the object of amusement. It was also very dangerous for a grown-up to be humiliated before mischief-loving children.

'I don't quite understand the point,' he said in an almost hushed voice. He was sad. Indeed apart from his trying to soft-pedal, the woman had unfortunately referred to a story in his life which people as a rule never spoke about. He thought everybody had either forgotten it or thought it did not matter. Now it had been mentioned at the wrong time and place. If he stayed in the house, he could not be sure what the woman would say. To leave suddenly too would imply that he did desert the army and that would bring about a loss of face especially to the children in the house. He had to say something. He thought hard and fast. He said: 'Maybe I deserted the army, maybe I didn't; but one thing everybody knows is that I've never attempted to murder people. You should know how to bring up your children!'

'Have you any yourself?' asked Mensa's mother, referring once again to another painful fact.

'I haven't, so what?' asked the bell man, cornered and in a desperate fighting mood.

'If you haven't, then don't instruct others how they should do it. If you could have had one, I'm sure your wife would not have run away from you. I know my boy has done something wrong, but why all this fuss, this malevolent grin, you nosy-parker? You must learn to mind your own business. Try to father a son and then everybody will know you're really a man and not a loosetongued detractor.'

'Jesus my Saviour! Do you hear what this woman is saying? Why do you allow women to talk like this? They use language like a knife. They don't only break the heart of man. They cut it!' He was near-hysterical. But he was a man and could not allow himself to break down for long. He recovered as quickly as he had lapsed and said what he had now thought he should:

'I didn't come here to be told by a household of fools and criminals how I should organize my life!'

'Then, please, walk out!' the woman ordered him.

For some time he half-sat and half-stood up. He did not actually know which he was doing, but he was in fact compulsively getting up, and he said: 'Before I walk out, I'd like to say that this house is a nest of wicked souls and incorrigible rascals!'

'Very good!' said Old Anang. 'You came here to complain about my son. You begin with a story you weren't sure of. Now you are complaining about my whole household. This is what I can't tolerate. The boy hasn't hurt you. He hasn't hurt anything of yours. There's the door. Make sure you get out quickly!'

'I'll go away all right,' said the village church bell man, 'but this is not going to be the end of it. It's the beginning, and I'll see it through. You'll be sorry for what your wife has said to me this evening. If God says vengeance is His, then we mortals must scrupulously execute it. Good night!'

'Agreed. The church bell is there. Go and ring it and ask God to bring back your wife to you. She has a handsome boy. The boy doesn't look like you. It must be another man's. So when it comes to vengeance you must leave God alone. He has been free with it and he hasn't kept you out. Go and have a good dinner!' said Mensa's mother, very pleased with herself.

The man did not say a word in reply and left the house. Old Oko was shocked at what had just happened. He turned to the boy's mother and said: 'What you've done is even more serious than the castration of my goat. I can tell you that. You see, you'll find it hopelessly difficult to prove that this man can't have children. Even if it is true, why say it? It's a serious thing to tell a man.'

'Yes, but don't you think it's even more serious for a man to devote all his energies to lying and seeking the downfall of other men because that's how he finds his pleasure?' she asked, looking as grave as ever. She continued: 'I don't like my boy's behaviour most of the time, but you can't make him any good by trying to make him feel he's the devil. It makes me angry. Here we are in a Christian village. There are far too many of us who happen to be regular evil-doers and yet we try all the time to make others feel they are the evil-doers for whom God has reserved a special punishment! This man thinks because he works for the church, he is above others. He sees nothing in any of us except our weaknesses. He laughs in his sleep because we have our weaknesses. He will plot our damnation in the name and service of God because we have some weaknesses. How can I best put it? Yes, he specializes in moral subversion. I fear most of our religious people because they are the agents of moral subversion. They use it as a means of barren spiritual entertainment. We have either to satisfy them or be damned. They neither have to help us nor satisfy us because they think they are only responsible to God and have his backing. I don't know whom God backs, anyway; but they are happy, yes, cynically happy, when someone errs. Because of their own shortcomings which they try to overlook, they are genuinely disappointed when someone tries to be good. You see, this man who rings our church bell is an idiot so he shows his own failings plainly. But others who are respected and influential in our society do it all the time imperceptibly and cunningly. Everywhere you turn, there is moral subversion of some kind. I'm fed up with it and I must say it. I'm never afraid of man born by woman no matter what he is or what he thinks he is!'

'You probably don't understand what we are talking about,' said Old Oko, very surprised and upset at the woman's outburst. 'You've actually slandered him. That's the issue. If he drags you to court, you'll have a lot to answer. Speaking for myself, I know well enough that we live in wicked times and we live by double standards. The man who says he's going to make life happier for you either here or hereafter is the man who is going to wreck all your happiness. He condemns others and tells you he has the mission and vision to help you. Very soon and too soon you find him immersed in the very things he condemns in others. But once it is being done by him, it is either right or it must be overlooked. You call it moral subversion. I have no name for it. I know it is there but I don't find it necessary to say so. There must be something basically wrong with creation, but that's not my business. The world is what it is. You're being funny to talk the way you do. You'll never be understood, so you have to be practical. The practical thing now is that the man is badly hurt. You've said things which we don't say in the open. I don't like the turn of events. Why should a castrated goat create this kind of trouble?'

'I'm not sorry for anything I've said,' Mensa's mother said, not in the least moved by the devastating seriousness of Old Oko. 'I wish I could be proved wrong. I'm prepared to defend anything I've said. I'm happy I've been able to thwart his evil designs. That's what matters to me.'

Old Anang lit his pipe. He knew his wife and could not agree with her more. He only deplored the fact that she said those things before the children. Besides, what she had revealed could set the whole village talking. It was painful to him that his son had brought this about. In any case, he had to get the truth and let Old Oko be satisfied.

Mensa too was not happy about the turn of events. He was especially moved by how his mother spoke and frightened by what Old Oko said to her. He felt he should say everything to his parents. Perhaps by speaking the truth they would be relieved of the uncertainty and distress that plagued them. He was prepared to take any punishment if only that could make his parents happy.

'Daddy, I didn't really mean any harm,' he began, 'the goat came and stole my food from me. I wanted to punish it but was not sure what I should do. Then I remembered what you once told me.'

'What did I tell you?' Old Anang asked, wondering whether his son was going to implicate him.

'You told me that if the two soft balls were removed, the he-goat was kept out of mischief.'

'But I didn't tell you to go and do it yourself, did I? Have you ever seen a boy do it or just anybody do it? People learn how to do it when they are grown up. An animal can be seriously harmed if it isn't properly done.'

'I'm sorry, Daddy, I don't know why I did it.'

'Who helped you do it? You couldn't have done it alone.'

'Okle, Darku, Otto, Odoi and Klu.'

'Did you ask them to come to the farm?'

'Yes, I did.'

'Why?'

'Because I couldn't have done it alone.'

'Do you know the punishment for this?'

'Yes.'

'What is it?'

'Caning.'

'Do you wish to be caned?'

'Yes.'

'Do you realize that what you've done is not expected of my son?'

'Yes, I do.'

'You go away and have your dinner.'

Mensa could not move. He did not know what to do or say. After some time, he walked slowly away to the kitchen where his mother, brother and sister were. Everybody was silent in the kitchen. Mensa was overwhelmed with remorse.

'It's a pity,' said Old Oko, who could find nothing else to say despite the many thoughts which had flashed through his mind.

'I think I have to pay you some money and take the goat,' Old Anang told Old Oko, thinking that financial compensation was the best thing he could do in the circumstances.

'No!' said Old Oko emphatically, 'I don't have to be paid. I don't need the money and I have no bitterness. I'm rather disturbed by something different. I can't understand how boys of their age could possibly conceive the idea and execute it. Nobody will believe they've done it; but they have. If they continue like this, I shudder to think what they'll do in future. You'd better see to training Mensa properly otherwise you'll have more sleepless nights before you die! I must go home now. I think we don't have to tell people about this. I'll slaughter the goat tonight and if anybody asks me why, I'll tell him off. Good night!'

Chapter Four

Old Oko left the house with no bitter feelings. He had been upset by what the new generation of boys was capable of doing. It was that they could violently and thoughtlessly get rid of what they found inconvenient. They were radical and dangerous. Any victory they could win over their earthly circumstance would be pyrrhic. On the other hand, he could not approve of the attitude of the man who rang the village church bell. He would want the boys, particularly Mensa, ruthlessly punished and humiliated not because punishment and humiliation were either remedial, deterrent, good or reformatory but because pain would be inflicted on them and that was to be his source of pleasure. He wanted to derive his amusement out of the boys' misfortune. He was also convinced that Mensa's mother had been far too ingenuous. She did not really understand either her world or the times. It had long been obvious, he thought, that in their kind of society the successful man was the morally crooked but he was ironically the efficient person who always managed to satisfy those in authority. Once he was accepted by those in authority, he must necessarily, in the eyes of the public, be good and humanitarian. Even if he were dangerously powerful, it did not matter because his society was too paralysed to produce a less efficient but more beneficial soul. Once such a crook gained power, he would twist and bend others to glut his ambition. And it was an ambition which was not all the time very well defined to himself. His whims were accepted as clever moves that would benefit everybody not today but in a distant unforeseeable future. Such a man became an institution that must be fostered. The church would not oppose him. It needed him because he was successful or so its flock thought. Indeed, everybody had to be like him to get on well in life. To talk about it like the way she did was to display gross childishness. It was a way of life and a standard that should be conformed to and not foolishly questioned. In short, he shrugged off, the woman had no understanding of the ways of the world just as he thought he had that understanding but was too impotent to do anything about it except to rely on his own little, isolated, personal uprightness which would either die with him or be carried on by another obscure person. 'She's guilty of indiscretion!' he said with conviction to himself and vanished into the darkness of the unlit street in the village.

The other boys had come surreptitiously to the house of Old Anang to learn from Mensa what had happened. They wanted to know first whether he had spoken the truth. When Mensa's brother, Tete, saw them, he ran and told his mother that the miscreants had come to their house. She went to the gate and asked them to go away. Tete's conduct irritated Mensa and awoke in him feelings of contempt and dislike. Mensa felt that Tete thought he was somehow superior to him since nobody heard of any misbehaviour on his part. Their mother and father frequently said that Tete would be a great man in future but Mensa would go to the dogs. Tete assiduously tried therefore to please his parents all the time. Mensa thought Tete a weak opportunist who would do anything to satisfy his parents so as to earn fine words of praise and flattery.

Just as the dismissed boys were leaving the precincts of the house, another boy, the son of the village catechist, sped by and entered the house.

He went to Mensa's father and told him that his wife and he were wanted immediately at the catechist's house. Old Anang knew what it was about. The man who rang the village church bell had been to report his wife and him to the catechist. He told his wife about it. She was not perturbed.

'You may be right,' counselled Old Anang, 'but you must choose your words carefully when we get there. If a matter of this nature is not tactfully handled, we'll get into endless trouble. I'm sure the village church elders will be there. Some of those people would like this case dragged on so as to get some evening diversion. Others would like the case snatched from the catechist and handed over to the local court so as to get bribed with drinks. We must go and make peace.'

His wife saw the wisdom in his weighing-up of the subject and their possible line of action. She knew they had no money for any local court where litigation was the spice of life. It was better, then, to nip any future trouble in the bud.

Old Anang and his wife were ushered in to the study of the catechist. The twelve church and civil elders were there. Some were trading harmless insults and others were seriously discussing the case they were going to try. They were sitting close to one another in a semi-circle. The catechist sat opposite them. Mr and Mrs Anang were asked to sit down on the left-hand side of the catechist so that they also faced the elders. The man who rang the church bell sat on the right-hand side of the catechist.

The catechist said: 'Let us pray!' They all rose looking as solemn as usual; that is, how they had learnt to look whenever prayers were said. The catechist said the prayer in a sonorous, mechanical voice: 'Almighty God, we thank Thee that Thou hast preserved our lives and fed us well this evening. Thou hast, through Thy word, taught us that women should humble themselves to men, and above all, control their tongues. They must also by word and deed set shining examples to their children so as to qualify for everlasting blessedness. We have assembled here tonight to have wrong righted, to have a loose tongue curbed and to exhort husbands to discharge their responsibilities in their homes efficiently. This Thou hast enjoined by Thy word and we have enforced by custom. O Lord, Thy guidance we seek in this serious trial. Amen!'

'Amen,' the gathering roared, that of the bell man being, of course, the longest and loudest.

'Lady and gentlemen,' the catechist began talking as he scanned the individual faces before him, 'we've come together this evening to look into a matter that is unique. Far too many people are involved in it. Things which ought not to have been done, have been done, and words which ought not to have been uttered have in fact been uttered. Christian conduct has been cast aside and it is our duty as leaders of the church and of our community to ensure that good conduct is maintained at all levels no matter what circumstances afflict us. Our friend, the bell man, who has been doing good Christian service without pay in this village, has reported a scandalous case to me and that's why I've asked you to come so that we can settle it amicably. Briefly, it is this: the food he took last night did not agree with him so he did not go to his farm below the hill this morning. Still, he needed some food for the day and he also wanted to inspect his other farm near our village. While he was going to this farm, he heard a boy asking another boy to cut the throat of a third boy. This may sound incredible but that was precisely what he heard. He was, as we would expect, naturally alarmed so he went to the farm of Old Anang to forestall any bloodshed. The boys concerned fortunately don't belong to my school. It is these untrained boys who often give trouble. We've got to have all of them in my school next year!'

'That's right,' applauded one of the elders.

'It happens that the boys complained of are Mensa and Okle,' said the catechist, 'but they bolted away when they saw our friend. Well, as a worthy member of our community, he went to Old Anang's house to report what had taken place. Unfortunately, Mensa's mother would not listen to him. She was downright unpleasant and told him that though he had had a wife, he couldn't have children. And to add insult to injury, she said he had deserted the army because he feared gunfire.'

The elders burst out with laughter which was later mingled with noisy chatter. Some said Old Anang's wife was historically correct. Others said even if it was true, it was not within the bounds of propriety for her to say so, especially in a household full of children.

'Well,' the catechist continued when the noise had died down somewhat, 'we are dealing with a grave matter. There is therefore no room for mirth or easy talk. It's a matter that should be looked into thoroughly and carefully. As far as my opinion goes, the time and place were not suitable enough for Mrs Anang to say those things. But I would like first to call upon Old Anang to tell us what he knows about the case.'

'I don't know who informed you about anybody committing murder. I have therefore nothing to say!' Old Anang said deliberately to see how the catechist would react.

'What exactly do you mean?' the catechist asked, feeling a bit disappointed with Old Anang's language.

'What I mean,' Old Anang began to explain, 'is this: there has been no attempted murder by my son so I don't see why I should be called upon to explain!'

The catechist clearly did not like the denial. It could make the meeting pointless, so he asked Old Anang: 'Did your wife insult the bell man?'

'Yes.'

'Why?'

'Because she couldn't see what he wanted in her house.'

'Are you implying that our friend is a thief?'

'I don't know of his past and I can't know about all his present activities.'

'I hope you don't intend to give cheek here!'

'I should be sorry to.'

'Did she tell him to go away?'

'Yes, she did.'

'Why did she insult him then?'

'Because he wanted to do your job for you.'

'Meaning?'

'He said she must raise her children in the way of the Lord. You've been telling us that.'

'And what was her reply?' the catechist asked, very convinced that Old Anang was as bad as his son.

'She told him to go and fetch his wife who had deserted him, bear his own children and raise a model family for everybody to see.'

'What about the army insult?'

'Well, that came in when our friend, the bell man, said my house was a haven for wicked souls. You see, he about covered everybody in the house including myself. In order that I might not get rough with him, she probably said that to make him leave the house.'

'I don't understand you,' said the catechist, not knowing what to ask next.

'What can't you understand, sir?' asked Old Anang.

'Don't ask irrelevant questions. We are looking into the case,' warned the catechist.

One of the elders asked permission to put a few questions to the bell man. The others were interested in the way the case was developing and were quiet. They never expected Old Anang to be so bold before them, especially before the catechist whom people addressed with the utmost reverence.

'Did you have a wife?'

'Yes, I did.'

'Where is she?'

'I'm not her keeper!'

'I see. She's not living with you, then?'

'That's true, anyway.'

'So what Old Anang's wife said is correct?'

'Yes. It is correct as an insult!'

'And it *is* also correct as a fact!'

'Yes, so what?' asked the man who rang the village church bell, fuming.

'I don't see why we should be asked to judge this case, then!' said the elder, not prepared to countenance any other interpretation. He stopped asking questions and sat back to hear what the others would say.

Another elder soon after begged to be allowed to ask his own questions. He had been smoking a pipe. But before putting his questions, he went out and spat and came back clearing his throat. His hygiene was questionable but he would not care. He was past changing his habits. He asked: 'Is it true you deserted the army?'

'Yes, but that was long ago,' said the bell man, who now wondered whether the elders were for or against him.

'Why did you do that?'

'Because somebody poured water into my left ear while I slept,' the bell man lied, hoping he could win the sympathy of the elders by doing so.

'Why did he do that?' asked the pipe-smoking old man, his eyes twinkling with curiosity and pleasure.

'He said I snored so loudly he couldn't sleep.'

'Did you consider that little incident a good excuse to quit the army the way you did?'

'You wouldn't know! I had to see the army doctor because

the pain in my ear was unbearable. Besides, the man said if I snored again, he would give me another water treatment. I wasn't particularly scared, though. The real reason was that I had a farm here. I also had my mother to look after. Naturally, I had to come home by ordinary transport to see to both. I didn't run away!'

'Why then did you have to run away into the bush behind the cemetery when some policemen came to this village soon after your arrival here? You see, I've no short memory!'

'Because I wanted to inspect an animal trap.'

'I see; but you'll probably recall that a search party was organized to search for you. You had vanished for three days and everybody was alarmed. The policemen too had left. They spent less than two hours here. We discovered you badly bruised and cut and starved. You were hiding in the barn of Carpenter Kodzo. Were you still inspecting a trap?'

The bell man did not like either the exposed facts or the last question.

It was clear he was being ridiculed by the old man. The truth revealed was also an unpleasant one. That bald, old, pipe-smoking man merely wanted to tease him. He was in no way conducting a trial. He, the bell man, too had a full right to make things unpleasant for him. He therefore asked a question instead of answering.

'By the way,' he asked confidently, 'is it not true that those policemen were in fact looking for you? Did they not, upon information, trace you to the place where you distilled illicit gin? Don't you remember that though you had boasted openly in this village that if any police-men came to your distillery you would hack them to pieces with your long knife, yet when you did see them you mysteriously vanished into the bush leaving your long knife, cudgels and unlicensed cap-gun behind? Don't you think cowards are made because they can't carry out the terms of their boasts?'

'So what?' asked the pipe-smoking old man without enthusiasm.

'So of course, you also are a coward. The only difference is that right now you've forgotten about yours but can remember mine,' said the bell man with uncommon insight.

Undoubtedly, there was, once again, an outburst of confused chatter, but this time, it was mixed with heated exchanges here and there. Arms were swinging widely and carelessly in the air. Somebody made a violent gesture of the hand and accidentally knocked the pipe out of the mouth of the elder whom the bell man had called a coward. The man was so exasperated that his body shook violently; but then that happened to be the tremors of a physically exhausted person. He was volatile and could have fought the assailant, but he had not the bodily resources; still he had in abundance the wiles of an old man which could compensate for any other defect and these he quickly called into play. He said he did not see the need for their sitting on the case any longer; it was obvious that Old Anang and his wife had no case to answer. He concluded: 'It's pointless we should sit on this case. There's no evidence of attempted murder. Anang's wife did not insult the bell man, she simply reminded him of his past. In doing so, she happened to speak the precise truth which the bell man himself has confirmed here before all of us. Everything is clear. We have to take a vote!'

'Are you the chairman?' asked the bell man, angry and intellectually more alert than usual.

'Whoever is the chairman should ask for a vote,' replied the old man, whose anger had in no way subsided.

'Is that how you refer to our catechist?' asked the bell man, smiling.

'Look!' cried the old man. 'He is not a minister. He is a human being and young enough to be my son! I'm asking him to put the matter to vote. I'm in a hurry. I want to go hunting this evening.'

'I'm afraid,' said the catechist with forced composure, 'we haven't done our duty by the bell man.'

At this, an elder rose immediately and said: 'I'm unable to see what duty there is in this matter. Nobody has been hurt in this village today. None of our boys can commit murder. We don't have time for imbecile stories. In your prayer, sir, you thanked God for having fed us well this evening. That kind of prayer actually compromises God. Some of us were going to have our dinner when your son came to call us to this place. I've listened to this case on an empty stomach and I'm not prepared to listen to it any longer!'

'Some of you people here are not alive to your Christian responsibilities,' said a pious-looking elder who had said nothing so far. 'We are here to foster brotherliness and love between man and man and not indulge in verbal tricks. If we feel both the Anangs and the bell man are wrong we should tell them so and reconcile them. If we think one party is wrong and the other right, we should say so with honesty and make sure that peace and love prevail. Our attitude now is more worldly than religious.'

'What's the man saying?' cried the pipe-smoking, bald old man. 'The catechist was religious before he gave us a biased review of the case. I'm old enough to know. Legality is legality and there are Christian judges. We try a case according to the evidence. Reconciliation comes after the verdict. Let's have a vote. When the minister comes down from Accra to administer the Holy Communion, he can reconcile them. He's paid to do that! You were a Christian before you went and stole a dog from the other village. I know you were sorry you did that and that's why you're a good Christian now. You were tried before you apologized to the owner of the dog. Why can't we do the same in this case?'

'I've always thought and will ever think you're a thoroughly bad old man in every possible way. Why mention this before the catechist?' wailed the pious-looking man.

'What's the man talking about?' asked the pipe-smoking, bald old man while his friends were roaring with laughter. 'I've always been bad. So people say. I've a free conscience and can die in peace. What happens to me later you and I can't be sure about! Let's have a vote!'

For eight full minutes, there was a complete breakdown of propriety and order. The catechist raised his voice and asked the venerable elders to keep quiet. Suddenly as if by magic there was absolute silence. The catechist knew that despite his own feelings he had to ask for a vote. A vote was taken. Seven voted for the acquittal of Old Anang and his wife and six voted them guilty. Those who voted for their freedom were the friends of the pipe-smoking, bald old man and those who found them guilty were those passionately devoted to the cause of the church and therefore could not but be with the catechist and the man who rang the village church bell.

Before the court rose, the catechist said: 'I'm glad Mr and Mrs Anang have not been found guilty. It is however my duty to give moral guidance. I've no right to fail anyone in this. In the performance of it, I have to follow my conscience and the teaching of our Lord. Some of the boys in this village who have not yet been put to school are rotten to the core. We've got to do something about it. At their baptismal, we pledged to be responsible for their moral and spiritual growth as prescribed by the church. They are definitely wayward now. I therefore appeal to Mr and Mrs Anang to send their children to my school after the Christmas holidays. They will be looked after by no one but myself. I'll neither spare the rod nor see them become delinquent. I promise to mould them into useful citizens of our country. Well, lady and gentlemen, I would like to thank all of you for the help you've given me in discharging my duties tonight. Though I'm not particularly satisfied with the conduct of the case, I'm glad it's all over. You used to behave well but tonight Satan has wrought havoc among us. Let us pray!'

Somebody laughed but everybody rose. Those in cloths adjusted them over their shoulders, stood erect and bowed down their heads. Those in European dress had nothing to adjust over their shoulders so they stood still, feet astride and their hands behind them. The catechist said a short prayer without inspiration and the elders left his house in batches of twos and threes. They were still debating the subject unofficially and non-committally. Anything could therefore be said for or against it as a matter of candid opinion. Some said Old Anang and his wife were spoiling their children and it was time something was done about it. Others felt the whole incident would have a sobering effect on the man who rang their church bell. All of them agreed, however, that the charge of murder was too flimsy and funny to be taken seriously. It was both fantastic and unbelievable. They were surprised the catechist thought it was possible. They thought he had the weakness of taking the bell man seriously. Any time he told him a story, his first reaction was to believe him and he would not try to investigate it later, so he formed wrong opinions about people which inevitably embarrassed those who thought the man of God should display better intellectual freedom and impeccable sagacity.

Chapter Five

'I agree,' said Old Anang's wife when she and her husband were alone on their farm, 'that our two sons should go to school; but I don't want Mensa to attend the school in our village. I don't think the catechist likes him. Mensa will never be happy if he becomes a pupil of that man. He will be caned unnecessarily. I've heard a lot about these teachers. Whenever they have a grudge against a pupil's parents, they use the child as a scapegoat and punish him unreasonably.'

'What are we going to do then?' asked Old Anang thoughtfully.

'I think we can send him to your cousin, Mr Lomo, the headteacher, in Accra,' she suggested.

'I don't want other people to look after my children,' Old Anang said, meaning every word of it.

'But we've only one school in this village. Mensa can't go there. Either he goes to your cousin or he remains at home with us. That's how I see it right now,' Mensa's mother argued firmly.

'I'll think about it,' Old Anang promised. He never liked to be forced into hasty decisions.

'You'd better think quickly about it,' his wife said. She knew if she allowed time to elapse Old Anang might not do as she had suggested. 'And when you've done so, we can write to ask him whether he'll have the boy. You know he'll have to consult his wife and she will also have to agree to have Mensa stay with them.'

Old Anang was hesitating not because his wife's suggestion was in itself bad but because basically he could not see how somebody else could look after his children better than he could do it. He thought that, although it was a common practice, there were far too many problems connected with it. First, it would appear as if he was shirking his parental responsibility. Second, he would have to have enough money on hand all the time to send to his cousin to cover his son's board and lodging. Third, his son was a challenge to him. The boy always roused in him his parental instinct to protect. He had to face the challenge and see him grow up as he would like him to. If he went away, how could he best help him and be satisfied with that help? He thought Mensa was not congenitally bad, he was just being too troublesome for his age. Time could help in moulding him into what a good man should be. On the other hand, to let Mensa remain in the village would not be altogether salutary. His education, he should have; and yet it was likely the catechist would so maltreat him at school that he would come to believe that he was unwanted. He was in a painful dilemma and did not like it. His pride was involved and yet he had to take a decision. He pondered the problem for some time and it became clear to him that he had to accept his wife's suggestion. He tried to console himself with the thought that it was possible God had His hand in that unfortunate situation and perhaps one day it would be possible not to have any regrets. He was never a coward but believed that the essence of things was to know when to compromise.

On the following day, after breakfast, he told his wife who, ever since they returned from the farm the day before, had not ceased from telling him to make up his mind: 'I think we can write a letter to my cousin in Accra. I'm not sure what he'll say, though.'

'The sooner the better!' replied his wife, delighted.

'But how are we to put the case? How do we explain why we're sending him to them? You see, you can't send your son to someone else to look after without just cause. We must have some good reason.'

'Well,' replied Mensa's mother, 'we've got to tell him the whole truth. That will make him sympathetic in training our son.'

'You can't, you know,' Old Anang argued, 'be sure of my cousin's ideas about how children should be trained. He may know the catechist here and consider him a good teacher and disciplinarian. He may get the impression that we want our child to be softly treated. I'll explain one thing to you. Be patient and listen carefully. I've over the years watched these mission- or church-trained teachers. Some of them are malicious and dangerous. They don't want anybody to progress in life beyond their own status because they think their profession is not as rewarding to them as they deserve. If they are down, everybody must be down. They therefore train their pupils to make sure they get stuck somewhere, presumably below their level, or, at best, at their level. Some of them by nature are heartless and wicked. They are impatient too. The only effective method they can use in training a child is the use of brute force. They get quick results but the child becomes docile, hypocritical and permanently cynical. Some of them think a good pupil is the one who is good at sweeping the teacher's house, washing the laundry clothes, fetching firewood, chopping firewood, running errands, keeping discipline in the classroom and managing with sixty per cent average in the terminal examinations. Such a pupil is nonpareil and is likely to get on in life. What I don't like about this kind of training, though I'm a farmer without any great ideas, is that such a pupil is trained to be an abject, cringing servant. To my mind, he leaves school uneducated because he can't be independent. He becomes in future a good storekeeper, or an obedient hard-working civil servant whose confident source of thought or action is what has been said or done before. He can't think for himself because his seminal mind is warped by routine thinking. Look at our catechist. He's a ridiculous robot. I can assure you that the bell man thinks for him and the bell man himself is a ludicrous, feeble-minded farmer. Imaginative men don't ring church bells! Such a pupil is nothing but a regimented doll who opposes change, sees in new dress fashions and other modern innovations a tragic betrayal of the national inheritance; sees in the young nothing but moral decadence while he himself may be unbelievably immoral. I had six years of formal education, but, at least, I'm free. People think I'm queer because I train my children differently. People think I'm queer because I use kerosene in burning bush on my farm. People have objected to my being made an elder of the church because I don't say what I'm expected to. I'm no

Christ and I do not wish to be. There are enough Jews; but do you think if Christ had said what he was expected to say the church would have been in existence? Look at our church buildings. They are all of the same design. You ask for a radical design and they say you are downright mad! I want my children to be free, bold, self-reliant and capable of changing the phase of that portion of the earth where they live. They may die in the process but what's wrong about such a death? Convention and conformity are the foundation-stone of decadence. I wish I had had more education, I could have shaken my country!'

'Are you drunk?' asked Old Anang's wife, who thought her husband was simply unleashing an abstruse diatribe that drunks spout in moments of mental vacuity.

'I'm not drunk, my wife!' he quickly replied, 'I'm just telling you some of the things I constantly brood over. I know I'm insignificant. I know there are one or two others in this country who know and think what I'm telling you now. They will die and be disposed of with these thoughts. What can they do? The machine which runs the social processes is indifferent, powerful and insensitive. It cannot hear the insignificants. It grinds them, pulverizes them, destroys them. One of my children should remove a nut in this machine. He may be hurt. I don't care. I've been hurt already and I know I'll bleed to death!'

'I can't see how what you're telling me can have any bearing on our sending Mensa to your cousin. I've seen a bit of your cousin. He's a good man. I'm sure he'll take good care of our son. All we have to do is to try. We can't waste words over it. We've got to take action.'

'Of course, we have to,' said Old Anang feebly, spent and dejected. He had spoken what he had on his mind and all life had suddenly become blank and empty. The real life he had to face was the one being presented to him by his wife. He was strong but powerless. He had in him charity but could not help being resentful.

In the evening he wrote the following letter in the vernacular to his cousin:

My dear cousin,

It's a pity you've not heard from me for so long. We farmers don't usually write unless we have something important to say.

You probably know I'm fond of my first son, Mensa, and I've made up my mind to give him the best education possible. What I haven't got, I can make up through him. I'm poor but I'm determined to do all I can for him.

I would rather let you know at once that Mensa is given to having his own way. This quite often gets him into trouble. Recently he castrated a fully grown he-goat unauthorized and this has disturbed the village a bit. Personally, I don't think this is a serious crime since his intention was to make the goat less mischievous. But he erred, I admit, in doing something that he shouldn't have done. Such daring too is not expected of a boy of his age. His conduct has led our catechist, your colleague, to believe that I'm not capable of training my children. He has therefore threatened to see that Mensa reforms as quickly as possible and has urged my wife and myself to let him admit Mensa to his school after the Christmas holidays.

While my wife and I don't doubt his good intentions, we feel, however, that from what we've seen in the past, he will subject our son to constant caning. We are unable to accept this method as the best possible way of keeping our son out of mischief.

My wife and I have therefore decided to ask you whether you'll be kind enough to have our son stay with you so that you train him with kindness and understanding. Naturally, you as a teacher will know better how to train him. I as a farmer can only suggest.

I'm prepared to send to you at the end of each month two pounds which, I hope, will be adequate to defray the cost of his board and lodge. I'm also prepared to pay any extra money that may be needed to meet any incidental expenses.

I'm sorry I have had to bother you but I've not been able to think of any other alternative course in the present circumstances. I trust you'll do your best for my boy.

Kindly write to let me know whether I can send him over to you.

Yours sincerely,
Anang

The letter was posted the following day and it arrived in Accra after twenty-four hours. Old Anang's cousin, Mr Lomo, was in the school office when the letter was handed to him. He was the headteacher of a primary school. He was, it must be said, a man whose personality had been dictated by his job. He loved children deep down somewhere but had learnt to distrust them. On the whole, he treated them impersonally. He would have liked them to be neat, well-behaved; but at first his strenuous efforts to make these a reality did not go beyond using words. There was no response so he had to rely on other methods. They could not be wholly effective but they got him halfway perhaps.

Mr Lomo was a tall man, born to look noble and easy, but his sense of moral righteousness had transformed him into a grim, formidable-looking man. He was neither lean nor stout and always wore cheap but well-kept clothes.

Already, he had four boys whom he was training. He did not like the idea because those boys could not and would not have the same facilities as his own children. He would like them to have them but his wife plus the lack of money thwarted any attempts in that direction. It was some parents who forced those children on him. He would explain to those parents that it was not easy but they would not understand. He would tell them that he lived in the school quarters which had neither spare-rooms nor beds; but those parents would press him to do something for them otherwise their children's future would be blighted.

There was another compelling factor working against him. Most of his colleagues were helping other parents by letting their wayward children stay with them. If he refused, then he would be called a bad, selfish man. He would be condemned as being un-Christian and perhaps as an irresponsible teacher of his religious educational unit. He had to do as others were doing to save his face. So long as the practice lasted, so long would he be a slave to it.

When he had finished reading Old Anang's letter he shrugged his shoulders and said to himself that it was going to be another burden that convention would force him to carry. Where and on what would the boy sleep?

Could Old Anang send the money he had promised regularly? Would his wife like the boy? If the boy was really spoilt, what influence would he have on his own children? Would two pounds be enough to feed a boy who was physically developing and therefore needed a lot of balanced diet? The cost of living was fairly high since items like milk, butter and eggs were being imported. The more he added to his family, the more the cost of living rose and the lower the standard of living of everyone in the house became. His wife was already over-worked in looking after eight robust children. Some would escape a wash in the morning and, sure enough, any time they escaped a wash their parents would call to pay them a visit. They would then gain the impression that his wife and he were not looking after their children properly. He would have no excuse because they looked upon him as a qualified teacher who alone understood the mysteries involved in raising children however difficult the children were. If their children were unwashed, it was nothing but wilful negligence on the part of both him and his wife. Severe words would be used against his wife because her children were well-washed so she must have been the source of the discrimination and the attendant negligence. Such complaints he would not be told directly by the parents but he would hear of them later in the town and he would be sad for a day or two. If his wife heard of them she would complain bitterly and ruin his appetite. This was a sacrifice that tormented him body and soul.

He was struggling through his adult life with four boys; now a fifth was to be added. The four boys belonged to parents who were not his relations. How could he refuse the fifth one who was the son of his own cousin, a farmer, who had great respect for him?

Reluctantly, as he had done before, he wrote a letter of acceptance to his cousin, Old Anang. As a matter of false charity which was uncalled for, he knocked off a pound from the two pounds, adding that he would have looked after Mensa without taking a penny but was compelled to take a token sum of one pound because of the exceptionally high cost of living in Accra. He was sure one pound a month was enough for board; lodge would be his own responsibility and he would charge nothing for it.

He made sure he posted the letter before going home to tell his wife about it because he knew if he had consulted her before posting it, she would have asked him not to take the boy as her hands were full. Experience had taught him that in matters of this nature he would have to take action before letting his wife know.

'Adzoa,' he called his wife in a forced cheerful voice when he arrived home, 'my cousin, Old Anang, is sending his son, Mensa, over to come and stay with us.'

'No!' protested Mrs Lomo, 'we can't have him. Where is he going to sleep? On what is he going to sleep? Some of these boys wet the bed. They eat late and heavily in the evening; the food makes them sleep so deeply that they wet the bed. I sometimes feel ashamed when we have visitors. Our lounge smells of urine and Dettol. When on earth are we going to be left alone to live with our own children in peace? We have to bring them up as comfortably as we can, haven't we? We have a duty to our own children, haven't we? Right now we don't have a home. We are running a kindergarten!'

'I do appreciate your feelings,' said Mr Lomo casually, 'but I've already written to Old Anang to tell him to send over the boy before the Christmas.'

'You shouldn't have done that!' Adzoa cried in anger.

'I should!' replied Mr Lomo firmly.

'Why?'

'Because we have boys in this house who were sent to us because their parents are related to you. Old Anang is my cousin. He is a respectable farmer, that's why we call him Old. He is as good as any of your relations!'

'Blackmail?'

'There's no blackmail in this. It's a fair deal!'

'It's no fair deal. It's treachery, short and simple!'

'You're wrong there!'

'Very well,' said Mrs Lomo, overwhelmed, 'let's have him. It's a simple business. We shall all suffer together. It's one thing to have these boys; it's another how they live! I shan't complain again!'

'Don't talk like that,' protested Mr Lomo. 'In the first place, if any of these children overhears what you're saying, they'll tell their parents we feel compelled to look after them. They'll tell them you don't want them. They'll be frustrated though they may not show it openly. When they've grown up, they'll tell ugly stories about you and me. Take the whole thing as a challenge and do your best for them.'

'You've always told me that,' Mrs Lomo said softly in her disappointment, 'but all I ask for right now is that there must be a limit to the number of boys we are going to have in this house. We've neither the means nor the genuine enthusiasm for so many boys. Why should we pretend it is all right to have them?'

When Old Anang received the reply letter from his cousin, he thought the problem had been resolved but not necessarily happily. He now had to think about how to get his son ready for the trip to Accra. As for his wife, she was very happy; her son now had the chance to escape for good the malice of the man who rang the village church bell and the unkind gossip of those who considered her son an enormity. Mensa, too, received the news with calm though he could not tell what great changes that would make to his life in future. He knew he would miss his playmates in the village. He was aware of a hopeful future but could not tell what that future entailed.

One evening when his mother was telling him to be a good boy when he went to stay with his uncle, he ventured to ask his mother some of those questions in the hope that she might be able to answer them.

'Will I get enough to eat when I go to Accra?'

'Of course, you will.'

'Are there any farms, mango trees and pawpaw trees in Accra?'

'There aren't any farms, but many of the trees we have here are there.'

'Will my uncle cane me if I break a plate? Daddy doesn't.'

'He'll look into why you've broken it before he'll decide on what to do to you. Everybody is not like your daddy.'

'Suppose he gets angry and doesn't ask questions and canes me?'

'I'm sure he won't do that. I know you are such a good boy and you won't be breaking plates, anyway, will you?'

'No, of course, I won't; but I'll run back home if I get badly caned!'

'That won't do you any good. Your daddy won't be happy if you run back home. You see, your uncle is going to make a gentleman of you. He'll make you become a great man in future if you behave and do as he tells you.'

'Is he a great man himself?'

'In his own way, yes. He's a headteacher and well respected.'

'But they say in this country only doctors, lawyers and ministers who preach are the great men.'

'I've heard about it but I don't understand it. In my opinion anybody whether a farmer or a carpenter who keeps out of mischief, helps his town or village not for his personal glory but for the good of all, is a great man.'

'Would you want me to be a farmer or a carpenter?'

'I want you to do well at school first, then the rest will follow.'

'I thought you said some time ago that you wanted me to be a doctor so that I could look after you and daddy when you are old?'

'That's what I'd have you be, but I'm not sure. It all depends on how well you do at school!'

'But suppose I want to be a lorry driver, would you like it?'

'Why?'

'Because I admire Mr Ako, our village driver. His lorry is nice and he tells the quarrelsome women to shut up when they shriek in his lorry.'

'I know; but Mr Ako has no respect for people who are older than himself. His words are vulgar and he lives from hand to mouth!'

'What do you mean by he lives from hand to mouth?'

'Our drivers, you see, spend too much money on unnecessary things. They have mistresses in every town where there's a lorry station. They don't save and easily get short of money. They are, in fact, mostly poor.'

'Who are mistresses?'

'Mistresses are the women they keep for fun. They don't intend to live with them like the way I live with your daddy.'

'Mamma!'

'Yes.'

'Is daddy rich?'

'Daddy is not rich because of his job; but he's never in debt and we are all happy. Don't you see that yourself?'

'Mamma, can I tell you one thing?'

'You can, my dear.'

'I don't want to go to Accra. I don't like teachers. I hear my uncle is a teacher.'

'Why don't you like them?'

'They only whip boys. When boys work for them they don't give them anything. Those who go to school in this village have told us. When we went and worked for Odoi's father, he gave us a penny each for the Sunday collection at church. You see, the catechist, Mr Yemo, always asks my friends to go and work on his farm and never gives them anything. But when it rains and they don't have any clothes to wear to church, he canes them mercilessly because they've failed to go to church. I don't like him because he is wicked!'

'Don't use such dreadful words! The catechist is a good man. He wishes your friends well.'

'Does one wish people well by whipping them?'

'Yes, if they are naughty!'

Old Anang joined them, lit his pipe and was silent for some time. Everyone was silent; then he broke it.

'I have some information to give.'

'Tell us what it is,' said his wife eagerly.

'My cousin mentioned in his letter that he would be paying us a short visit tomorrow.'

'That's splendid!' said Old Anang's wife.

'Mensa, won't you be glad to have him here?' Old Anang asked his son.

'I will!' the boy answered. He knew that was what his father would like to hear.

Mr Lomo arrived at the village at dusk the following day. By local standards, he was well dressed and distinguished. Though his shoes were slightly cracked here and there, it appeared they were accustomed to good polishing. His dress sat on him like a man who would not look awkward in Ghanaian cloth. He spent some time with the local catechist whom he went to see before coming to Old Anang's house. Such was the strength of the professional bond that held those teachers together. When he came to the house, he was in high spirits not because he was drunk but because he may have tasted something which, whether it was locally distilled or decently manufactured gin, no-one could really look into as teachers were not as a rule expected to drink.

Old Anang's house had been well tidied up and a lavish meal prepared for him. After the meal Old Anang engaged him in a lively conversation. He enjoyed talking to Old Anang who, he thought, could speak better sense than many educated men he knew. As they were talking, Mensa passed by. He was completely naked and had his clothes bundled under his armpit. He was going to take his cloth for bed and did not see why he should wear again the clothes he had worn all day long. That was what he used to do. When he got to where his father and his teacher-uncle were sitting, he turned to his father and said airily:

'Daddy, I feel so refreshed. I've had a cold-water bath and it's so nice!'

'Very good,' his father responded with love, 'now go and get your cloth and go to bed.'

But suddenly his teacher seized him by one arm and spanked his bare buttocks with the other, growling: 'Children don't walk naked before their elders! Get out and dress up properly before you come in here, will you!'

Old Anang was ashamed and embarrassed. But his son was furious. He turned on his uncle and cried: 'Who are you at all? I'm in my own house and you come here to beat me. It's just foolish!'

He ran away immediately.

Mr Lomo's indignation knew no bounds. He turned to his cousin and said in measured tones: 'I don't think you've done anything whatever to train your children. I've never had a child of his size insult me before. This boy is a challenge to me. I'm going to take him over and see what I can make of him!'

Just before Christmas, Mensa was despatched to Accra. He was entrusted to the village driver, Mr Ako, whom he admired and who treated him kindly while he was taking him to Accra. As Mr Lomo did not live in Accra itself but lived in the suburb, it took some hours before the boy was finally handed over to his would-be mentor.

Mensa was quiet during the trip. He never asked questions and when the women on the lorry asked him inquisitively what he was going to do in Accra, he gave the short answer that he was going to stay with his teacher-uncle. The women liked the idea. They wished their children could have the chance and advised him to be a good boy in Accra and uphold the good name of their village. One or two gave him a few pence to keep in his little savings wood-box. The driver bought him a fat loaf of bread when they got to a big, sprawling, dirty, noisy, jostling, crowded and complex market in Accra.

As soon as the lorry arrived, several Zabrama headporters with shaven heads, wearing khaki shorts and smocks, raced after the lorry each pointing at the load he would carry. Mensa was surprised at the abusive language virtually everybody used on the good-humoured headporters. He was also surprised at the headporters' proficiency in the use of the local language. In thirty minutes' time, all the words his mother had taught him never to use either in private or in public because they were vulgar, had been freely and uninhibitedly used. They were bandied to and fro with relish and everybody was gay because they had been used.

One incident interested him most. As the headporters were unloading the baskets of tomatoes and sacks of cassava from Mr Ako's lorry, another lorry arrived. It had on it about fifteen passengers, men and women, who began to climb down as soon as the lorry stopped. Once more, the omnipresent Zabrama headporters appeared indicating and picking their headloads. One of them picked on a suitcase belonging to a male passenger in cloth. It was clear the man did not need the services of a headporter and he did his best to tell the headporter that he did not want his services and to leave his suitcase alone.

'Why should I leave it alone?' asked the headporter, rather disappointed and in a tone that indicated that he had not had any training in how best to address people when frustrated.

'You just leave it alone and go away!' replied the man, also in a tone that showed that he had no respect for the headporter.

This the headporter sensed so he said: 'You can ask me to leave it alone but you shouldn't tell me to go away, you stupid bushman!'

The man's lower jaw dropped, his eyes bulged out of their sockets and his cloth hung limp over his shoulder. It was a serious matter; for he could not understand why the headporter should describe him as a stupid bushman. Nobody ever respected those headporters and the qualities that recommended them were no more than their bad manners, dirty clothes and skin, and their general backwardness. How did it come about that one of them should dare call him such a name? But he did not know one thing. Those headporters, no matter what the society in which they lived thought of them, usually and goodhumouredly applied the very epithets of scorn which were poured upon them to the very people who did that, and watched the dramatic effect it had on them with delight. In this particular case, the headporter was so pleased with the effect of the epithet on the man that he was grinning broadly ready, meanwhile, to see what the man would say or do next because everybody around was delighted and interested. True, the man would have gone away but he felt that would be interpreted as an admission of defeat inflicted by a lowly headporter; so he asked:

'Have you washed this morning?'

'I haven't,' replied the headporter, more amused than ever and emboldened by the apparent aivety of the man, 'but I have one question to ask you in turn. Are you circumcised?' The lorry drivers laughed their belly-full, the market women yelled with glee, clapping their hands and indulging in their own obscene interpretations of the question. It was impossible for the man to be angry; he was not merely surprised or shocked; he was sad; for the headporter had asked a sore question. The fact was that he hailed from that part of Ghana where circumcision was not compulsory and he in particular had been spared the trouble. Normally all the people who were natives of the city had been circumcised and for some reason or other, found sport in teasing those who had not been circumcised. It was therefore necessary not to let anyone know how one stood in the matter when one was in Accra. Now that nuisance of a headporter was determined to disgrace him in such a crowded place for no other reason than the simple one that he would not let him carry his suitcase for a small fee of threepence. He racked his brain and thought of a question that could enable him to get his own back. He asked: 'How many of you sleep in one room, you dirty mouse, twenty or thirty?'

Unfortunately, nobody was interested in his question. Everybody was looking forward to what answer the head-porter would give.

He did that by way of a question: 'Why do you ask about twenty or thirty? Eighty of us sleep in one room and my dear, darling girl who loves the room, is from your bush area. She has refused to go back home. She enjoys the way I manage her. I won't be surprised if she's your real sister whom you've come to look for! I'll do what I can for her for the last time tonight so that you take her home tomorrow!'

The man was now shaking with anger because everybody was enjoying every syllable of the headporter's words. He thought of punching him but he realized there were three serious impediments. He was in cloth and he would have to remove it before he could feel free to engage in any scuffle. He had six hundred pounds in the briefcase which he held in his right hand. He was going to use the money as a deposit to take delivery of a one-and-a-half-ton lorry which he was going to buy on hire-purchase. If he put the briefcase down and fought, anything could happen to his treasure. Finally, those headporters were communal. As soon as one of them engaged in a fight, the whole lot of them would not only give moral support but would give physical aid if they thought their brother was taking a beating.

He said nothing therefore and strictly speaking did nothing. In grief, he adjusted his cloth over his shoulder, paid the driver who brought him to Accra his fare, held his suitcase and briefcase firmly, and left the place. One of the market women asked him whether he was not tough enough to box the ears of the filthy headporter. He shook his head to indicate that he was not keen. He never uttered a word; he simply walked away scowling while the bunch of headporters on the spot hooted at him and shouted that he was a coward. This was what they liked and would have done to everybody especially the market women; but it happened that they were no match for those women who could insult them in the most imaginative obscene language. The women could also fight if it came to it, and had a way of getting hold of, and torturing the most painful, sacred and vital parts of the headporters' physiology. Whenever they realized they were going to be beaten, the headporters as a rule shunned a fight with them. As might be expected, then, whenever the headporters tried and found themselves out-matched verbally by the market women, they stopped and went about their business diligently.

Chapter Six

What Mensa saw and heard at the Accra market made a deep impression on him, but he however had little time to ponder it as there were so many things to look at as the lorry drove awkwardly through the city. He tried to register every detail, no matter how minute.

The lorry finally stopped in front of the house of Mr Lomo. He could not, at first sight, believe that his uncle stayed in such a house. The building looked the same as many of those in his village. Though many of the buildings in the area were quite modern and were built of cement blocks, this one was undeniably built of swish and stone. The corrugated-iron roofing was brown with age and rust, the wood rotting and the entire structure looked incongruous and tired of human habitation. If there were buildings like this in Accra, why did people consider Accra exceptional, he asked himself in disappointment.

As soon as the lorry came to a halt, four young boys rushed out of the house to see who had arrived. Immediately they saw that it was only another little boy, their interest promptly shifted to what would be unloaded. Apart from his small tin trunk in which he kept a few clothes, Mensa had brought along several tubes of yam and cassava, plantain, banana, a bundle of firewood, pawpaw, mangoes, and fat balls of kenkey. The four boys started carting the edibles only to the house without being told and Mensa who knew little of human motives thought they were disciplined and serviceable. The driver who because of his profession and age was better equipped to read into the motives behind this unsolicited help, was amused and apprehensive.

Soon, as he had expected, a quarrel arose over who should carry the ripe banana to the house. The driver thought he should intervene but before he could do so, two of the boys were already rolling on the ground in a desperate fight. One of them had not properly fastened on his tiny, leather waist-belt. His shorts broke loose from it in the mêlée so that while he had to pull up his shorts to cover his nakedness of that unseemly part of his body with one hand, he had to dislodge the boy who sat astride his chest with the other. He accomplished neither and in sheer fighting fever started kicking the air. It was not the air he wanted to kick, in fact; he wanted to kick the backside of the boy who sat astride his chest. Meanwhile one of the non-fighting boys had run into the house to report that a domestic riot had broken out. While he was reporting, the fourth boy had vanished completely from the scene with two mangoes, one banana and a half-crushed pawpaw to devour in peace behind the thorn hedge that served as the wall of the house.

The driver separated those who were fighting; in other words, he lifted the one who sat astride the chest of the one who lay helpless and half-naked on the ground. He asked the two panting boys whether they had had no breakfast that morning. One replied that they had eaten something but he felt his stomach was empty. The other, who was adjusting his shorts and breathing with difficulty, said that he had not had any breakfast at all; he was sent to buy the morning's newspapers and, while he was away, the other three boys cheated and ate his share of the food.

He had hardly finished talking and had not had the time to wipe the sand from his hair when Mr Lomo suddenly emerged from the gate of the house.

'Who were fighting?' he asked in a loud voice that completely frightened the boys and nearly frightened the driver.

'Badu and Antwi!' the informant boy quickly pointed out.

'Who started the fight?' Mr Lomo asked expertly. He knew exactly which question to ask whenever boys got on the wrong side of rule and order.

As might be expected, Badu said it was Antwi and Antwi said that it was Badu. Both were now panting heavily out of exhaustion and fear.

'Each of you will get four lashes for fighting at all!' said Mr Lomo grimly.

Mr Ako, the driver, out of human compassion pleaded that for his sake the boys should be spared. Mr Lomo gave him a ridiculing smile and told him firmly that he was essentially a lorry driver and should not go about pleading for boys under special training. He substantiated his stand by saying that those boys were always either doing mischief or on the verge of it. The surest and only effective method known to him to cure them was to whip them severely and promptly as soon as they gave trouble. The driver, however, was unimpressed but did not say so, for he knew it would be pointless to express his opinion. Still he wished he could tell Mr Lomo that the boys had told him that they had not been well fed that morning and that was why they were exceptionally excited at the sight of the fruit; but he realized that if he said it, it would probably complicate matters for the unlucky boys so he held his peace. When Mr Lomo left the place, he gave each of the dispirited boys threepence. The boys received the gift with mixed feelings because of the punishment that loomed ahead.

Mensa watched how those boys scrambled for the fruit and was sorry for them. On the other hand, he enjoyed the way the two boys fought and was quite convinced that he could give the two of them combined a sound beating in any free fight. He had heard stories of how boys in Accra excelled in fighting because of the cinema but the demonstration that took place under his nose was so appalling that he dismissed any preconceptions. He thought the boys could never throw effective well-directed punches. To him, they didn't fight; they wrestled.

Indeed, the confidence he had lost while coming to Accra was restored the very moment he was at Mr Lomo's house. First, there was the house which did not look any different from what he had seen before; second, there were those four boys whom he could bully at will. After all, they had fought because of the fruit he brought and their strength was negligible. If he had missed Odoi, Klu, Otto, Okle and Darku, he was, as fate would have it, in another manageable company.

He followed the boys to the house. The one who ran away with the two mangoes, one banana and the half-crushed ripe pawpaw which he ate behind the thorn hedge, was back; his lips were carefully wiped and he was looking as innocent as ever. The other boy who had reported the fight was as happy as a young goat because of the ordeal which awaited his unfortunate friends.

Though all the boys did not know who Mensa was, they were nevertheless happy he had come because apart from other remote considerations, he had brought food in great abundance. Consequently each one of them was very nice to him and made sure he became his best friend at once. They asked him where he had come from and when he told them, every one of them lied that he had heard of the place before and that the place was famous for the many different kinds of fruit that could be had there. They therefore expressed the hope that since he had already eaten so much fruit because of his long association with the place, he would surrender his share of the fruit that he had brought to the house to them.

Now while the boys were engaged in flattering and generally befriending Mensa, two of Mr Lomo's children were studying him from the distance. They had already taken possession of some of the fruit and nobody told them they should not do that. They were better clothed and looked more intelligent and contented. But Mensa took an immediate dislike to them because he vaguely felt they looked proud and snobbish. He never liked to acknowledge that another boy was better than he.

He was engrossed in studying them and thinking about them when Mrs Lomo came out of the kitchen. Though Mensa had never seen her before, he knew she must be the mistress of the house because of her bearing and her somewhat close resemblance to Mr Lomo. He thought it would be proper to give her a smile, so he did so. She returned the smile and asked him if he was well and whether he was happy to be in Accra. Mensa said yes to both questions. She then asked him about the health of his father and mother and about all the other members of his family. Mensa replied they were all in good health and thanked her.

After the civilities, Mensa told her that when he was leaving the village his mother instructed him as to how the various kinds of fruit and food should be distributed and to whom they should go. He would therefore implore her to stop those boys (meaning her children) from either stealing or picking some of them to eat. What immediately struck Mrs Lomo was the articulateness of Mensa. She had all the time believed that boys from the rural areas were bashful and tongue-tied whenever they came to the city. This one was different and she wondered what manner of boy he was. In any case, this being her first encounter with him, she tried to be as affable and as condescending as possible. And to evade Mensa's request as tactfully as she could, she told him that she would look into what he had complained of later and that in the meantime she would provide him with something to eat as he must be hungry.

That something to eat was to her some kind of heavy food. To her knowledge and belief, a boy from a village considered bread and tea either a rarity or at least a delicacy which could never pass for an ordinary sustaining breakfast. Despite what she thought on the matter, she was in practice not accustomed to giving those children who had come under her protection and guidance, tea and bread and butter in the morning. It happened that on that day, whatever heavy food there was in the house for breakfast, had already been gobbled down by those four perpetually hungry boys.

To give Mensa some of the food he had brought would be improper for obvious reasons. It would detract from her prestige which she was anxious to build. In order that Mensa should realize that he had arrived at a superior place, she decided to give him some tea. Mensa was therefore served with tea, not in china or in an earthen-ware teacup but in a big aluminium bowl. Only two lumps of sugar were put into the sea of tea and just a few drops of grudging milk were put into it to make it look like mudwater. The transparent, quarter-inch thick slice of bread provided had no butter on it. The bowl of tea was placed on the floor; the slice of bread tucked into his hand; a low kitchen-stool placed near the bowl and he was invited with pleasure to enjoy himself.

Mensa lifted the bowl from the floor and tasted the tea. He was disappointed. The tea tasted like boiled herbs seasoned with smoke.

'Please, madam,' he called out.

'Yes, Mensa!' Mrs Lomo responded. 'But don't call me madam, call me Aunt Adzoa.'

'Aunt Adzoa, I'm afraid your tea is no good!' Mensa bluntly told her. Here was Aunt Adzoa who had made a big effort and here was Mensa who had dismissed that effort with one little sentence. Aunt Adzoa was naturally displeased but she suppressed any outward sign of it and asked politely: 'What's wrong with it?'

'There's hardly any sugar in it. The bread is also too thin and has no butter on it.'

'Do you have tea, bread and butter at your village for

breakfast?' she said, having thought she could silence the boy with the question.

'Of course, I do. I sometimes have Ovaltine, bread and cheese. Whenever Mr Ako, the driver, is coming to Accra, my father gives him money to buy these things for us.'

The other boys who at first envied Mensa his breakfast but now found that Mensa was talking up to Aunt Adzoa were pleased but did not believe his Ovaltine story, so they cleared their throats noisily and said among themselves that Mensa was lying. Mrs Lomo heard them and shrieked at them in exasperation to keep quiet.

'If you do have such a decent breakfast at home,' said Mrs Lomo without the tact she had previously displayed, 'why have you chosen to come here?'

'I didn't choose to come here. It was my father who asked me to come!'

'Do you want to argue with me?'

'Of course not. You asked me a question and I gave you an answer.'

'Are you a spoilt child?'

'I'm not a spoilt child. I don't steal fruit like your children do.'

Mensa, it was clear, was unconventional. He did not talk like a mission-school-trained child. A mission-school-trained child must hesitate and, if necessary, beg for forgiveness whenever his elders were angry with him. No matter whether he was right or had a good excuse to give, once his elders, whether rightly or wrongly, thought he was wrong and were displeased with him, he must cower in tears and plead that he would never do anything wrong again. He must start every sentence with 'please' whether or not the word was idiomatically or contextually appropriate. He must not look an elderly personage straight in the face and tell him no, if that were the truth. The truth was what his elders wanted to hear and he must say it in abject self-abasement. No doubt there were many grownups who had been so trained in this way, who said yes, when they should say no. Men who tried to please anybody in authority and inevitably carried through life a personality which was colourless, futile, spineless, timeserving and oft-times dangerous.

Mrs Lomo, as might be expected, was nearly hysterical; she was neither crying nor talking. She was babbling something and heaving sighs. She made her way into the lounge where her husband was sitting reading the morning newspapers and waiting for Mensa to finish his breakfast, so that he could have enough time to give him some brainwashing induction talk, on how he should behave in the house. He was also waiting to mete out punishment to the two boys who had fought before Mensa so that Mensa could see for himself that he was capable of backing his words with action. This would put Mensa on a good footing right from the beginning; God having provided him with the right setting. He did not in the least like how his wife looked when she entered the lounge. He asked:

'What's the trouble?'

'I told you we shouldn't have that boy!' she shouted at him hysterically.

'No! No! No!' Mr Lomo protested. 'Don't talk like that!'

'Don't talk like that, you say, but he's already used insulting language against me!'

'Insulting words? Good heavens! That's impossible! What did he say?'

'Do you want to suggest I don't know when I've been insulted?'

'By no means, but it's difficult to believe the boy could have insulted you so soon. What happened?'

Mrs Lomo was at a loss as to how to reorganize Mensa's words to constitute a grave insult that her husband would believe. She nevertheless succeeded in concocting something.

'He says I'm a lazy housewife!'

Mr Lomo was at once reassured and amused because what she said could not be true. And yet his wife was shrill, strident and insistent. He realized, however, that if he dismissed this as frivolous it would mean that he was going to take sides with the boy, and this he would not do. Not that he had much conscience in being unfair to the boys, he was used to doing whatever was necessary to keep his household going.

He called Antwi, Badu, Mensa and the two other boys to come and see him at once. His own children, who were almost always free from parental interference and punishment, divined, from experience, that there was something afoot. So they trooped into the lounge to watch whatever was going on. When the boys entered the room and Mrs Lomo saw Mensa she left the room saying as she went out: 'Justice must be done.' Mr Lomo was sitting on a sofa, looking very grave. His gravity was faked but it worked on the boys. Antwi and Badu were naturally tearful because of the fight. They had been caned the previous day and were going to be caned again. Mr Lomo had become a bogy before whom they trembled.

'Danso and Dua,' Mr Lomo called the other two boys 'I want you to help me judge these boys and say where they went wrong.'

Danso and Dua were in no way jurors at all. It was the practice in the house that whenever some of the boys were in trouble, the rest of the boys who happened to be innocent were called upon to help judge those who were thought to have committed the domestic crime. Very often, the jurors ended up by being caned themselves if they showed the slightest sign of trying to discharge the accused because of insufficient evidence or because of conflicting evidence or because of doubt. An eager attempt to discharge the accused meant that they themselves might have taken part in the commission of the crime at a certain stage, or that they were blindly trying to condone and connive at what, to Mr Lomo, was obviously wrong. It must, however, be said in fairness to Mr Lomo that quite often those boys who happened to constitute the jury had the natural itch to acquit the accused because crime in the house was committed in rotation so that a boy who happened to be a juror one day could quite easily be the accused the next.

Yet in directing the jury on the merits of a case, Mr Lomo did his best by facial expression, intonation and stress of certain points to impress upon the jury that the accused, they should note, had to be found guilty. All the boys had therefore learnt the hard way that once there was a trial, there would be caning and it was the business of some of them to hasten the process and not impede it. They could only attempt to impede it at their own risk. The trials were always staged, then, to instil fear into all the boys, to inculcate into them a sense of justice and righteousness and to make them realize that if they erred they could be sure of the consequences.

Danso and Dua therefore paid particular attention to every word that fell from the lips of Mr Lomo: 'I was reading this morning's newspaper when Dua came and told me that Badu and Antwi were fighting. Now Danso, I want you to ask Badu and Antwi what the rule is regarding fights in this house.'

Danso passed on the information to Antwi and Badu and there was silence for a minute. Each boy was trying to remember the exact wording of the rule. Antwi started but could not continue so Badu quickly took it up to make Antwi realize that sitting astride people's chests was one thing and a reliable memory that could be called into service at a critical moment was another. He recited: 'All fights, even if in defence, are prohibited in this house. Whenever a boy is provoked, it is his duty to report the provoker either to Master or to Aunt Adzoa who will deal with him.'

'Now, Badu and Antwi, were you aware of this rule when you fought?' Mr Lomo asked.

'Sir,' Badu started his defence, 'when Antwi knocked me on the nose, I didn't know why, but I also knocked him on the mouth before I remembered the rule; so I didn't want to fight and wanted to go away but something must have gone wrong because all I knew was that I had been thrown on the ground and stripped. I could not get away from Antwi without throwing a punch or two at his stomach. I thought if my punches hurt him he would stop the fight; but it appeared they did not, so I thought of giving him two or three kicks in the back but these too only hit the air. It was when I had about finished kicking that, I think, you came and saw us. It was never my intention to fight, sir.'

'Very good. But the fact is that you fought. Tell me: where was your self-control when Antwi first hit you?' asked Mr Lomo.

'As I've said before, sir,' the boy answered, 'I had thrown the punch before I remembered the rule. I don't know why I forgot the rule, sir. I beg your pardon, sir. I won't do it again, sir.'

'Dua and Danso, is Badu guilty or not guilty?'

'Guilty, sir,' both boys said in unison.

'Now that we've finished with Badu, we'd like to hear Antwi,' said Mr Lomo.

'Sir, my case is simple,' Antwi began.

'How do you know it's simple?' interrupted Mr Lomo.

The boy ignored Mr Lomo's question and continued with what he had to say.

'This morning when I went to buy your newspapers for you, Badu, Danso and Dua ate my food. When I returned I had nothing to eat. I didn't come to report it to you immediately. I wanted to make sure, so I asked Aunt Adzoa whether the food was meant for all four of us. Just then, this boy arrived in that lorry and we all rushed out to welcome him. I went to help with the unloading of the luggage. I chose the bananas. While I was trying to adjust them properly in my arms, Badu came along and said he would help me carry them but I refused. He therefore tucked his right forefinger under my armpit and tickled me. I felt like laughing and contorted my body so the bananas dropped down. I was angry when I saw that some of the bananas had been crushed and others made dirty. I pushed him to go away but didn't intend to knock him on the nose. I think he must have got angry because he suddenly punched me on the mouth. I was badly hurt, sir, and in trying to stop him from hitting me again, I tripped him but unfortunately both of us fell on the ground. It was never my intention to fight, sir. I wanted to keep him on the ground so that if he got tired I could leave him without further trouble and report him to you, sir.'

'I don't think I can believe your story, Antwi. By the way, Danso and Dua, is he guilty or not guilty?'

'Guilty, sir!' both boys said with alacrity.

It was not for nothing Danso and Dua said 'Guilty, sir' with alacrity. They were badly scared because Antwi had said that while he was away to buy the newspapers they had eaten his share of the breakfast. There could be trouble for them too if Antwi's complaint was looked into, and so by shouting 'Guilty, sir,' with speed and emphasis they were sure Mr Lomo would overlook this. True, Mr Lomo was so intent on finding Badu and Antwi guilty that he forgot entirely about the jurors' crime.

He cleared his throat and said: 'Badu and Antwi, you've been given a fair trial. If I cane you without going into why you fought, you will probably tell your parents when they come to visit you that I have been caning you all the time as if I was either mad or foolish. Right now, you've been found guilty by your own friends and I cannot but agree with them. You should get ready for six lashes each! But before I whip you, I dare say it is possible you'll get another fellow to share your sorrows with you. I mean your new friend who has just arrived!'

Mensa thought it was a joke. The other boys were shocked and dismayed. They could not see why Mensa should be punished so soon. To them, Mensa was a source of so much to eat. They liked him. They felt no pain should be inflicted on him.

'Well, I know you're surprised to hear what I've just said. But it happens that I've known Mensa for some time and he's as bad as each and every one of you!'

Mensa was so angry and upset that he said involuntarily: 'This man is funny! He's only seen me once and he's so cruel to me! Now he says I'm a bad boy. How did he know?'

The boys feigned great indignation and cried: 'Hei! Hei! Hei! Stop, will you? We don't talk like that here!'

Mr Lomo would have boxed Mensa's ears mercilessly as soon as he spoke, but he felt he should control himself lest he would confirm Mensa's charge that he was cruel. What he did, then, was to ask the other boys in the light of what Mensa had said whether Mensa was guilty or not guilty. There was a thunderous response of guilty which was followed by giggling and titters more directed at Mr Lomo's disgrace than at anything else.

While these things were in progress Mrs Lomo was hiding behind a door within earshot. She heard Mensa utter those damaging words and was very pleased because she had been vindicated. As soon as the boys declared Mensa guilty, she burst forth from behind the door and asked her husband pointedly whether he needed any proof to substantiate her complaint that Mensa had called her a lazy woman. Mr Lomo said she was quite right but Mensa in a sudden surge of boldness said she was another liar. At this stage, Mr Lomo was so cross that he slapped Mensa in the face, then boxed his ears with both hands and then kicked him out of the room. He then turned to the other boys and ordered them to leave the lounge at once, adding that he was so much beside himself that if any of them stood there in that room, he would murder him!

When the boys had left the room, his wife wanted to say a few words to cool him down, but he was so upset that he left the room for the school office; but before leaving the house, he was forced to tell his wife out of propriety and habit that he had some business to attend to. Mrs Lomo was not happy. She did not like the way the whole affair ended. What she wanted her husband to do was to punish Mensa, but now it was apparent her husband was downcast; exactly why she could not tell.

As Mr Lomo sat in his office, one thought exercised his mind. Why would Mensa speak the way he did? Was it because he was an incorrigibly bad boy or was it how he naturally spoke? He brooded over the last question for some time and suddenly an idea occurred to him. He wanted to find out for himself whether that was the real problem. He came to the house and asked Mensa to come along with him to the office. He was pleasant and affable. He asked Mensa to sit down on a wooden bench placed against the wall. Normally boys never sat down when they were in his office. They always stood erect in military fashion, their hands behind them, the feet placed astride; neither at ease nor attention; they stood on the alert and in obeisance.

He smiled and asked Mensa: 'Why did you hurt that goat in the village. Didn't you know it was a bad thing to do?'

'No, I didn't know. That goat was a nuisance. All the boys in the village hated it. It ate my food. It fought the other he-goats and worried the nanny-goats. My father had told me that if a goat was troublesome and it was castrated, it sobered down. Moreover, it would grow fat and the flesh tasted excellent when served.'

'Thank you,' said Mr Lomo with a smile, 'you can go back to the house.'

'Is that all you want to hear from me?' Mensa asked him without any fear or inhibition.

'Yes, that's all,' his uncle replied, still polite and cheerful looking.

But Mensa had more to say: 'My father asked me to tell you that he's well. He gave this two pounds to me to be given to you. He says he'll send some more at the end of next month. He says the big yam is for you and the small ones are for the children in the house. While I was coming the women on the lorry gave me some money. Here it is. Can I keep it in my wood-box savings bank? I want to show it to you before I save it.'

'Oh, yes; you can do that; you can save it in the wood-box. But won't you like to keep some for yourself and buy some candy with it?'

'No, sir. My mother doesn't like that. We always keep such monies in our savings wood-box, then when it is Christmas time, it's checked and we get fine clothes bought with it. I'm told there are fine clothes in Accra. Will you buy some for me?'

'Of course, I will.'

Mensa rose and left the office.

The idea which dawned on Mr Lomo had now been proved right. The boy was ingenuous and spoke freely like an uneducated boy from an uneducated village. He had nothing to hide or fear. He saw everything in either black or white; and would give vent to what he thought was true without a second thought. This was perhaps good, Mr Lomo vaguely felt, but all the same it could not be countenanced. It was a sign of simplicity, naïvety and total backwardness. If allowed to flourish, it would give a lot of trouble to a civilized society. No good educational system, he was sure, would tolerate it. A good educational system should, no doubt, make a boy as docile as possible. It should make a boy a good diplomatist who would say he was not aware of something, not because he was not really aware of it, but because he could not be proved to be aware of it; he must be the kind of boy who should specialize in manufacturing white lies as a means of profiting from life. For example, the defence put up by Badu and Antwi was preferable to any blunt statement of fact that they fought over the bananas. Such truthfulness was anathema. It fetched punishment. It was illiterate to speak the truth and be punished. The good life demanded lying. It had been so, it should be so and it must remain so. Who could go through life successfully without it? Abstruse philosophy is woven by great men to support it, not in all circumstances, but in some circumstances. Mensa could, when he had the mind to, say why he had done the wrong thing, even if saying so would incriminate him. The four Accra boys would do the wrong thing and say that it was never their intention to do it and that something beyond their control must have compelled them. To Mr Lomo, those four boys, no matter how black their lying was, were using the right language. It showed that they were responding successfully to correction; they were becoming trained and disciplined; they had discretion. Mensa's natural honesty was not to be tolerated; it was not to be fostered; he needed training to get rid of it otherwise, in future, he would embarrass organized society and organized society must survive not on occasional honesty but on endemic subtle lying.

Thus having diagnosed Mensa's essential weakness, he became confident that he could train him to become a Christian gentleman who would, in future, be a shining testimony to his dedication to moulding children into responsible adult citizens of his beloved country.

When he returned from the office at noon, he called Mensa and asked him whether he had been well fed. The boy told him that the food should have been enough for them but certain strange things happened. First, the food was rushed upon by his friends who bowled large morsels into their mouths and scarcely chewed them up before swallowing them. Second, before they started eating, Antwi meticulously removed all the meat from the stew and placed it aside saying that it would be shared out not on the basis of complete equality, but in accordance with seniority, which was reasonable because the seniors in the house did more work than the juniors and they needed more meat to keep them fit. Yet when they finished eating, there was a great deal of argument about the size and delicacy of each piece of meat. The argument was in progress when, in a flash, there was general looting and all the meat vanished from the plate, each boy making away with what he could get to go and eat in perfect tranquillity behind the thorn hedge. When he protested to Antwi, Antwi told him with a mouthful that the whole thing was a ritual and that he would get used to it in due course. In the meantime, he should go and collect the two empty plates and wash them up. He should make sure he got a share of the meat next time.

Third, when he took the plates to go and wash them, he saw Mr Lomo's children eating decently at their specially laid table. Each of them had his own plate to eat from and enough food to himself. That was how he took his meal when he was at the village. Since he had had no meat he asked the children to give him some of their meat but they told him to go away and wash the plates. They threatened to report him to their father if he played the fool.

Mr Lomo listened patiently to Mensa in despair but not in defeat. He told him: 'Whenever I call you and you come before me, stand upright with your hands behind you! If I ask you questions, give short answers. Say "Yes, sir" or "No, sir" according to what answer you have to give. I don't want long-winded stories. If there's any misunderstanding between you and your friends, report it to me directly in two or three sentences. If there's any trouble between you and my children, tell Aunt Adzoa about it. However, I would like to warn you that she doesn't take much nonsense; so before you go and report her own children to her, you must satisfy yourself that your complaint is unquestionable otherwise you'll get into trouble. I must make it plain to you that a lot of activities of boys in this house are childish. I'm a busy man. I don't want you to come and tell me every silly thing that happens between you and them. You can only report any of them to me if he breaks a rule of the house. Here are the cardinal rules in addition to the one on fighting which was recited ably by Badu: first, no boy shall steal in this house or take anything into his possession or for his own use without first asking Aunt Adzoa or myself.'

'Suppose what he takes is his and not yours. After all we're all in the same house?' asked Mensa, not particularly impressed by the first rule which Mr Lomo thought sufficiently water-tight.

'Fool!' roared Mr Lomo. 'Ask no questions while I'm talking. I can see you're determined to make firm friends with the cane!'

Mensa kept quiet. Mr Lomo sat down. It was on a fairly dirty veranda that overlooked the fairly dirty compound of his quarters. Mensa drew near him and he droned on: 'The second rule in this house is that every boy shall wash twice a day: once in the morning and again in the early evening. A hot-bath is generally not allowed. It wastes fuel and may only be had during sickness. Moreover, no boy shall have his hair cut or trim his nails or iron his clothes on Sunday. By the way, this rule is fully supported by the church so it requires special attention. Third, every boy in this house shall go to church on Sunday, rain or shine, and, after the church service, be able to give a reliable summary of the sermon if called upon to do so. Fourth, when a boy in this house is sent on an errand, he must run and never stop on the way either to chat with other boys or take part in a soccer game no matter how tempting that may be. Fifth, none of you has the right to report to anyone whether it be his parents or just anybody at all that he's not being properly fed in this house. Three offences are committed at once if this rule is broken: subdivision one—such a boy, if he does that, has shown gross ingratitude which is against the teaching of our Lord; subdivision two, he's learning to tell-tale which cannot be tolerated in this house; and subdivision three, he's finding an excuse to go begging which can be a sure sign of his future degradation. Sixth, no boy is expected to shout in this house or make an unwarranted noise. Seventh, whenever a boy is wronged, he must report the wrong-doer; he has no right to take action himself. This is a key rule because it's the easiest to break. Eighth, no boy has the right to attempt to argue either with Aunt Adzoa or with myself. Both of us know what is good for all of you and what we say is final. Ninth, no boy shall neglect any domestic chores assigned to him. Only one thing can cause this rule to be broken: laziness! Finally, every boy in this house must, at all times, show both by word and deed that he appreciates what Aunt Adzoa and myself are doing for him. If he doesn't, he'll lose favour with us. I'm sure you understand the eleven rules, don't you? I hope you'll do your best to abide by them!

'But uncle,' said Mensa.

'No! Call me master!' Mr Lomo cut him short.

'But master, how can I remember all these rules?' Mensa asked with some frustration.

'Aha! There you are!' cried Mr Lomo. 'You've already broken the eighth rule. You want to argue. You want to argue, don't you? I've finished with you. All you have to say is "Yes, sir" and go away. Go away at once!'

'Yes, sir,' Mensa obeyed and retreated from his presence.

Chapter Seven

After the Christmas holidays, Mensa started going to school. He was one of the biggest boys in his class. In all, there were about six big boys in a class of forty-five. The big boys were either older or physically more developed than the other boys were. He was very happy indeed at the beginning of his first day at school and he had every reason to be: he was in his sacred, new khaki uniform.

His full name had been entered in the school register and he felt important when the class teacher mentioned it during roll-call in a martial voice. He watched the teacher closely to see whether he was an ordinary mortal or a special breed of man reserved only for schools. Already the personality of the teacher had profoundly impressed him and curiosity forced him to know why. The teacher was undoubtedly an old man probably between sixty and sixty-five. He had a spare body and was of medium height, his face long and somewhat wrinkled. His smile was kind and infectious; but his frown could make a class-one boy cower so much that if he did not screw up a little courage, his knees would buckle completely under him. Strangely enough for those days, he always came to teach in a khaki suit which, unfortunately, was a badly tailored one. It was always well-washed but never well-pressed. Whenever he arrived at the classroom, he would carefully and painfully remove his very tight-fitting coat which he hung on the back-rest of the chair behind his rickety table.

Mensa, before coming to school, had learnt that his teacher's real name was Mr Akushi but no pupil ever called him that. His popular nickname was 'I'll-twist-you.' The nickname derived from the first words uttered by him whenever he wanted to cane a boy. The words were then followed by a gymnastic exercise which justified the use of them. By way of illustration, when a boy arrived late for school, 'I'll-twist-you' would say: 'Haa! Hum! Hei! Yes! Haa! Hum! Hei! Yes! You're late for school, aren't you? Now where's my cane? (which a boy would dash forward to go and fetch, for boys delighted in nothing more than to see their fellow boys in mortal pain). Now get ready! I'll twist you!' He would then grab the boy by the trunk of his body, lift his entire human frame up, hook his neck under his armpit so that his face stuck out behind him, get his knee under his lower abdomen and jack the buttocks up by placing the feet under the loaded knee on the seat of his chair. In this way, the buttocks of the boy, who would be screaming under the strain of the complicated process, would be available at close quarters like a convenient plateau. He would finally whack the boy's buttocks and backside generally by giving a series of strokes in very quick succession. When he had finished larruping the boy, he would be panting distressingly because of physical exhaustion, and then mumble feebly; 'Haa, hum, yes; haa, hum, yes. I'm sure you've enjoyed the caning. You'll definitely not be late for school after this pleasantry.'

It happened, however, that though boys would be

screaming their soul out during the complex operation, as soon as 'I'll-twist-you' set them down from his extraordinary and ingenious pillory, they would begin to giggle. If 'I'll-twist-you' still had enough wind in him, he would repeat the whole process to ensure that he inflicted the necessary pain to make the urchin come to school early enough. If, on the other hand, he had not had a satisfactory breakfast and consequently was tired beyond human endurance, he would pretend he had not seen or heard the boy laugh.

It may be wondered, perhaps, why the boys laughed after going through such an unorthodox man-handling. The easy answer is that 'I'll-twist-you' was so feeble and skinny that his caning never hurt at all. Moreover, the canes he used were never vicious ones; they were little dried twigs which could not disturb the nerves in any way. On the whole, his caning punishments were more enjoyed than dreaded. If anything, it was his frowns that really scared the children to death.

Having thus taken a good look at his teacher and having heard so much already about him, Mensa was quite sure that he was going to get on capitally with this frail, old man who always walked three miles to school. It happened also that 'I'll-twist-you' was in turn eyeing him surreptitiously. Mensa caught him once in a fleeting moment and wondered why the old teacher was doing that. After all, there were many other boys in the classroom. Why did he pick on him and eye him? He thought about it for a few moments and finding no good answer to it, forgot about it entirely. There were so many things that attracted his attention.

His first morning at school was perhaps the most interesting; he was among a motley collection of children, some looking lugubrious because of the enforced separation from their dear parents, some were noisy, fidgety and given to free fights, some were quiet but busybodies and reported any misdemeanor promptly to 'I'll-twist-you' who hardly listened to them or heard them as he was busily doing registration work. The work he was doing was definitely clerical and if he allowed the slightest disturbance, there would be errors which would be bothersome to rectify. As a rule, then, whenever he was engaged on such clerical duties he hardly paid attention to the general noise, restlessness, the deep sleep of overfed boys and the occasional fist-fights that broke out in his classroom.

The school bell went for the mid-morning break which in those days was called 'recreation' and which none of the boys understood. Those boys who had lost their front teeth and were impatiently waiting for replacements did their best but managed to call it 'licreathon'. Anyway, as soon as the bell went, all the boys vanished from the classroom shouting, pushing, laughing and tripping one another. They did not stop until they got to the women who sold food to them.

Various kinds of food were being sold: rice and stew, yam and stew, fried plantain, roasted groundnuts, oranges, bananas, doughnuts and so on. Many of the boys were armed with pennies, tuppences, threepences, fourpences and even sixpences to buy any of the appetizing items displayed. It was the practice that a lot of the boys did not have breakfast before they went to school. Their parents could not manage to feed them at home early in the morning. The break therefore assured them of a pacified stomach. There were a number of children, however, who had had breakfast and were therefore given little or no money. Naturally, such children too would have liked to have a bite during the mid-morning break for the very good reason that their colleagues happened to be eating.

One academic upshot of this arrangement was that the last lesson before the mid-morning break was clearly a futile undertaking, simply because the pupils were more interested in what they were going to put into their stomachs, than in what their teachers were trying to make them get into their heads. During that lesson pupils were terribly busy, having engaged in clandestine negotiations. Those who had no money would bargain with those who had on the basis that if they bought something, no matter what, just something and they gave them some, they would manage to pilfer something from home the next day to compensate. The stolen thing could be two or three lumps of sugar or a piece of dried bread (since it kept long and un-aired in the thief's pocket) or a piece of crumbled cake that demanded turning a pocket inside out to unload it or a guava or an orange (particularly a small one that would not make a pocket bulge) or just any eatable at all that currently happened to be available in the supplicant's home when he was going to school. Such negotiations were tough, for children were more interested in immediate benefits than in future rewards. Besides, there had been disappointing cases in which the supplicants, on the following day, had either reneged on their promise or had simply been unable to bring something along because there was no suitable eatable available in the house to be stolen. For a boy to be successful therefore at the negotiations, he must use all the imagination God had endowed him with, and paint a very rosy picture of what the one who gave would have in return. He must impress upon the giver that the next day would not take long to arrive and that his big cake would be the most delicious ever eaten by man. A business of this nature automatically precluded profitable teaching and class discipline was taken care of by business pupils not by the teacher.

Another upshot was that after the mid-morning break, 'I'll-twist-you', being a wise and experienced teacher, would let his pupils do some activity, say, singing or reciting the vowels of a language. In those days nobody bothered about which language vowels were being taught. What mattered was that Mr Akushi would make the children recite seven vowels. The children loved those vowels, especially when their stomachs were full and would sing or shout them with such enthusiasm and force that it was a miracle the roof over their heads did not collapse. It was an appropriate lesson nevertheless, for if it was not carried out in this way, many of the children would sleep off the effect of the heavy food during the lesson.

Mensa was among the lot of boys who lined up in front of the women who sold food to the children. He had no money but had followed the crowd. He was surprised to find that Aunt Adzoa was among them. Unlike the other women, she had more things to sell, the notable ones being rice and stew, fried plantain, fried cocoyam and confectionery. She was watching Mensa to see if he would buy anything; she knew Mensa had no money right there. If he bought anything he would have to explain later in the house how and where he got the money. Mensa did not like the way she watched him so he had to withdraw from her sight; he was sad and disappointed; for he noticed soon afterwards that Aunt Adzoa had called her two children who had started school with him that day and had given them something to eat though all of them had had their breakfast before going to school that morning.

He went and sat down at a corner, and for the first time since he came to stay with his uncle, he wept. He felt nobody had any love for him and life was devoid of joy. Not that he fully understood his plight but he knew that those who loved and cared for him had posted him to an alien spot where human beings existed not for him but for others.

His face was still wet with tears when, turning his head, he noticed a boy he had never seen before come to sit by him. The boy was lean, very dark and extremely handsome. His features were clean-cut. He spoke softly and asked him: 'What's your name?'

'Mensa,' he replied.

'Somebody told me you were staying with our headteacher, Mr Lomo, is it true?'

'Yes it's true.'

'Why have you chosen to stay with him?' the strange boy asked with surprising assurance.

'I don't know. It was my father who asked me to come,' Mensa answered, not knowing why he said so. Then he asked the strange boy: 'What's your name?'

'Torto,' the boy told him, and smiled gently displaying a fine set of clean, white teeth. He had dimples and his face was smooth and well-washed.

'Look Mensa, I've bought more fried plantain than I can

eat from the headteacher's wife, you'd better have some,' Torto said, pushing some of the fried plantain into Mensa's hand.

Mensa accepted Torto's fried plantain with gratitude and thanked him. They both ate in silence. After some time, Torto suddenly asked him: 'Do you like the wife of the headteacher?'

'I'm not quite sure yet. Why did you ask?'

'We don't like her.'

'Who?'

'All of us boys!'

'Why don't you like her?'

'She's selfish and wicked!'

'Are you sure?'

'I'm very, very sure. All of us are very sure! Can't you see that for yourself?'

They continued eating in silence. Torto looked serious and appeared to be more interested in what he had to tell Mensa than in the plantain he was eating. It appeared also he was rather disappointed Mensa would not confirm the popular opinion about the headteacher's wife. Mensa, for his part, was a little puzzled. Was the boy really speaking the truth when he said his aunt was selfish and wicked? Could he take a boy whom he had never come across before into his confidence? Perhaps he ought to keep his thoughts to himself and let the boy do the talking. On the other hand, he had the strong urge to know why the boy said she was not a good woman.

'Why do you say she's selfish and wicked?' he asked.

'Don't you see she's selling most of the things there?'

'What's wrong with that?'

'There is a lot wrong with that!'

'Why?'

'I'll tell you,' Torto said, drawing bodily close to Mensa to make sure he was not overheard. 'When we go to buy from those women, she'll watch boys who don't buy from her. She'll ask their names from other boys and then report them to your master. He'll then find some excuse from time to time to punish those boys. Can you believe your master whipped a boy until he urinated into his pair of short trousers? Your master said that boy had not combed his hair, so he whipped him so severely before the whole school; the boy, I tell you, soiled his pair of short trousers. Usually, a boy is given two strokes of the cane for not combing his hair; but this boy—it was because he always refused to buy from your master's wife!'

'But why shouldn't he buy from her? She's selling so many things?'

'You see, many of what she sells are not very tasty. They're also expensive. Her slices of plantain, cocoyam and so on are so very thin! One's got to buy so many before one feels one has taken something at all. Formerly, women from the town came to sell to us, but they were all stopped. Now it's only the wives of the teachers who come to sell to us. Their things are very expensive but your master's wife's are the worst!'

Mensa was quiet for some time. He was thinking. He broke the silence and said: 'The headteacher is my uncle, and his wife is my aunt. You've been saying wicked things about them. I'll report you to them!'

'Come on, have some more plantain! It's very good!'

Mensa accepted the plantain and ate it with relish.

After Mensa had finished eating the lot, Torto said: 'Now I'm sure you won't report me, will you?'

'Of course, I will!'

'Here, have some more plantain!'

Mensa accepted it and ate it.

'Mensa,' Torto called sadly, 'you know we are friends, don't you? Don't tell anybody what I've just told you, you understand?'

'I will!' Mensa said firmly, looking away from Torto's pathetic gaze.

'Please, don't!' Torto pleaded, about to cry.

Just then the bell rang to indicate that the joyous mid-morning break was over. All the boys rushed to the open space before the school block. It was a multi-purpose place. It was used as the school chapel, gymnasium, parade ground, inoculation theatre, football field, volley-pitch, rounders-pitch and when the school was not in session at night, it was used as a lovers' meeting-place.

The school's rickety and half-dead fife-band was in full session. Each class stood in twos in rigid military fashion. All the teachers, six of them, were standing on the school's veranda, in the shade, while the children took the scorching sun. Each class teacher stood in front of his class and barked orders. The newly admitted class-one boys were unruly and noisy. They had not yet been initiated into the military discipline which prevailed on such occasions. It was only a matter of time.

While they were so engaged, Torto, who was in another file, was looking intently in Mensa's direction; he was trying to wink and smile at him, hoping that Mensa too would wink and smile reassuringly back at him. Unfortunately Mensa would not look his way; Torto therefore had to persist, and he was so taken up by the fruitless effort that when the teacher on duty bellowed 'Mark Time!' he did not hear him. Mr Lomo, the impressive headteacher, who stood aloof both from pupils and teachers, noticed Torto's inattention but waited for more evidence. Meanwhile, Torto was still winking and smiling. The teacher on duty yelled again 'Right Turn!' and then 'Quick March!' Torto was standing without any intention of moving when a boy immediately behind him, marched and bumped into him. The boy who bumped into him was so startled that soon after the bump, he nudged Torto in the ribs to get moving so that they would not be caught. Torto was so startled by the well-intentioned nudge that he squealed.

'Halt!' cried Mr Lomo. The whole school came to a dead halt. The boy playing the bass drum was so taken aback by the thunderous cry of halt that he gave the already tired drum a big superfluous bang which marked time for nobody. He had to pray to God at once that no ill should befall him for striking the bass drum when it should have been silent. It was the kind of thing the headteacher did not like and he had been warned before. He had been accused before by the head of the school of playing the bass drum not to keep time, but to satisfy his juvenile lust for hitting things.

'Torto! Come forward!' Mr Lomo thundered.

Torto, thinking that Mensa had reported him, decided to run away at once, never to return. But the shock he had had on hearing his name mentioned paralysed him.

'Torto! I say, come forward!' cried Mr Lomo, this time brandishing a stout cane he held in his hand.

The whole place was as quiet as a courtroom just before a judge pronounces sentence.

Torto once more thought of bolting; but he knew too much about that school. Just as he had been told in detail that the wife of the headteacher was selfish and wicked, so also had it been explained to him in graphic language that it was hopeless and indeed dangerous for a class-one boy to run away from school; Mr Lomo would order the big boys to chase and catch him; and if they caught him, they would so secretly nudge and twist all parts of his body that they would give him hell before the worse hell followed.

He therefore obeyed and went forwa"d. B' the time he reached the headteacher, who stood tight-lipped and overpowering, his mind had become completely blank. Mr Lomo spoke out aloud and said: 'Attention, everybody! This boy Torto standing before me, while the master on duty was giving orders, was laughing and winking. When you were all ordered to march, he was so engaged in naughtiness that he wouldn't budge. What shall we do to him?'

'Whip him!' the whole school roared to the skies.

Since the class-one children did not know about Mr Lomo's judicial procedure, they were at the time the question was asked, completely at a loss what answer to give. But when they heard their comrades shout whip him, they naturally and belatedly yelled in their tender voices 'Whip him!' This delighted the hardened teachers who laughed copiously. Mensa however cried, 'Don't whip him!'

'Who said, "Don't whip him"?' Mr Lomo demanded,

completely annoyed at the attempted subversion of school discipline. All the children near Mensa proclaimed in various discordant voices, 'Mensa! Mensa! Mensa!'

'Will he come forward at once?'

Mensa hesitated; he did not want to go forward; but the boys who stood behind him pushed him enthusiastically forward. He left his line and climbed on to the veranda.

Mr Lomo then said: 'Here are the bad boys in this school! What shall we do to them?'

'Whip them!' the school crowd authorized him.

Of course, this time, there was no dissentient voice and Mensa and Torto were given that dose of medicine which had succeeded in keeping school children healthy into their adult lives.

When Mensa returned home after the morning's session, he realized that word had already reached home about the morning's incident. Mrs Lomo was cold towards him and made unkind indirect references to his chronic misconduct while talking to her own children. She told her children to behave at school and never do anything which would make their father whip them in public; that would definitely be a disgrace to them. She knew they were good boys, and, unlike other boys, they would always do what was expected of them.

When Mr Lomo came home for lunch, he called Mensa to the lounge and told him: 'Although you're young, I'll tell you a proverb which you'll find useful: "When in Rome, do as the Romans do." I know you don't know where Rome is but what I want you to learn from this proverb is that while you're here do as everyone else does and you'll be happy. For example, if everybody washes his face and feet and combs his hair before going to school in the afternoon, you just do the same and straightaway you'll be spared the cane during the personal hygiene inspection. Similarly, if your teacher expects you to say "Whip him", you simply say "Whip him" and you'll find life pleasant. I was very disappointed this morning when you said "Don't whip him". It showed that you didn't respect me. It's my responsibility to make all the boys respect me and all the teachers and all other grown-up people in the world. Only a bad boy will try to say anything unpleasant or unexpected to his teachers or seniors or those in authority. At this stage of your development, you do not and cannot know better than your seniors. You go away and don't repeat this morning's conduct in future.'

'Thank you, sir,' Mensa said and left his presence.

That afternoon at school, Mensa was not as happy as he had been early in the morning. He sat quietly at his desk watching 'I'll-twist-you' carry on with his clerical affairs, his spectacles perched somewhat loosely on the bridge of his nose. Once when 'I'll-twist-you' raised his head to survey the room which was reasonably quiet this time, as most of the children were taking an illegal afternoon nap after the copious midday meal, he saw Mensa looking at him. 'I'll-twist-you' studied him closely for a minute or so not looking through his glasses but from above their rims. He called Mensa to come forward. Mensa went and stood close to his desk, then he said: 'Look here, my dear boy, I was born and bred in the countryside myself. In my time, life was easy and free. Nobody was taught honesty. Indeed, people were not sufficiently crooked to be dishonest. Now everything is not simple, my dear boy. You see, you got into trouble this morning because you said what you felt you should say, not what everyone expected you to say. My dear boy, if you want to survive in this world always say the things people would wish you to say or wish to hear and not what you think should be said. For example, if someone says "Good morning" to you and you think it's bad morning, you don't have to say "Bad Morning". If you said that you'd be considered lunatic. My dear boy, that's how the trouble starts until you have injustice being paraded as justice. You probably don't understand me, but you'll learn in good time. My dear boy, I don't have to say much; you'll learn in good time. You see, I'm paid to do this or that when I'm here. At home, I do what I like provided I don't hurt anybody. You have also come here to do this or that. When you've finished with schooling, you can do what you like provided you don't hurt anybody. Is that not funny, my dear boy? It is, it is! Life is funny, my dear boy. I've seen a bit of it, my dear boy. Whenever you're in trouble come and see me. You may go back and sit down but don't look that sad again, my dear boy!'

Mensa did not know what to say in reply. 'I'll-twist-you' continued with his work and looked as if he had not said a word. He was working hard and assiduously, clearly bent on finishing what assignment he had for the day. On the surface the incident did not seem to have touched him but it was these minor incidents which had formed him as a teacher. After all, he had earned his teaching certificate on the job. He never went to a teacher training-college. He started as a Pupil Teacher, took an external examination, and the education department was condescending enough to send him a certificate. He never dabbled in matters concerning educational policy; he simply carried out instructions.

He was not a scholar and never wished nor pretended to be. The various headteachers under whom he had served thought him rather funny but good enough for the first class, where his diminishing strength would not break bones and where his frown would bring wayward children into the fold of discipline. He was aware of what other teachers thought of him and was more amused than disturbed.

Once in a while, he would impart his philosophy of life to those children in whom he had boundless faith and confidence; but he knew they would not understand him because they were so young. He trusted that if those children's memories served them loyally long after they had finished with their basic education, they would remember his words and weigh them for what they were worth.

He believed that the end-product of education was man's realization of what the life he faced was worth and his relationship with it; his rational grasp of his environment and of himself; his developed intellect that enabled him not to be committed necessarily or even at all to what all other men on earth thought and said; his freedom to seek the truth, the spiritual happiness or whatever faith he desired, upon which he could anchor his life which was buffeted because the whole of creation was founded on treacherous restlessness and had ever remained restless and was full of dismal uncertainties; and that the only certainty he could have would be the certainty of a never-ending battle in a settled style, to adjust his life which would be extinguished one day and would be lost to a dark nothingness. He had an inward contentment and was at peace with himself and his world. He sought after no economic efficiency upon which to base his happiness; he sought after hard thinking which made him free from the cobwebs the modern man had woven over the earth. He was left alone and alone he stayed; he never tried to be at the top, and desperate ambition did not becloud his destiny.

Whenever he came to school, he never said a word to his colleagues unless he was spoken to. He normally did not take part in lengthy conversations. He always stood erect before the headteacher, his hands behind him, ready to take instructions. His comportment pleased the headteachers because it was a sign of his submissiveness and also of their great importance.

Since he had never been to a teacher training-college, nobody thought much of his opinions and his observations on life which, being so unorthodox, were considered out-of-the-way and ludicrous. Those young teachers who had arrived fresh from college and possessed highly valued certificates, used to provoke him into conversation because they had nothing worthwhile to do and needed some amusement. He had long before detected this and not to hurt any of them he dismissed them politely by telling them that he had some teaching notes to revise before the next lesson. When he had done that once or twice, they stopped coming along. None of them really valued his excuse or his existence in the school or in the world except that he was a popular teacher (not really in the best sense) with class-one children; he could be tolerated until one day, which would not be too far off, he would get displaced by a better qualified teacher with a glorious certificate.

When Mensa returned to his desk and sat down, he was overwhelmed by all that he had heard. He had so far had a lot of talking to, interspersed with caning. He knew he was now in a world which was not easy. He could only distinguish between those who were good to him and those who were hostile to him. Why those people were what they were, he could not tell; he had neither the intellectual capacity nor the time for it. He sat down quietly not knowing how to manage to look cheerful, though at that moment he had some peace of mind because 'I'll-twist-you' had been nice to him.

Looking round, he saw a boy with a large head and small legs making faces at him, sticking his tongue out at him and then grinning in the most provocative manner. He would follow up with an accurate demonstration in pantomime-fashion of how Mensa was whipped in the morning and how he contorted his body in agony. Mensa was at first amused and disposed to laugh; but he realized that the boy did not mean his actions to have any theatrical effect on him; for he continued to imitate Mensa's facial distortions soon after he had received a stroke of the cane. If he had himself been good-looking, Mensa might not have minded. He tried to make all the signs and signals he could think of to make 'Bighead—small-legs' Odorlu realize that he did not enjoy the joke. But 'Bighead—small-legs' was delighted and thrilled when he discovered that he had achieved the desired effect, that is, to make Mensa uncomfortable and irritated.

When the class was given the mid-afternoon break,

Mensa went to Odorlu to protest, but he was surprised to find the boy in the company of four other boys who appeared to know already what he was going to protest against. He had hardly finished what he had to say when 'Big-head—small-legs' said: 'You go away! You're but a dirty country boy; what can you do? And look at your head, too!' The other four boys laughed and laughed. One of them laughed so much that he zig-zagged about, half-bent, fell on the ground, got up, coughed and coughed and said he had laughed so well that his ribs were aching. Mensa was in a rage by this time and so he brandished a clenched fist to show that he was ready for a fight.

As soon as his tormentor saw it, he said: 'Look at the fool! He wants to fight! Country boy, let me tell you what I've already heard and seen. In this school, we don't fight in the open. Come, let's go to the hideout behind the school lavatory and I'll teach you how to fight! What's the use of my living in Accra and seeing the Joe Louis boxing pictures? Come! You'll have to cry again this afternoon!'

After he had uttered the last threat, he once again imitated the way Mensa received the cane. Mensa would have released a punch but he felt like looking round first and when he did so, saw 'I'll-twist-you' in the classroom window, so he followed the boys to the hideout.

When they were near the place, his heart sank for he remembered the threats of 'Big-head—small-legs' afresh and wondered whether it was wise to fight him. Could he really fight him when he had heard so much about the wonders boxers could perform? Maybe it was better he avoided a bout altogether. On the other hand, he was already too much committed to withdraw. If he did the boys would only make his life miserable in future.

As soon as they reached the place, and one of the boys said they could have a go, Mensa was quick, like lightning, to throw a punch with all his weight behind it at the pointed and proffered nose of 'Big-head—small-legs', thus hitting him before he could assume the stance of an experienced boxer. The punch hurt Odorlu so badly that he screamed in agony and when he saw the blood ooze from his nose, he cried like a baby, calling upon his mother (who was not there anyway) to come and deliver him from the pain and murderer.

One of the onlookers who had supported the bleeding boy ran off to Mr Lomo's office to report that Mensa had hurt a boy behind the school lavatory. While this doubledealing informant was away, 'I'll-twist-you' suddenly appeared at the scene. Both he and the boys had a shock from different causes; he, for the bloodshed, and they, that they had been caught. 'I'll-twist-you' was not openly disturbed; he was in full control of himself. He asked one of the boys what really happened and the boy, because of fright, told him the whole story without suppressing any part of it. 'I'll-twist-you' gave poor 'Big-head—small-legs' first aid with his personal bunch of keys which he had chained in his pocket. The bleeding stopped.

Just when he had stopped the bleeding, Mr Lomo burst on them breathing hard. He roared: 'Where's Mensa, I'll cane him! I'll give him twelve lashes! He's broken the most important rule! Fighting is forbidden and he knows it!'

'Sir, Mensa hasn't fought. It's just a case of nose bleeding,' said Mr Akushi calmly and confidently.

'All right! Mensa, you'd better thank your stars! Now, everybody here, go back to your classroom!' he ordered. So both 'I'll-twist-you' and the six boys went quietly and quickly back to their classroom.

Chapter Eight

The six years Mensa spent at Mr Lomo's house and at school were significant because certain aspects of his character were greatly transformed. He tried as much as he could to avoid physical punishment and in the process became adept at breaking rules without being caught. His friendship with Torto grew; for after they had both been whipped and disgraced publicly they took to each other. But it was plain that Torto was more fond of Mensa than Mensa was of him. Torto thought all the time that Mensa was in hell as long as he stayed with his uncle and that he had to do his best to mitigate the stresses to which his friend was subjected.

One day he invited Mensa to lunch. At first, Mensa did not find it easy to accept the invitation; that would mean his not going home during the midday-break. When Torto however told him that they were going to have chicken-stew and rice and other delicious food in addition, Mensa accompanied his friend home.

He was profoundly impressed by what happened there. It was a clean and happy home. There was no inquisitiveness or nagging. When Torto told his mother that Mensa was his friend and that he had brought him along to share his lunch with him, his mother asked who Mensa was and when she was told he was the nephew of their headteacher, she was so pleased that she gave them a very generous lunch.

Those were the days when headteachers enjoyed a great deal of prestige; they were just one step short of being ministers of religion. After serving as headteachers for some time, they became catechist headteachers and in due course were ordained as ministers of religion to shepherd Christ's flock to Heaven. Then, ministers of religion were not only highly respected but were freely given gifts to ensure that they did not devote too much of their precious time to seeking the wherewithal of their daily sustenance. Moreover, ministers of religion had the licence, once they thought they were professionally inspired, to say anything they wished and whether damaging or otherwise to their erring flock from the pulpit. Whatever they said was divine and went unchallenged by the well-behaved members of the congregation which so diligently listened to them. Human nature being what it is, it was necessary for members of the church to be on the best of terms with the ministers so that direct or oblique references to their errant ways might not be made by the servant of God from the pulpit. And the ministers with due humility and decorum that befitted their calling accepted those gifts with pleasure.

Thus as Mr Lomo was on the right path to being a minister of the church, and there was no reason to believe he would ever embezzle school funds which could disqualify him, Torto's mother had every incentive to start in advance showering kindnesses on him through his nephew. But this was only one of the reasons why she was prepared to be kind to Mensa. It was the practice that everybody was kind to headteachers, so she also had to be. Basically, she was a good-natured, generous and sympathetic housewife and her son, Torto, had inherited these virtues.

Throughout his short stay in that house, Mensa closely observed the behaviour of the inmates and the atmosphere that prevailed. He felt he was in a different world altogether where there was peace and love. Torto spoke freely and frankly about what happened that morning at school to his mother. His mother listened to him with unfeigned interest and asked him what he did and how he behaved generally. Torto told her everything and she encouraged him to be a good boy always. When they were leaving for school, Torto's mother gave Mensa threepence and Torto a penny; she asked Mensa to call again some time.

The two boys were very happy when they returned to school. However, during the mid-afternoon break, Antwi sought Mensa, found him and asked him where he had been. Mensa told him. Antwi then informed Mensa that Mr Lomo was annoyed when he could not be found for lunch and that he should expect trouble. After imparting the uncomfortable information, Antwi made it clear to Mensa that he had had a generous lunch because the food which was meant for the five of them was enjoyed by four of them. He then advised Mensa to go to Torto's house the next afternoon so that the four of them could have more to eat again. This did not please Mensa but he had more to worry about.

After school, in the evening, and as usual, Mr Lomo asked Mensa to come and see him in the lounge. When Mensa went in, he saw Mrs Lomo sitting close and snugly by her husband quite happy and smiling. Her own children were sitting or lying on the carpet some eating toffee and others doing their prep. Badu, Danso, Dua and Antwi had gone to fetch water to fill the big drums in the house. Mr Lomo immediately started firing questions at him. Mensa was determined to be evasive at every turn and twist.

'Where did you go this afternoon during the midday-break?'

'I went to Torto's house, sir.'

'Did you ask permission?'

'I thought of asking, sir.'

'Did you in fact ask?'

'I don't think I did, sir.'

'Mensa, be careful! Did you or did you not?'

'I didn't, sir.'

'Very good! What did you have for lunch?'

'Nothing, sir.'

'Are you sure?'

'Yes, sir.'

'Very sure?'

'So very sure, sir.'

'Look here, Antwi has already told me everything you told him this afternoon. I know this piece of information will disappoint you and spoil your lying. You make things worse for yourself if you continue lying. Now, tell me, what did you have for lunch?'

'Rice and stew, sir,' Mensa replied, more disarmed by treachery than by the detection of lying.

'Is that all?'

'And rolls of sweet pancake, sir.'

'Is that all?'

'And orange squash, sir.'

'Is that all?'

'Yes, sir. That's all.'

'What about the threepence?'

'Which threepence, sir? The one I have in my savings wood-box?'

'Fool! What did you collect from the place?'

'I was not asked to collect anything, sir.'

'Idiot! Were you given threepence by Torto's mother?'

'Yes, sir.'

'Where is it?'

'Here it is, sir.' Mensa handed the threepenny piece to his master.

'That's right!' said Mr Lomo. 'Since you got this threepence in the wrong way, I'm going to keep it for good. Now hear your sentence. You'll not be fed by your aunt this evening and tomorrow morning, you understand?'

'I understand, sir.'

'Leave the room!'

'Yes, sir.'

Before Mensa reached the door Mrs Lomo called him back and started asking him her own questions.

'What did you tell Torto before he took you home to give you lunch?'

'I told him nothing.'

'Why did he invite you, then?'

'I can't tell.'

'Why did you accept the invitation?'

'I felt I could.'

'What made you feel?'

'I don't know.'

'Look here, boy, if you don't want to eat my food any longer, I'm prepared to stop cooking for you. As far as I'm concerned, you're completely insignificant in this house! Your father pays a pound a month for your board. I can give you cash every day so that you find food for yourself. You're a disgraceful and ungrateful boy! I'm fed up with you! Get out!'

Mensa stood stunned after Aunt Adzoa had finished with her tirade. Mr Lomo thought if Mensa continued standing there, his wife might be tempted to say everything that was on her mind. That definitely would not do; it could have serious repercussions, so he said: 'Didn't I ask you to quit this room?' Mensa replied mechanically, 'You did, sir,' and left the lounge.

Though unhappy, Mensa was somehow relieved it was over. He weighed the sentence passed on him and felt he could weather it. The sustaining lunch he had had that afternoon would be all right for him until well into the next day provided he went to bed early that evening. In the morning, he would drink a lot of water which could give him a feeling of satisfaction until the mid-morning break when Torto would provide him with something to eat.

When he had finished thinking about when and what he would eat next, two things immediately exercised his mind. Why should his uncle take possession of his precious threepence? Did he take it to keep for some time or did he mean to make it his own? He felt the money belonged to him and could not see how his uncle could be justified if he permanently kept it. Then there was the question of Antwi's conduct. Why, on earth, did he report to Mr Lomo everything he had told him about his afternoon's absence? This was the sort of thing Antwi, Badu, Danso and Dua were doing most of the time. One of them would inform against the other though each had thought of the other as his friend and comrade in hardship. In this particular instance, it was Antwi who told him that his uncle was angry with him and even advised him to repeat the visit. Why then did he go back to tell his displeased uncle all that he had told him?

Mensa could not find satisfactory answers though he gave them a good deal of thought before going to bed. One thing he was sure of, however: Antwi had made him lose a threepenny-piece and earn the terrible displeasure of his guardians.

In the morning, he told Torto what happened to him the night before. Torto was shaken by what had taken place and felt he should do something to make life easier for his friend. He had a good idea. He told Mensa he would tell his mother he would like to stay at school and study during the midday-break. He would suggest that his mother gave him packed lunch. There were other boys who did not go home during that period because they wanted to stay and work; some of them, in fact, came to school from very far away and it would have been impossible for them to go home and have lunch and return before the afternoon session began. He would make sure his mother gave him enough food to satisfy the two of them. Mensa should go home quickly during the midday-break and eat a token lunch before returning to school to have the real lunch with him. This arrangement proved satisfactory and benefited not only Torto and Mensa but also Antwi, Dua, Badu and Danso who had more to eat since Mensa ate so little. And naturally, once they had more to eat they never stopped to think why Mensa ate almost nothing at lunch-time every day.

Torto and Mensa were enjoying their lunch one day when Odorlu saw them. He had been in great fear of Mensa since the fight and had wanted desperately to establish the most cordial relations between Mensa and himself. When he saw them, he thought he had finally got the opportunity. He proposed to the two boys that he should join them at lunch because he also did not go home and had brought his lunch to school. He was accepted and the three formed a club of happy lunch-time diners. Whenever a boy provoked Mensa, it was 'Big-head—small-legs' who would warn that boy in time that Mensa's blows could cause actual bodily damage, so he should leave Mensa alone. Very many boys were warned in this way and in course of time, Mensa became famous in the school for his fighting prowess.

It happened also that the boys staying with Mr Lomo developed skin rashes because they never really washed well. One effective remedy, it was supposed, was to have those boys bathe in the sea. They were ordered by Mr Lomo to do so. At first they were reluctant since they had heard ugly stories about how the sea was cruel to boys who took it for granted. But once the order had been given, they had to go.

When they first visited the beach, they went to that part where the fishermen were working so that they could have people to save them if the sea decided to swallow them up. They really enjoyed the afternoon at the beach, for the life they saw there was an active one indeed. There were the women fish-mongers who were shouting at one another; there were also the great fishermen who were, as could be expected, good-naturedly trading insults in obscene language while working on the ropes with which they tugged the dragnet to the shore.

When the last section of the dragnet landed, everybody, men, women and children rushed to see the catch, so Mensa and his friends also went to see. They noticed that the boys there were not idle; they were seriously and brazenly stealing fish from the meshes of the dragnet. The fishermen tried to stop them in two ways. One was an exercise in verbal mastery and the competent use of lively imagery. The fishermen did not use old, wornout, abusive terms; for before they abused a thieving boy, they would first study both his physiognomy and physiology to find out whether God had made a mistake somewhere. If the boy were unfortunate and they found what they considered to be a defect, they would base their abuse on a vivid description of it. Such an abuse was calculated not only to cause despondency in the boy but also to amuse the man who hurled it, and his colleagues roared with laughter only when it was considered a successful abuse and the hapless boy should be prepared for another which could make him question God. Of course, if such a boy were wise, he would ignore the abuse altogether and go on stealing the fish which were more important; and if the catch was good, the fishermen were likely to be more interested in their own verbal fireworks than in the few fish they would lose.

On the other hand, if the catch was poor and the fishermen were disappointed with it, an open theft of their meagre fish could be a disastrous undertaking. They would not only abuse but would hurl missiles. Their kind of missile consisted of a handful of watery sand which could have a stunning effect on its target. The fishermen, needless to say, were a strong people, particularly in the arm, and a good throw could knock a boy straight into the breaking surf. If a boy were fragile and he got paralysed by it, he was bound to take mouthfuls of sea water before he could stagger out of the water possibly to go and lie prostrate on the dry sand for some time to recuperate. Sometimes after such a recuperation a boy would abandon the search for fish and go home cursing yet frightened.

Still fish stealing could be definitely attempted by hardy boys despite the risk involved. A boy would have to watch the glum fishermen while disentangling fish from the meshes. As soon as a handful of watery sand was thrown, he should be agile enough to duck it while giving the fish a final pull out of the mesh and then make away with it at top speed. Once a boy bolted away and got mixed up with the crowd, that was the successful end of a daring venture.

Mensa watched the boys who were stealing fish for some time and then decided to try his luck. He went near a fat, short boy who was pulling out a sleek, medium-size eel from a mesh. Mensa bent over and grabbed a sole by the head and tried to break it loose. Another boy with a pot-belly was working on an attractive dogfish which he was determined to have at all cost. But the fat, short boy had been noticed by a deep-throated, hefty fisherman who barked: 'Hey, you boy, leave that fish alone! You remind me of a short, thick boar running after an anaemic sow!' That, as it happened, was not a particularly serious or successful abuse, but the fat, short boy stopped pulling at the eel to study his body to see whether the description was apt or not. This, the fishermen enjoyed and started laughing. While they were thus occupied, Mensa got his fish plus the one the disheartened fat, short boy was trying to get and ran away with both. While he was away the fishermen had laughed off the abuse, the pot-bellied boy was noticed by another fisherman who cried: 'Pot-belly! Do you know the difference between you and an over-fed puppy on a short run? And your legs? Bamboo sticks!' This time, Antwi, Dua, Badu and Danso joined in the general laughter.

And while the laughter was in full swing, Mensa returned and repeated the predatory act several times until he caught the eye of a fisherman who shouted at him: 'Drop that fish, you son of a witch! Go and look at your head in a mirror, then study the shape of a deformed coconut!' It was simply the kind of reference Mensa had traditionally disliked. When Okle referred to his head on the farm, he fought him; but Okle's reference was mild and this one was original and capable of being remembered by his friends. If he continued stealing the fish, worse things might be said about his head so he gave up and went back to see the fine loot of which his friends were proud. Antwi removed his shirt and the fish were tied in it. They went back to the surf and washed and swam to their heart's content. Then they decided to go home. They collected the bundle of fish and arrived home elated.

When Mr Lomo saw Antwi half-naked, he said, 'Antwi, did you go through the town half-dressed?'

'Yes, sir.'

'Why?'

'Because we wanted to bring some fish to you, sir,' he lied.

'Where's the fish?'

'Here they are, sir.'

Antwi untied the bundle. When Mr Lomo saw the fine, fresh fish, he was so pleased and excited that he called his wife: 'Darling, come and see!'

His wife came, then he said: 'Look at these! Wonderful fish! Wonderful fish! Aren't they really nice? We're going to have a good dinner tonight, aren't we?'

'Oh yes, we surely will have a good one!' his wife assured him having been also very impressed by the attractive collection of fish.

It appeared the fish had been sacrificed to save Antwi from trouble. The boys were not perturbed because they thought when the fish was cooked, they would have some. Soon it was dinnertime and Antwi was called by Aunt Adzoa to collect their meal. There was not enough light where the boys ate in the evening and so each boy had made his own plans how he would steal the cooked fish unobserved while they were eating; and they would have plenty to steal since they had brought so many fish home for dinner.

But when Antwi arrived with the food, he was sad.

'Antwi, what's the trouble?' Danso asked.

'We've not been given fish stew,' he replied feeling hopelessly guilty and disappointed. He set the food down and declared: 'Look at this! Aunt Adzoa has prepared two different kinds of stew, one of rotten meat and the other of our fine fish! She's going to enjoy our fish with her husband and children! Why is this woman so cruel?'

'Antwi, don't worry! None of us should worry yet,' said Danso, his eyes sparkling with ingenuity in the half-lit darkness, 'I have an idea. You can go and tell master that we stole the fish after all. He'll get angry and reject the stew prepared with it. Then we'll have the stew to eat!'

'But suppose he decides to whip me for stealing, for lying and also for coming home half-naked?' Antwi asked, not satisfied with the possible consequence of such a confession.

'No, I don't think he will whip you alone just like that,' Danso said with conviction. 'He'll think of whipping all of us. We are five. He's likely to give us two lashes each. We can easily take them and have the stew!'

'I think what Danso has said can work,' Dua pointed out.

'But are we really prepared for two lashes each?' Mensa asked. He said further: 'It's the first stroke that matters. As soon as any of us receives it, he should scream as if he's going to die. That frightens him, you know. So the second stroke will be soft and won't hurt at all. Now, everybody, as soon as you get the first one, jump and scream and rub your buttocks vigorously with both palms. He'll think he's done it, and the second one will be just fun!'

'I think the plan will work,' Badu said excitedly. 'Antwi, if you can't go I'm prepared to.'

Antwi said he would. He rose and went to the door of the dining-room and knocked at it.

'Yes! Come in, whoever you are!' said Mr Lomo casually

and cheerfully and then continued enjoying the fish. He was normally a dour fellow with a sour humour but on that night he was rather somewhat expansive.

Antwi entered the room and went close to Mr Lomo. As he watched the fish his mouth watered and, for the first time, he was sorry he was not the son of Mr and Mrs Lomo. He told his master, 'I've come to make a confession to you, sir.'

'Out with it, my dear boy!' Mr Lomo said affectionately. He had never called any of those boys my dear before, but, for that moment, the unusual meal had altered his normal disposition.

'I want to tell you, sir, that the fish we brought home this afternoon was stolen.'

'How?'

'We got them from the net without asking the fishermen, sir.'

'Ah, my dear boy, that's not stealing at all. It's the practice at the beach. Any other thieving is forbidden and an honest confession welcome. I'm thoroughly enjoying your fish. It's not a stolen item. You may go and tell your friends they need not worry!'

While Antwi was trying the ruse on Mr Lomo, the other boys were huddled behind the door of the dining-room eavesdropping. When Mr Lomo spoke, they would not believe their ears, but when Antwi left his presence, they realized their plan had failed. When Antwi came out of the door, they all trooped behind him, went back to the unwholesome meal that had been given them, and ate it with heavy hearts and in absolute silence.

Another incident took place when Mensa was in his fifth year. One widespread craze among boys in those days was the writing of a special type of love letter which boys called *billets-doux*. It was not clear who originated the writing of them but young boys between ten and twelve were expecially fond of them. Most of the contents of those letters were stereotyped and were copied freely without any acknowledgement to the original author.

It was Badu who mysteriously acquired one such *billet-doux* and secretly showed it to Danso. Danso's imagination was fired and he decided to make practical use of it. There was a girls' school nearby, so he decided to copy the letter to a girl who he thought would readily share his love. He did not in any way want the girl sexually. No. If the girl happened to approach him, he would definitely run away. That was how the game was played. The love-affair was conducted mentally and was more of an imaginative exercise than a physical enterprise. Sometimes it was brought down to earth by an exchange of one or two flimsy gifts, such as a bar of chocolate from the boy, and, from the girl, an embroidered handkerchief which would be more suitable as material for decorating the top of a coffee-stool than as a convenient thing for wiping or dabbing the face. The consummation of love was the idea that one had a girl somewhere, far away, whose beauty was abstract and the best in all creation.

But, to the religious school authorities, any form of love-affair whatever between a young boy and a young girl was the most sacrilegious offence ever committed since Adam and Eve were said to have put the entire world on a permanent evil footing, against which the Church had battled for several hundreds of years. Indeed, it was a sure forecast that the boy or girl caught practising it was going to be in future the worst sexual degenerate whose relationship with the Church and with God was assuredly bound to be hopelessly unholy. It was a sure sign also that such a boy or girl was hankering prematurely after the pleasures of the body which would not only interfere with the wholesome working of the mind but also hinder the proper working of the soul. And when both body and soul were fouled or tainted, what was left of the man but his brute existence which the religious organization could never accept in any circumstance? Any boy or girl caught with a letter of this nature was declared to have committed a first degree offence known to the entire religious educational set-up, and the punishment that went with it was nothing short of wilful murder under the banner of the Christian crusade for the salvation of the soul which had no need of the human body anyway. Consequently, the boys who wrote those letters or conducted those juvenile love-affairs were as secretive and desperate as illicit gin distillers in the dark forests of the Akwapimian hills.

Danso therefore copied the letter which ran:

My sweet, darling, darling until death!

When I see you walking to school, I fall into a trance and see you as an angel whose beauty is beyond the powers of human description!

My love for you knows no bounds. It is so deeply rooted that I am prepared to die for you!

Your face is as round as the full-moon, your cheeks as attractive as a fresh harmattan pawpaw!

I shall be the happiest man in this world if you can but say you love me with all your heart and soul!

Day and night I dream of you and I shall die if you do not say you love me!

Yours till death parts us,
Danso

Danso folded the letter which he put into an envelope. He took his tin of lavendered toilet powder and poured some of the powder into the envelope to make the letter smell sweet. He then went to the school garden and tore a sweet-smelling rose petal and put it into the envelope. Finally, he gave the letter to Badu for onward transmission to the girl.

Badu dutifully went and waylaid the girl, crouching under the hedge on the path that led to the girls' school. When he saw the girl approach, however, his heart sank and he seriously thought of abandoning the mission altogether; he had nothing to lose. Danso was, in the meantime, standing behind a tree in the far distance watching the proceedings with a trembling body. Somehow, Badu pulled up courage when the girl was near and suddenly emerged from the hedge and accosted her. He gave her the letter saying, 'Danso asked me to give this to you.'

'Are you sure it's from Danso?'

'Yes.'

'What's in it?'

'I don't know. He asked me to give it to you.'

'All right,' the girl said and took the letter.

When Badu returned to Danso's hidden observation post, Danso asked him: 'Was she angry when she received it?'

'I'm not sure. It's very difficult to say. I'm afraid she didn't look particularly pleasant!'

'Do you think she'll report me?'

'Your guess is as good as mine. It will be just too bad if she does!'

'I'm sorry I copied that letter for her, Badu!' Danso said regretfully now that the deed had been done.

One thing, however, was not known to either Danso or Badu. The girl already had a boy-friend. He was the bass-drummer of the school's rickety band. What she did was to hand over Danso's interfering letter to her boy-friend for advice. Her boy-friend, the bass-drummer, was furious at the whole idea. Danso was more handsome and infinitely more attractive than he was. If he did not act, anything could happen. He therefore advised his darling to hand over the letter to Mr Lomo and tell him that though she did not want to be corrupted, Danso had persisted. At first, the girl did not want to because she saw nothing in it; but the bass-drummer threatened that if she did not do as he had directed, he would scrawl on the school lavatory wall what Danso had written to her and that she had agreed. He reminded her of the consequences if her headmistress and Mr Lomo got to know. She must therefore send the letter immediately to Mr Lomo without further doubt or protestation.

The whole school was on parade after the mid-morning break when Danso saw the girl enter the office of Mr Lomo. Danso's stomach turned to water and he felt like going to the toilet, but he could not leave the lines. The girl stayed in Mr Lomo's office for a few minutes, came out and then went away. Mr Lomo strode out of his office looking grim. He stood erect, chest out, his chin up and surveyed the whole school. He said nothing as he did the scanning but a few moments later, he called Danso to come to his office immediately. Then he called four other boys including the bass-drummer. The school therefore had to march by the time provided by the solo side-drum.

When Danso and the four hefty boys had taken a rigid, solemn stand before Mr Lomo who sat behind his desk with six vicious canes carefully stacked on it, Mr Lomo silently read over the letter, then showed it to Danso and asked: 'Did you write it?'

'No, sir!' Danso denied out of sheer mortal fright.

'Very good! The four of you, mount him!' he ordered.

One boy got hold of Danso's right leg, another grabbed his left leg, another seized his left arm and the fourth boy clutched his right arm. He was then heaved up onto a table which Mr Lomo had already cleared for the corporal punishment.

Danso was given thirty-one lashes on his bare back. The beating was so noisy and severe that the whole school was hushed for the rest of the morning.

The pain and injuries Danso received were such that he could not walk and had to limp and crouch back to his classroom. He could not sit on the chair for he was sharply hurt by the cuts the canes had made on his buttocks. When he went to bed in the evening he could not lie on his back and he lay awake groaning and weeping till day-break.

When other boys in the school got to know why Danso

had suffered, they tore up all specimen copies they had and marvelled at what harm a *billet-doux* could cause.

Badu was so scared that he could not eat the afternoon and evening meal and spent the rest of the day and the whole of the night, whenever it was opportune, to plead with Danso that he should never mention to anyone that he was the one who delivered the letter. But Danso's existence had been so temporarily interrupted and shattered that he never knew what Badu spoke about.

For three days, Danso was very ill, and Badu, Mensa, Antwi and Dua thought he would never be active again. The wounds hurt him and Mrs Lomo grudgingly nursed him. The boys always sat by him whenever they had nothing to do, saying nothing but caressing his limp hands.

Mr Lomo wrote a lengthy and characteristically high-sounding letter to Danso's father making several points about how Danso, instead of being submissive and hard-working, had become precocious and was practising sexual promiscuity with the careless abandon of a rabbit. He took the trouble to remind Danso's father that his son's conduct was exactly the kind of thing both church and school would vigorously suppress since it put a boy on the easy road to hell. His father should, however, thank God that his son was caught in time and dealt with in the most fitting manner. He was aware that as he (i.e. Danso's father) had had two wives before the church had persuaded him to dispense with one, it was absolutely necessary that the greatest effort must be made to ensure that his son did not repeat the error.

He would be honest to admit to Danso's father that the

beating he gave his son had been somewhat severe; but the severity was demanded by the magnitude of the offence, and he was quite sure a most effective deterrent action had been taken. On the whole his son was in safe hands and a good foundation had been laid for his future happy Christian life. He concluded the letter by assuring Danso's father that all was well with his son and he should not have the matter weigh on his mind.

Danso was able to recover fairly fully both from the shock and the injuries after two weeks. He had now developed a psychopathic fear of Mr Lomo. All along, he and his four friends had hated and feared him, but now they were so obsessed with the fear of what he could possibly do to any of them that he seemed a malevolent and destructive force. They now had two Mr Lomos: the physical one they feared and tried their best to please to avert danger and harm to themselves and the spiritual one who haunted them in their sleep, dreams and thoughts.

They thought and dreamt of Mr Lomo as a demon wanting to destroy them. They had all types of tortuous hallucinations in which he was the principal character. They would imagine or dream they were being chased over a precipice or being flogged to death by him, their parents looking on but unable to help. They would then be shocked into real life and if it happened in a dream while they were in bed, they would lie awake panting for some time before they would sleep again out of sheer tiredness, when there was about two more hours before day-break.

Chapter Nine

Mr. Lomo had long ago recommended to Old Anang that Mensa should go to a particular middle boarding-school in Accra. There he would have available the best education a Christian gentleman could have. Old Anang readily agreed because he had not had that kind of education and it was welcome if his son could have it. He thought also that if Mensa went to a boarding-school, it would be a great relief to the Lomos who had looked after him during the past six years. Above all, that boarding-school in particular had turned out a cluster of pupils who in later life had done extremely well, and there was no harm in letting Mensa seek his fortunes through that institution. Mensa was himself happy he was going to break away from the Lomo family and go to a school where he would be free to study in peace.

Mensa had the whole dry, uncomfortable December free before starting his new and interesting life at boarding-school. In this month he could see his parents whom he had not seen for six years, and get the money and other things he would need for boarding-school. The desire to go home was intensified by a letter Mr Lomo received telling that Old Anang was seriously ill. Mr Lomo was alarmed for he was fond of Old Anang in whom he saw a constant attempt at independent thought and action. This he admired but would not cultivate, because his calling as a Christian teacher precluded it. Mensa was told but he could hardly understand how serious the illness was. He was overcome by the pleasant thought that he was going back home after so long a time. He wondered what the village looked like now and whether all his friends were there. He imagined himself an adored hero from Accra who would tell them fascinating stories about the city. Old memories which had never been erased flashed through his mind, and he spent a sleepless night in excited anticipation.

He returned, as he had come, by lorry, and was surprised to find the village just the same as he had left it except for the addition of a few buildings here and there.

Even the durable bell man was there and had not aged in any way. The catechist too, had not been transferred from the village. All his boy friends were extremely happy he had come. Like him, they had grown a lot bigger, and they had many stories to tell him.

His mother wept when she saw him. His brother, Tete, though grief-stricken, was happy he had come. When his mother wept, his younger sister cried too. So he was in a state of confusion when he went to his father's bedside. His father was satisfied that his son had come but he was too feeble to talk much to him. He took his hand and pressed it gently and affectionately. Then he said in a surprisingly clear, if not strong, voice: 'How are you, my son?' Mensa said he was quite well but before he could say anything again, his father had a relapse and he had to withdraw from his bedside and room. Old Anang's state affected his wife and the few relations who had come to help and console her.

In the evening, after a good dinner unlike any he had had for a long time, Mensa's old friends called to see him. They were so very happy and had so much to say, that Mensa's father's illness took second place in their feelings. As soon as they managed to lure Mensa out of the hushed house, Odoi started his story at once.

'Mensa, I've something to tell you!'

'It's a very interesting story,' Darku chimed in.

'I'd like to hear it,' Mensa said enthusiastically.

Odoi started the story right from the beginning to make sure he did not leave a single detail out. 'A year or so after you left this village, an Ewe hunter came and settled here. He is still here with us and is called Gadago. This man, Mensa, is a very good hunter and a first-class marksman. He's been hunting down all sorts of animals: grasscutters, wild boars, antelopes, deer, pythons and, once, a panther. He's so good that some people, taking his background into consideration, wonder whether the whole thing is natural. We used to have our doubts, to be frank, Mensa; but now we believe the man uses no supernatural powers. He likes to be thought to but he's simply an exceptionally good hunter. That's all!

'Somehow, our friend, the bell man managed to make friends with this hunter. He's a mean fellow; he probably wanted free bush-meat. We were surprised to find that the hunter decided to allow him to accompany him on a hunting expedition one night. Their destination was far in the thick forest; it is a place where there is a stream. Many animals go to drink there at night and Gadago had shot many fine bush animals there before.

'Of course, the bell man had no gun, he still hasn't. So he took along a stout club with a lethal knob with which to protect himself and also deal the last lethal blow to any animal which had been shot but was wasting time dying.

'He was extremely tired by the time they got half-way to the place; he was also scared by the general silence in the wide big forest and, at a certain stage, he asked Gadago if he could be allowed to return home. But Gadago told him that that was impossible because once they had started, they should do their best to get through with it so that they could give a reasonable account of themselves when they returned home. To make him feel a little happy, Gadago took him to a nearby farm belonging to another Ewe man. These Ewes, Mensa, are a hard working people and they have the most impressive farms in these parts. I know your father has a very good farm, but what I'm saying is that these Ewes also have very good farms!'

'You go on with your story,' Mensa told Odoi. 'I'm not interested in a comparison of farms!'

'I will,' Odoi said, chuckling in the dark, having been amused by Mensa's lying denial. 'They branched to this farm and stole some fresh corn. They made a fire and roasted the corn. As they ate it, the bell man forgot his fright and became talkative. He told lying stories about how he used to be a superb hunter but had to stop hunting when somebody out of envy which, he said, the church had strongly condemned, stole his gun. Gadago asked him if he was sure he could kill a panther. He said he could easily do that and was surprised the people in north Ashanti could not kill the elephants that destroyed their crops and sometimes had to run away from their villages because they feared the huge, flabby animals. Gadago listened patiently to him and said nothing.

'After they had finished eating the corn and had warmed themselves by the fire, they resumed their trip. It was a quiet night. The dew was falling and the forest smelt sweet. Mensa, you may not know, but there's something one can experience in the forest; it's as if one is in a different place altogether. One is either afraid or one is happy. If one is in good company and one is not afraid, one feels like staying there all the time never wanting to return home. I had the feeling once when my father took me there. But the bell man, though he was in very good company, was terribly afraid when they reached the thick forest near the stream.

'Gadago was walking in front of him and they were getting near the spot where all sorts of animals went to drink water. Suddenly, something like a red glare shone from the distance. The bell man saw it and said, already panic-stricken: "Look, Gadago, what's that?"

'"I can't tell what it is," said Gadago. "It's not an ordinary animal because the eyes of an ordinary animal shows differently against the glare of the hunting lamp. These are different. I can't understand!"

'"Why not shoot it at once!" the bell man said, having stopped dead.

'"Why should I shoot when I don't know exactly what I'm shooting?" Gadago retorted.

'"Please shoot!" the bell man said, in a hushed trembling voice.

'"No, I don't want to die!" Gadago said, also apparently scared stiff.

'The glaring eyes approached and there was a deep rumbling sound. The bell man's legs buckled under him and he clutched at the poor hunter dragging him down with him. Gadago forcibly broke loose from him, dropped his gun and ran for precious life. He grabbed the trunk of an old wild orange tree and tried to climb it thorn and all. The bell man followed close at his heels and also tried to climb the overloaded tree. Gadago was not happy about his joining him up the tree because he would have preferred the unidentified animal to kill and devour the bell man first. So he watched the approaching head of the bell man, aimed his foot at it, and stamped it vigorously down. The bell man lost hold and fell to the ground. He ran hell for leather and then got hold of the trunk of a banana tree. He didn't realize it was a banana tree; all he wanted was a tree. He climbed the slippery stem with trepidation and agility, got to the top but the juicy plant could not bear the weight so it gave way and broke! Down came our friend crashing to the ground! He didn't die or even faint; he was stunned and lay helpless.

'The animal growled again and drew nearer. The bell man had partially recovered his senses. He saw it and ran wildly about calling on various sources for help: his father, his mother (both are dead, you know), the catechist and finally the one he should have called first, God. The animal was so frightened by his savage screams and his strange theatrical performance that it turned round and vanished into the bush. Meanwhile, the bell man was shouting, yelling, crying, throwing his arms about until he fainted dead away.

'Gadago stayed on the fruit tree for some time flashing his hunter's bright lamp in all directions to see whether the animal was really gone. It had. He climbed down and came to the bell man. He saw that he was coming to, so he went to the stream and fetched some water in an enamel drinking cup which he carries in his bag whenever he goes hunting. He splashed the cold water on the bell man's face. A few moments later, he came round. He asked feebly, "What was it?"

"'It was a stray domestic pig!" said Gadago laughing.

"'Are you sure?" asked the bell man, not believing his ears.

"'Very sure, Ataa Quashi!"

"'And why didn't you shoot it?"

"'It took me long to recognize it. It must have been wallowing in the mud so it was difficult to make it out!"

"'Thank God I'm alive!" the bell man said, and heaved a sigh.

"'I also thank heaven I'm alive," Gadago told him, "but make sure you don't get panicky again when you see a harmless pig in the bush. You should have known right away it was a pig when you heard the grunt of the swine. You were bragging and mouthing how you were a bold and a good hunter in your time. Which time was it? You nearly frightened yourself to death because of a wretched, stray pig. I knew it was a pig when I heard the noise it made. It is kept on an Ewe farm some quarter of a mile from here. It must have taken a long time to reach here. Anyway, when I heard its grunt and hoarse squeal which was more like a growl than anything else, I pretended I was afraid to see how you'd take it. My friend, life is for cowards who keep quiet but act effectively when faced with danger and not for brave men who trust in God and boast freely but collapse before the slightest sign of trouble! Get up, will you, and let's go home. You're for ringing church bells, not hunting!"

"'I don't quite understand," said the bell man, embarrassingly confused.

"'You will never understand," said Gadago. "There's one thing I'll do to deflate your confidence which is based on words, and your imagination which is founded on an empty confidence in God. I'll tell every bit of what happened tonight to the young boys in the village whom you've worried for so long! This is the kind of story they'd like to hear about you!"

"'Please don't!" the bell man begged.

"'I will. It's a true story, after all!"

"'I'll supply you with free cassava and yam for two months if you don't tell anybody about this," the bell man tried to bribe Gadago.

"'Aha! There you are! In our conversations you condemn in strong language bribery and other evils you say you find in people, but now that you are in trouble, your first impulse is to offer a bribe. If everybody bribes just once, you still have bribery rampant!"

"'Gadago, you're not a Christian because you've not been baptised and confirmed. In fact, you're illiterate! Why do you try to talk like an educated Christian?" asked the bell man, his deep-rooted feeling of contempt for uneducated non-Christians asserting itself.

'"I don't understand you. What's wrong is wrong," the hunter told the bell man flatly, and added: "I'll tell the boys!"

'Well, Gadago called us one evening and told us the whole story. We were naturally very pleased to hear it and thanked him warmly for telling us. The next day, late in the afternoon, we all went and stood near the path which led to the farm of the bell man. We made sure we would clearly be seen by him, and decided that when he got near, we would clear our throats in an uncommon way. We were determined that if after clearing our throats he tried to ask ugly questions or reprimand us in his usual authoritative manner, we would make both direct and indirect references to how he behaved during the hunt. We were very happy when we saw him coming along the path loaded with farm produce. When he saw us, he had a bad start, and that was the signal! We started clearing our throats with all our might. But his reaction to what we did surprised us; indeed, it was a pleasant surprise, for he said: "Hello, boys, how are you today? Come on, each of you, have some cobs of corn! I've more than I can cook or roast for tonight and I've a lot more on my farm."

'As I say, Mensa, we were pleasantly disarmed and accepted his gift. In fact, that was how it worked out that we became friends with the bell man. He realized, as you probably have noticed, that the hunter may have told us everything and there was no point in his trying to tempt, badger and bully us any longer. We've been on the best of terms with him ever since and he always asks about you. He flatters us now that we are no more boys and, from time to time, he'll tell us things that will reveal the secrets of life to us. We find him a good story-teller, though; but we don't always follow some of the things he says about life. He's an interesting man!'

'I should be glad to see him,' said Mensa, thoughtfully.

But Darku would not let the conversation flag. He said: 'Mensa, you haven't heard all about the bell man yet. Something happened which is even more important to me. That day your mother told the bell man he should go and find a wife and bring up his children properly for all to see, I happened to be around lurking behind the gate to hear what would be said because I wasn't at all happy. I think the bell man took what your mother said to heart and he took action later on probably to spite her.'

'Did he succeed?' Mensa asked.

'I don't know,' Darku replied, 'but I think the problem with the bell man is that he attempts what he knows he can't or shouldn't do, and then fails completely!

'Even when he's failing and he's being ridiculed, he doesn't see it! Could you believe the bell man took a wife again?'

'That's impossible,' Mensa said.

'But it's true,' Odoi confirmed.

'But everybody said he couldn't keep a wife,' Mensa recalled.

'That's what everybody said or thought,' Darku agreed, 'but the bell man thought differently. All he wanted right then was a wife but none of the girls here would have him.

I can't tell you why they wouldn't because it was the girls who said they wouldn't have him!'

'Nonsense! Why pretend you don't know?' Odoi protested.

'Odoi, don't be silly, women must know when a man is suitable!' Darku argued and went on with his story: 'Anyway, strange stories were circulating, all of them to the effect that he couldn't father a child. No girl in this village would have anything to do with him.'

'I don't understand these women. When they're going to have babies, they cry and weep and swear they won't have babies again; and yet, when they have a man like the bell man who wouldn't give them children, they refuse him!' said Odoi, grinning contentedly in the dark. But nobody was apparently listening to him and Darku was still talking.

'He defiantly decided to take a wife from the other village. There was a plain woman there with a child who had been deserted by her husband. The bell man picked on her. He has more money than he needs. You ask anybody, Mensa, and you'll be told. So he used his money generously and impressed the woman and her parents. The woman agreed to have him.

'When the preparations for the wedding had gone quite far, the woman's father said he would have none of the wedding. I think somebody may have informed him about the bell man because he was unable to say precisely why he would not have the bell man marry his aged daughter. Moreover, it was too late to stop the wedding since the banns had been called three times in the church and though people shook their heads in disapproval, nobody came forward to protest or to object to the marriage. In short, Mensa, the wedding took place!'

'And who rang the church bell?' asked Mensa, cynically.

'The hunter! Gadago!' Odoi replied, laughing.

'Did the catechist allow him?' asked Mensa again. 'According to you he never goes to church and has not been baptised.'

'Why, everybody was happy that day and nobody cared about what somebody was, or what he did,' Odoi explained. 'In fact, the hunter was dangerously drunk that day and rang one of the bells so violently that he broke the rope that worked it. The catechist, I suspect, was also drunk because he said nothing. Instead he was grinning and smiling all the time and gave a lively sermon.'

'I've never heard of a drunken catechist or minister before,' said Mensa, not believing Odoi.

Mensa's naïve doubt forced Odoi to lapse into one of his lengthy explanations. 'I know when the catechist is drunk. There are some people in this village who when drunk, deliberately shout and abuse others who, at some time or other, have wronged them. Such people are seen by everybody to be drunk. Sometimes they're not even drunk; they pretend to be, so that they can be excused when they use abusive or improper language. In any case, once a person shows publicly that he's had a drop too much, he's likely to be given a lot of trouble by the catechist and the elders. As for the catechist and the elders, they also drink hard whenever they can. You know, they drink the same stuff as anybody else. However, when they're drunk, they try not to show it and go to bed. So you see, the catechist and the church elders get drunk like, say, Gadago, but they don't misbehave or break the ropes that work church bells so people say they don't drink at all! Ordinary people get drunk and play the fool so people say they drink too much. I don't see the difference!'

'Of course, there's a difference,' said Mensa, who felt he could enlighten Odoi on the not-so-simple dichotomy. 'If you drink often and you're publicly seen to be drunk, then people say you're a drunkard; but if you're often drunk and few people notice it, then according to the public you don't drink. For example, my uncle, Mr Lomo, has hidden bottles of whisky and illicit gin under his bed. At lunch time he takes large quantities of illicit gin as he has reserved the whisky for distinguished callers before whom he takes orange squash. And when his wife complains, he says he's taking it to have a good appetite. Yet by the time he's had his lunch, I can tell you he's drunk. He plays a trick by sucking at peppermint lozenges to kill the smell. He sweats copiously and woe betide any boy who breaks a rule at home or at school! He whips hard to drive his drunkenness away. Whenever I find him sucking at the lozenges in the afternoon after lunch, I know there's a rough time ahead and watch my steps. Anyway, Darku, you can go ahead with your story.'

'Well, the wedding took place and everybody was happy or pretended to be.

'Most of the girls were openly amused and ridiculed the whole affair among themselves. I was watching your mother and she too appeared amused when the two took the marriage vow!'

'How did you know?' Mensa demanded.

'Because of the way she smiled. The bell man looked rather handsome for once. He was in rich Kente which he later told me cost him eighty pounds!'

'Eighty pounds? Incredible!' cried Mensa.

'Mensa, you don't quite understand,' Darku began to explain. 'The bell man has worked for a long time. He has always been hoarding his money and can easily afford expensive things if they take his fancy. He was quite splendid on that day. We all flocked to his house and had plenty of everything. It was the first time I got drunk and I regretted it later. I stole into the room where the girls were pouring the beer and wine into the glasses …'

'And his girl friend was there!' Odoi revealed smiling.

'Whose?' asked Mensa to be sure.

'Darku's, of course!' Odoi confirmed, now laughing audibly.

'That's true, Mensa, but it's not the whole truth. I thought she was my girl and was dreaming of how I would marry her in twelve years' time when, to my surprise, a stupid, ugly-looking teacher came from nowhere and married her! I thought the man was wicked because he was so old and my girl was so young. I couldn't understand why he should have decided to make such a young girl his wife. The whole mess was supported by the girl's foolish parents. I wasn't happy about it and of course Odoi didn't like it either. One evening, Odoi and I went and hid in a nim tree. The old fool passed by to go and court my girl. We simply stoned him. Somehow, the stones missed him, probably because of the dark and the distance; they hit somebody's window. A man in the room insulted the mother of whoever threw the stone. Meanwhile the fool had suspected trouble and had ran away. We also took fright because if we were caught it would be too bad. The catechist would murder us because the man was a teacher. We climbed down quickly and ran away. I had to give it up. He married her and took her away. I don't even know where they are now!

'It was that girl who gave me the drinks and I gulped down anything she offered me. I got hopelessly drunk and it was Odoi who noticed how bad I was and helped me home. After he had removed my shoes and clothes, I had a complete blackout until the following morning.

'Really Mensa, it was a very successful wedding and the couple looked quite cheerful. For a week or so, there was good feasting and merriment in the bell man's house. Still, it was being whispered all over the village that sooner or later the marriage would break up. We thought it was bad people made their married life a constant subject of their conversation. We often visited the couple and they fed us royally.

'However, after six months, we noticed that the bell man was losing weight and was definitely less cheerful. We didn't like it because it appeared he was no longer interested in us and we were anxious to make him as happy as we could. Mensa, we saw him as one of us, you know. Klu thought we should cut our frequent visits to see how he would react. In fact, we expected him to complain but he didn't. We didn't lose hope. We decided to go and stand at the most conspicuous places where he could easily see us; he did see us but never said a word to us. We were very disappointed; we pitied the sad man.

'One day when we were going to fetch water and were walking close behind the girls …'

'Why did you walk close behind the girls?' Mensa cut in to find out.

'I'll tell you why,' Odoi quickly volunteered to answer the question. 'The girls in this village, all of them, are interested in us but they pretend they're not! So we always walk close behind them to tease them!'

Darku then added: 'And we've also observed that the girl who abuses you most and is always eager to pick a quarrel with you is doubtless the one who loves you! You see, these girls are hypocrites. They love us but will make us uncomfortable before we get anywhere with them!'

'I see,' said Mensa, determined to probe the subject, 'but if you're not interested yourselves, it is neither desirable to walk so close behind them nor even to take the trouble to tease them.'

Darku blandly evaded Mensa's point when he said: 'I don't at all understand what you're talking about, Mensa! Odoi, do you?'

'Ha! It's for Klu to answer. He's the one who walks closest to the girls!' Odoi too shifted the responsibility of explanation.

'You don't harm a girl if you walk close to her, do you?' Klu asked, with rare philosophical evasiveness.

'Now, Mensa, answer that question! It's a very good question! Answer it!' Odoi challenged Mensa now that there was the possibility of their being able to circumvent Mensa's point entirely.

'I've nothing to answer,' Mensa said coolly. 'The point is

this: you talk as if it is the girls who are fond of you and that you're not particularly fond of them; but by the way you're behaving, it appears you're perhaps more interested in the girls than the girls are in you! After all, you've just told me that Darku had one of them for a girl friend until a tired, old teacher snatched her away! Now who are the hypocrites? I want to know!'

'By the way, Mensa, I didn't tell you the teacher who married that girl was tired,' Darku protested promptly, his real intention was to try to divert the trend of the probe.

Klu got the hint so he also said: 'Mensa, you always ask funny questions. When are you going to stop?'

Odoi saw a clear opening and tried to make it as wide as possible by saying, 'As for me, I don't like the girls in this village. I saw a picture of some pretty girls of Achimota College. I can tell you they are the girls I want!'

'And they are the girls you'll never get!' Mensa teased him.

'Mensa, you're a goat!' Odoi said half-hurt.

'All right, Odoi, we don't have to call Mensa names the first night he's with us after six years,' Darku intervened. 'The Achimota girls are there; you can run after any of them if you like! I have to finish my story. We walked close behind the girls. One of them asked the other whether she had heard that the bell man's wife had run away. The other girl said she had not and asked whether it was really true. The girl said it was true and laughed. We also laughed and cleared our throats loudly to make them realize that we had overheard what they had been saying. After that Odoi told the girls point-blank that it was a serious thing for them to talk about and that we were entitled to report them unless they told us everything. At first they wanted to show off and tried to be saucy. But Klu coolly explained to them that if it was heard they were discussing such a subject along a public path, they would have a lot to answer for. This, and Klu's expert manner of talking to girls made them reasonable and the one who first asked the question told us what she knew.

'According to her, the bell man's wife ran away to her father because she was not happy as the bell man treated her coldly. Odoi wanted her to explain what she meant by that but the girl asked him to go and ask the bell man.'

'I hear Ghanaian women don't stay with their husbands if they can't have children,' Odoi said laughing and rubbing his hands.

'Who told you that, Odoi?' Mensa asked him.

'I hear,' was the lame reply.

Darku therefore continued: 'What the girl told us was true as we found out later. The bell man's wife had deserted him and he became disheartened and disappointed. He got drunk almost every day and shunned the company of everybody and everything except the church and the bells. We were extremely sorry for him; his wife was such a very good cook and she was very kind and nice to us. It's a pity the bell man has so many things wrong. I can't understand it at all!

'Now, Mensa,' Darku concluded, 'we've told you the two most important stories we've reserved for you. It's your turn now. We've always discussed what wonderful stories you'll tell us about yourself and Accra when you return to this village. We learn strange and interesting things happen in Accra but we never can tell.'

Just then, Mensa's sister came to where the boys were and told her brother that their mother wanted him in. Mensa had to leave his friends who were used to staying up late in the night. He promised them a lot of stories he would tell them the following day.

Mensa was asked by his mother to go to bed. He slept in the same room with Tete, his brother. Naturally he would have to have another conversation bout with his brother; but it was soon apparent that his brother was more interested in himself than in anything else. He bombarded Mensa with his own achievements and never stopped to ask him how he had found the life in Accra; nor did he even appear to be conscious of the fact that Mensa too, would have something useful to tell him. Nothing ever mattered to Tete but himself and his own world. As a boy, he was already beginning to see the world in terms of himself; and at school, if a boy in his class was praised, then it meant that something was wrong with the teacher; but if he was praised, then it was as it should be.

He told Mensa how he had been at the top of his class every year and never scored below seventy per cent in any subject. He had been a class prefect every year and he did not like boys who aspired to be prefects, because those boys were undoubtedly more interested in toppling him than in the prefectship. Surely, he was far more capable than any of them; they knew it, every pupil knew it and, above all, all the teachers including the catechist were aware of it. He had his own farm now, and was quite sure Mensa could not farm. Mensa pointed out to him casually that in Accra it was impossible to have farms. There were gardens and those were what they looked after.

'Ah, but we have gardens here, too!' said Tete, in a vain tone, 'and Section Blue of which I'm the captain had the best plots.'

'I suppose the soil here is better than that of Accra,' Mensa said quietly to indicate to his brother that there was no point in trying to boast. But his brother had no time for subtle hints especially when he was gloating over how he excelled others.

'You see, Mensa, with gardening it is not a matter of soil really but what you actually make of the soil despite its quality. You must have been told this by your teacher. We are taught how to handle every type of soil here.

'My Blue Section is the best and I received the annual garden prize on behalf of its members!'

'I see,' Mensa said, and then flattered and dismissed his brother by saying, 'Tete, you're very good. Now let's sleep; I'm very tired.'

Tete sincerely enjoyed the praise and replied, 'Very good, Mensa, I'll tell you more about what I've been doing with myself tomorrow. Father and mother are always impressed by my achievements.'

At dawn, at about five o'clock, the boys' mother came and roused them from bed. Tete jumped to his feet and was ready. Mensa rolled in his bed and protested he had not had enough sleep; his mother could come and call him later. His mother said he should not talk like that and should get up because their father wanted to speak to his children. Mensa jumped out of bed at once at that piece of information, really very anxious to hear his father speak. He had missed him for so long.

When they stood round their father's bedside, they thought he was not in any great pain; he was calm and composed and appeared happy and contented. He said in a feeble but clear voice, 'Are all my children here?' Mensa's mother said yes.

'Is Mensa here?'

She said yes.

'Very well,' he said, and went on to speak slowly, softly and clearly:

'I've one or two things to tell you, my children. Though you may not see or know it, I'm now very sick and tired but I'm not afraid to go. I'm not sad; I'm happy. I'm an uneducated farmer and can say plain, boring things; but I believe in them otherwise I won't waste time and the little strength I have in saying them. You can take or reject them; but I, as your father, would strongly urge them on all of you. Are you listening to me, my children?'

'Yes, father,' his children replied. Old Anang went on: 'Though I've been poor, I'm not in debt; I've no grievance. I've no malice against anyone and I've never expected anyone to work my ruin. I'm grateful to all for everything. Note this point, my children: never make friends. Never make friends. People are more often ruined by their friends than by their enemies. You have to be nice to people; you should co-operate with people in a cause for the common good; but withdraw when people want to be too close to you and start telling you everything about themselves. Don't tell people all about your disappointments and your successes; they like the former and are alarmed by the latter. Try to do good for its own sake. If you've nothing to offer to charity, don't go and borrow to impress people; charity becomes taxation if you do that. If you have, give freely but never expect any reward. If you do, you'll get disappointed with people and if you're constantly disappointed, you'll become bitter and see the world in terms of the unpleasant and the negative. Most of the people I've known don't give anything freely. They give something for something. They don't share; they invest. Don't expect any gift from anyone for whom you've done some good and never think about him or a gift. Love mankind more than individuals. If you think a man doesn't like you, avoid him. Always attempt what you think you can do well and not what everybody is doing but which you can't do. Take pride in your own loneliness and comfort in the happiness of others. Never think about those who are supposed to be getting on in life. Life is too slippery for anyone to know who is getting on for good or ill. Seek the sick, the humble, the dejected and the supposedly down-and-out; they're wonderful people. Do them good, cheer them up and feel you're one of them in a world in which there's always something blatantly and radically wrong. If anyone praises you, withdraw from him. Speak your mind freely; but if you think there are too many people around who will destroy you because they don't or can't understand you, translate your ideas into that harmless personal way of life that makes for peace, hope and light in your dark corner. Don't advertise yourself and never take anyone seriously. Nurse no ill-will. Nurse no ill-will. My children, life is wrong, funny and full of ironies. You may achieve happiness by getting what you never really worked for desperately. If you get it, thank your stars and keep quiet. You're supposed to believe in God, but if you happen to be unable to do as He wishes, you may end up in hell. What I have said is all I wish to say. It is all I offer you. I'm tired. You may leave me so that I can rest a little.'

While his father spoke, Tete was thinking more about how he was going to be greater than his father. He was so preoccupied with that thought that he heard little of what was said. He saw life as a matter of being down or up. He was on the upgrade and could not listen to everything.

Mensa thought his father was somewhat too stern and lonely. He could not see how he could drop such a good humanitarian friend as Torto who had helped him while he was being starved and ill-treated. He could not indeed digest at once all that his father said. He was, during that moment, more sorry about his father's state than about the possible harsh difficulties that the future could entail. Little did he know, however, that the sympathy he had for his father had made it possible for his father's words to sink deep into his mind.

As for their mother, she had heard most of those ideas before and if she did not agree with all of them, at least she knew her husband was a man of great integrity and could be relied upon. He did not only supply her material wants but also with sustaining spiritual courage, independence and hope. She wept as he spoke.

Her daughter wept also and felt helpless. Indeed, she was

so emotionally carried away that all she knew was that life would be barren without their great dependable father.

There were two sources of light in the room as Old Anang spoke to his family. One was a lantern which had kept wake with him while he lay in pain and helplessness; the other was a candle which was lit by his wife to provide better illumination during the family meeting. Now that Old Anang was groaning and struggling with the little life that remained in him, a whiff of air blew out the candle. The half-darkness returned to the room because of the feeble illumination provided by the more adapted lantern.

Mensa could not bear the groans of his father; he felt his father must be suffering from a fatal illness and that his suffering must be unbearable. He had been told vaguely that the cruel illness was in the stomach but what exactly it was, nobody ever told him. He knew that no matter what it was, it must be intent on doing grave damage otherwise his father, who had been so robust before he left home, would not have been left so weak and helpless under its relentless mission.

But he was not allowed to hang about his father's room. He was called away by one of his aunts and was told to go with Tete to their farm near the village to get the day's supply of cassava for the house.

When they returned two hours later, their father was dead.

Chapter Ten

After his father had been buried and the house began to feel empty though there were still a few relations left behind to cheer up mother and children, Mensa was full of one thought: could it be possible for him to go back to school? There were three of them and he doubted if his mother could look after them all. In his case the difficulty would not be so much the school fee as the catering fee which ought to be paid for at the end of each month. It was perhaps possible and easier to send him to the middle school at the village but he did not want to go to that school. The middle boarding-school in Accra had captured his imagination; it was the school he yearned for; there he would have his classmates and school mates with him again; there he would be free from domestic chores and bother; there as soon as he finished the four-year course he would have a job waiting for him at the government secretariat in Accra.

Nobody really knew how disturbed or unhappy he was, for a sad face in the house could only possibly mean mourning for the departed. His friends, especially Odoi and Klu, did their best to cheer him up; but once an activity was over, the haunting, depressing thought took possession of his mind.

One evening, after dinner while his mother was sitting

alone by herself deeply immersed in thoughts which he felt would never be pleasant, he went to her and said: 'Mother, are you sad?'

'No, I'm not.'

'Then why do you look so sad?'

'I'm thinking about what we're going to do next.'

'Mother, will it be possible for me to go to the middle boarding-school in Accra?'

'I've been thinking about it all the time. Your father wanted you to. I don't see why you shouldn't.'

'Can you pay the fees?'

'I can't tell now, but I'll do my best. Once I get you there, God will help us with the rest. We have to make sure you've passed the entrance examination and the school is ready to accept you.'

'I'm very happy now, mother. I don't want to go to any other school but that one. The boys there are neat and well-behaved. Everybody admires them and many of the people who pass through it become lawyers, doctors, engineers and distinguished civil servants. I feel I might have a chance of being distinguished too.'

'Don't be too sure, my son; just work hard when you get there and leave the rest to time.'

'But mother, father worked hard, nobody heard of him and he's now dead.'

'Yes, that's true; but he died without disappointment, my son.'

'Yes, but when a man is great and he has a lot of money and everything, he shouldn't die disappointed. Can you tell when the rich die disappointed?'

'I can't tell. I can speak for your father because he told all of us he wasn't afraid to die; he was not in any way in debt to anyone. I myself knew that was true and felt he was happy despite the pain. Were you happy after you had castrated that goat?'

'No, mother; I'm really sorry about it!'

'Well, life is sometimes like that. There are so many worries, problems and difficulties for everybody. It's how you get rid of them, your attitude towards them, how you think about the way in which you get rid of them or have got rid of them that matters. What people feel about your actions is one thing; what you think about your own actions however great or distinguished you may be, is another. Disappointments are personal, but some people sometimes tell us they're disappointed or make us feel they are, particularly when they're going to die and we're sorry for them. It's not a question of being rich or poor or being this or that.'

'Since I've already had one disappointment because I castrated that goat, do you think I'm going to get some more?'

'Don't talk like a child! You're fourteen now and must begin to think like a man. Your father has told you enough. Think about what he's said to you and make your own decisions. You've got to face life and feel satisfied you've not treated it crookedly. I can't tell you don't do this or that. I have to leave you to yourself. Think before you act. Still, you can never be too sure!'

It was getting to the end of January and soon the holidays would be over. Those relations who had come to help Mensa's family through the strain and stress caused by the death of Old Anang had gone back to their homes to make what they could of their own lives.

Mensa's mother was never idle. She tended the farms that had been left to her, and her children helped her as much as they could. But she knew that the children would go to school and that she could not work the farms alone. There was an alternative occupation which she thought of very much and which if she could successfully manage would be rewarding financially. That was trading in wax print. But then that required an initial outlay of money, a working capital; where was she to get it? Her husband did not leave her much in cash. Whatever cash was left she had spent on the funeral, most of it having gone into a liberal provision of drinks and food for those who came to mourn with her. Even the little cash donations she received from the poor sympathizing villagers had to be used on those two without which, as decreed by a crippling custom, no funeral gathering could ever pull through.

A bold idea occurred to her; she could ask the bell man for financial help. At first she thought the bell man might by cynically happy that in the long run, she was going to be financially indebted to him. Upon second thoughts she realized that the money, if obtained, was not going to be a gift. The education of her children was far more important to her than the adverse regret of people.

Early one morning, she went to the bell man's house. As was his practice, the bell man was sitting in a deckchair on his veranda, apparently lost in deep thought. When she saw him, her courage melted and she wondered whether her mission was wise. But the bell man had already seen her and was getting ready to receive her. She took a deep breath and went to him.

'Good morning, Ataa Quarshi!' she said boldly, and that was the first time she called the bell man by his real name for more than fifteen years.

'Good morning! How are you?' the bell man responded, cheerfully and eagerly.

'Quite well, thank you.'

'How are the children—Mensa, Tete and their sister?'

'They're all well, thank you.'

'Thank God. Anything I can do for you?'

'Yes. I've come to see you about a pressing subject. I hope you don't mind the bother?'

'Not at all! Not at all! I'm prepared to help you in any way I can!'

Mensa's mother doubted whether the bell man was sincere, the man seemed unaccountably polite and obliging. Yet she was already committed and events must take their course.

'Well, as you know, my husband is no more,' she began, a sudden fit of sadness having momentarily seized her.

'Don't talk about it! Don't talk about it!' the bell man said passionately. 'It's been a terrible blow to all of us. He was a good man who understood life better than many of us. He did understand life, I can assure you. I can! Some of us take everything for granted; he never did. I never realized what a giant he was until he died; then I had a sudden revelation and was quite sure this village would never be what it was again. When he told us we should have our own health clinic and post office, we opposed him because we thought he wanted to throw his weight around when the chief, elders and catechist were there. Some fools even said he wanted the health clinic because of his chronic stomach ailment; they didn't think it could kill him in the long run, let alone so suddenly. Now I know better! I know better! We're the poorer! I miss him! I miss him!'

Mensa's mother was not only wiping the tears off her face but was also completely surprised to hear the bell man pay such tribute to her late husband; for it was the bell man who was often used as a tool in intrigues against any move her husband made to push the village forward a bit into civilization. It was true the bell man was not altogether conservative; still it happened that whenever he had to choose between thwarting the moves of Mensa's father and the good of the village, he chose the former with pleasure and shelved the latter. Now that the man he enjoyed opposing was dead, he was forced willy-nilly to see the paramount importance of development and the futility of all that he had done to withstand it by making things difficult for its exponent. It was now clear to him that, all told, it was the entire village that had lost and not the more easily perishable Old Anang. He was anxious to do anything to atone for his former malice and misdeeds, hence his eagerness to help the woman, although she was unfortunately not aware of this yet.

She said, 'I think you know that Mensa will be going to a middle boarding-school in Accra. Tete, his brother, will attend the middle school in this village. There's their sister who has also been going to school. I need the money to pay their fees but I can't work the farms my husband has left alone, and make enough money to pay all the fees of my children.'

'That's true. That's true. You're quite right,' said the bell man thoughtfully and somewhat apprehensively. He would like to forecast what would be said next.

'I've decided to become a trader in wax print and need some money as security. I can start with a hundred pounds. So I've come to ask if you can lend me a hundred pounds to start the trade. I'm prepared to pay it back with interest; that is, any interest you'll suggest. I'm sure I'll be able to make the money and refund your hundred pounds and the interest on it to you. I expect to work hard and sell it fast in the neighbouring villages. I'm quite healthy too.'

For some time the bell man did not utter a word. Mensa's mother could not guess what he was thinking so she said nothing. It was the bell man who broke the silence. 'I'll be back in a moment,' he said as he rose from his deck-chair with an exuberance of sudden energy that astounded the woman. He went to his bedroom humming the tune of a church hymn. He stayed there for five minutes and returned smiling. He was holding in his hand two bundles of pound notes. He gave the two bundles to Mensa's mother and asked her politely to count the money. She did so carefully with trembling hands; it was a hundred pounds, all together.

Mensa's mother could not easily believe that all that money was for her because she had acted on hope and not on expectation. And now she had got what she at first merely dreamt of. The bell man was also overwhelmed, for it never occurred to him for a moment that he ever would be called upon to do good to a woman who had tried to mock and ridicule his physical failing. Now it was charity that had replaced intentions of revenge. Both had little to say to each other. Mensa's mother, like the bell man, was overwhelmed and spoke briefly. She said: 'Thank you very much for this. I'll do my best to refund it to you before the end of the year.'

The bell man replied: 'What matters is your children's education. Make the best possible use of the money, and when you genuinely feel you can refund it, do so. I don't insist on any time limit!'

Now that Mensa's mother had cash in hand, she was sure Mensa could be sent to the middle boarding-school; she told Mensa and he was very, very happy indeed. For some two days, he could not sleep and imagined all kinds of things as he lay awake. He worked himself into believing that one day, he would rise in the world and perhaps hold a top post in the civil service. He had seen and admired so many great civil servants in Accra who were said to be financially buoyant and socially acceptable. They always looked grave, those top men; and the secret of their lives was a mystery to him. They were people who hardly spoke their minds without caution or a highly guarded phrase. It was possible that he too could also rise from the ranks and become like them; definitely, he wanted to be one of them in future. He had once been told rather casually by 'I'll-twist-you' that if one wanted to be successful in life, one should read a lot; just read anything at all that came one's way. Reading could be boring when one started to make it a habit, but when one became used to it, it could be a wonderful, pleasurable activity that would have to be satisfied everyday.

He told his friends about his going to the middle boarding-school in Accra.

Some were delighted, others could not see any significance in his going to that school. Odoi in particular had his own ideas. Where he got them from, none of them could tell except himself. He told Mensa in his characteristic frank style: 'Mensa, if you go to that school, you'll be sorry, I can assure you! There are millions of bedbugs there and you'll not sleep for four years. They'll suck all the blood out of you! And I shouldn't be surprised if they brought your corpse here one day for burial!'

'Nonsense,' said Klu, 'I've never heard of bedbugs sucking anybody's blood till they died.'

'Not when they're one or two,' said Odoi looking dangerously serious. 'Mind you, in this case, they're not in the thousands but in the millions!'

'Who counted them? You?' Mensa asked more amused than alarmed.

'Can you count a million bedbugs?' Odoi asked, breathing audibly with excitement. 'Look, if you are in bed, and just when you're going to sleep, you smell something travelling in front of your nostrils, then you wonder whether it's a bedbug and you quickly catch it and squeeze it between the tips of your two fingers, then smell your finger tips to be sure, then you say, "Good heavens! It's a bedbug!" Then you get up, strike a match and find several of them, brownish, anaemic, scurrying away, then you lie down again about to sleep and then you feel under your feet there's a bedbug, across your thigh, there's a bedbug, over your stomach, there's a bedbug, by the sides and under your buttocks, there's a bedbug, and on your fore-head, there's a bedbug, and then nearly under your armpit and almost in every other part, there are bedbugs, what will you say? I want to know! They're many! You just can't count them! I hear there are twenty boys in a dormitory, each of them earmarked by a battalion of bedbugs; and there are four or five dormitories all together; don't you think there can be millions of them in the whole school?' Odoi asked, completely out of breath now; he could not stand still and was swaying from side to side, sweating, rubbing his hands and wearing a confident smile that served notice to his friends that he was an unassailable authority on what he was talking about.

And while his friends were thinking of how to discredit his exciting piece of information, he went on: 'Over there, the bathroom has no roof. Boys have their bath at five-thirty in the morning; they shiver and the cold is biting to the bones! And, you know, when it rains and they're in their bathroom, they can't finish washing, they've plenty of nat-ural shower nonstop! Their towels are useless because they get too wet and remain showered so long as it's raining and so long as the boys are in the bathroom. Yet if a boy runs out of the bathroom naked to the dormitory to squeeze the water out of his towel and to wipe the wet off his body, he is in trouble. He's whipped for going nude which this coun-try doesn't like! Mensa, I'm sure when you get there, you'll check up on what I'm saying now. I know you think it's a bunch of lies and that I'm joking; but that's why I'd like you to check up. If I were you I wouldn't go to that school. My own uncle was there; he's now a branch manager of a bank. When he comes home on leave, he talks a lot about his experiences in that school.'

'But it's said it's all right to suffer a great deal at school so that when you leave school you can enjoy life better,' said Klu, who wanted to comfort Mensa who was seriously engaged in weighing up the points made by Odoi.

All of them were silent for a brief spell, thinking; then Mensa said, slightly downcast, 'I can't understand you, Odoi. Everybody else I know says it's a good school. I've seen a bit of it from the outside myself. I'm sure if I go through it, I'll be a great man in future.'

'A great big boss in future?' Odoi asked, cynically. 'You just don't know what you're talking about! I don't know of anybody who has been a great man on an empty stomach! Do you understand me? On an empty stomach! In that school, boys don't have tea and bread for breakfast. They take ordinary drinking water! I tell you, they take plain drinking water and by eleven in the morning, boys who have a weak stomach faint straight-away. My uncle told me everything; they faint straight-away! And before that school gets through a year one of the boys must be dead!'

'This is a lie!' Klu cried, with great vigour. 'You simply want to discourage Mensa!'

'A lie?' asked Odoi, with vehemence, the perspiration streaming down his chubby cheeks. 'I'll tell you more. A boy who had the money and could afford to buy some breakfast from one of the wives of the teachers, died two days after eating what he bought from her. Even the specialist doctors at Korle Bu Hospital could not save him. The stuff he bought from her is called "soaked". It's overfried cocoyam into which the rancied palm kernel oil has soaked beyond measure! Such a piece of cocoyam was so hard that the boy couldn't chew it up. The sharp splinter bits got into his stomach and pierced through the stomach wall like deadly shrapnels! He died. All the boys knew it was the "soaked" that killed him and yet they could not say so openly because they would have been whipped if they did. So they all fell back on water and many fainted at eleven in the morning when it was time for reciting long verses of church hymns! I must admit it's possible some of those rascals fainted or pretended to have fainted because they hadn't memorized their long hymn verses! And, by the way, my father says only a fool won't fill up his stomach in the morning before he works!'

'True! Everybody in this village knows your father is a heavy eater!' countered Klu, who felt Odoi was dangerously brainwashing Mensa if not both of them.

'Do you mind if I tell my father what you've just said about him?' Odoi asked, his eyes ablaze with mischievous delight. Of course, he knew his father could eat a lot, but it was, in any case, none of Klu's business to blurt it out just anywhere.

'Odoi, you can go and tell him!' said Klu defiantly. 'Your father knows I'm a good boy. He knows that even long ago, I volunteered to weed his farm free of charge. He has once or twice asked me to buy him some tobacco; that was when you were being naughty and complained about a sore foot which wasn't sore in any way! He knows I'm a better boy than you are, so he simply wouldn't believe you if you told him. And, mind you, it will be insulting to tell him such a story. You may get a dirty slap somewhere if you tell him! Even if he decided to look into the matter, I'll mention Mensa as my witness after I've denied it completely. Mensa will also deny it and you'll get into awkward trouble. You'd better drop the idea!'

Odoi was not pleased with the way Klu wanted to bluff his way out of possible trouble. He thought fast and said: 'Look, Klu, you have to choose between two things. The bananas on your father's farm are ripe. Bring me a bunch of them and I'll drop the matter. If you refuse, I'll tell your mother what you said about my father. I know she'll take a serious view of it and you'll get a hurting slap in the face before you'll have time to explain yourself! Now talk yourself out of this one. I'd be glad to hear you!'

Odoi was enjoying life at this stage because he could see the painful confusion into which he had plunged his friend. Klu's face showed it. He was black, so it would be incorrect to say he blushed, but the expression on his face changed. He was annoyed; he did not like the way Odoi used words to make life uncomfortable for his friends and then to blackmail them on top of it.

He recalled that Odoi dreaded physical violence. He was a coward in that respect, so Klu decided to exploit it. He said, feigning a very furious look: 'Now let me tell you one thing, Odoi! Only one thing! If you play the fool with me, I'll punch you in the mouth, like this!' And, whang, Klu threw a demonstration punch which missed Odoi's lips by a fraction of an inch. Odoi recoiled in fright; he was speechless and immobilized where he stood. But his brain was working red hot. He saw two alternative courses of action before him: either he ran away by simulating threats that he was going to report Klu or he should force a laugh and reprimand him for taking the joke too seriously. He decided on the second alternative and so smiled cheerfully and said: 'Klu, you don't have to take everything seriously, do you? I was joking, you know. How can I tell my father or your mother such a silly story? Come, you know we're friends and I can't do that! You're too easily excited and you make me forget all I want to tell Mensa about that hell of a boarding-school!'

'All right, Odoi,' Klu said, trying to hide his feeling of triumph, 'I was playing the fool and didn't mean to hurt you. Let's forget about it, but make sure you don't tell Mensa any more silly stories about that school. You know how the catechist treats us here; it's the same thing everywhere. But you know we all like to go to school because apart from the spelling, the recitation of hymn verses and the mental drill in arithmetic, it is really very nice. And you know how happy we are when we get our own back on the catechist! Have you forgotten the story you told me?'

'I don't remember telling you any story!' Odoi denied, to frustrate Klu; he could not easily forget an injury.

'Never mind,' Klu said, ignoring his spurious denial. 'It's a story you, Odoi, told me and I liked it because it was against the catechist.'

'Tell me. What did Odoi tell you?' Mensa asked eagerly.

'According to Odoi,' Klu offered to tell Mensa, 'the catechist asked three of them to go to his cassava farm and clear the weeds because they couldn't spell the word "develop". They spelt it with an "e" at the end. Odoi said he thought it could be spelt like the word "envelope". In fact, he couldn't see why the one had no "e" at the end of it and the other had.'

'But at least the two words sound differently, don't they?' Mensa asked, attempting to be and looking clever.

'All the same, Odoi and the other two boys couldn't spell it. So by way of punishment, the catechist asked them not to come to school that afternoon though he would mark them present in the attendance register. They should go to his farm instead and do the weeding in the hot sun. Mensa, I hope you know what weeding in the hot sun is like; you sweat and breathe dust; the sweat mixes with the dust and this irritates the skin; you get stung by the tsetse fly and curse the whole of creation. Anyway, they went to the man's farm and did the weeding, but they made sure they didn't cut the weeds to their roots so that they would sprout vigorously in three days' time. Moreover, they uprooted a few cassava plants, cut off the tubes of cassava and put the cassava plants back into the soil. Then they went and made a fire with dried twigs and roasted the cassava and had a good meal.

'When they returned to the school at about four o'clock and the school was about to close for the day, they told the catechist that they had discovered a few of his cassava plants uprooted and were dying. They explained to him it was likely it had been done by that half-mad tramp, Odotei. They told him Odotei had done the same thing on their fathers' cassava farms. The catechist said they were quite right and that Odotei was becoming a nuisance and should be sent to the mental hospital in Accra and locked up. He ended by saying that Odoi and the other two boys were very good boys though they couldn't spell and that if it had been any of the other boys, they would have been happy about it and would not have cared to report it to him. He said if they continued to behave so well he would write a good conduct report for them at the end of the term. Odoi and the two boys were happy they had fooled the fool!'

'Odoi, is it a true story?' Mensa asked, absolutely impressed by it.

'Klu often lies but this one is true! I uprooted four cassava plants myself,' Odoi confirmed, feeling very proud by rubbing his hands while shifting his trunk from side to side.

'How I wish we could have done the same thing to my uncle, Mr Lomo!' Mensa said wistfully.

'Ah, but in Accra you don't have cassava farms,' Klu reminded Mensa.

'I know; but we do have some gardens which have mostly crops like groundnut, okro and garden-eggs. Something could definitely have been done to those garden crops to teach some of those teachers some sense. You go to school and they make your life one long hell! They even let blood sometimes! Why are teachers like that? Did God create them like that?' Mensa asked, angry and disappointed.

Odoi had a quick answer to part of the question at least: 'My uncle tells me it's all the fault of the white missionaries, especially the German missionaries. He knows a lot about those German missionaries, you know; and says that although they were ministers, they could whip boys like slaves. For example, if a boy was sent to one of them for insulting his mother, he would strip the boy's backside naked and give him twenty-four lashes; then before he gave the twenty-fifth, he would shout "And one more for the Kaiser!" And, thud, the boy got it. My uncle says, once a boy was whipped like that he never insulted his mother again and would be a good boy for ever. I think most of these teachers were so treated by the German missionaries that they wanted to treat us in the same way.'

'But if they didn't like it, why should they do it to us if they're sensible?'

'You'd better ask them. I don't know,' Odoi said, not interested in the reasons behind it.

'Of course, Mensa can't ask them a question like that without getting badly caned. They never smile and hate awkward questions from boys,' said Klu, with resignation. He went on: 'According to the catechist, what was done to them when they were young is good for any other child today. There's nothing we can do about it. But there's one thing that puzzles me, Odoi. I can't believe a white man will give a human being twenty-five lashes. They look so nice when they come to this village.'

'I can't understand it myself. You can ask my uncle when next he comes here on leave. All that he told me was that there were Basel missionaries; they were hard working and they didn't like naughty children so they would give them twenty-five lashes, the last and severest one, according to them, was for their Kaiser!' Odoi tried to explain.

'But where are they now?' Mensa asked, finding the story difficult to believe.

'Ask my uncle, will you?' Odoi said firmly, but then went on to say what he had been told: 'I don't know where they are now. My uncle said there was a great war and the British collected those missionaries and threw them out of the country. He said the British were wrong to do that but I can't tell.'

'Did the British send them out because they whipped boys?' asked Mensa, hoping Odoi would say yes.

'Maybe they did, maybe they didn't; what my uncle said was that the British secretly feared the Germans. I don't know the Germans, so I can't tell!'

'I wish I knew those missionaries,' said Mensa, wondering what sort of people they were.

'I wish I knew them too, you know,' Odoi took it up, 'because my uncle said they were very, very hard working and practical. They wrote several books in our languages and put up several strong, airy bungalows which are now being used as school buildings.'

'One for the Kaiser,' muttered Klu to himself. 'That's a funny idea.'

Chapter Eleven

Mensa arrived at the middle boarding-school in Accra during the last week of January. It was late afternoon and several other boys had already arrived. There was nothing he could think of in particular and his mind was more or less blank. The place was strange and new to him; and yet it was the place which he had thought of and heard so much about.

The buildings of the school were impressively old; they had lasted for over a hundred years without any radical renovations. The ground-plan of the school was based on that of a monastery, if one may be allowed the comparison. There was the front two-storey imposing block. It was imposing because it was built on the brow of a sharply rising bit of ground. This block was carefully quartered for various functions. The four rooms on the first floor were used as classrooms and the headteacher's office. The three big rooms on the ground floor were used as two dormitories and a classroom. Form One occupied the big classroom on the ground floor and Forms Two, Three and Four used three rooms upstairs.

Connected to this block, on the right-hand side, were quarters for teachers and a curious place that was used both as a backyard and as an all-purpose store. Then connecting the quarters on the right and left in the northern wing of the establishment were two dormitories for boys. Between the two dormitories was a huge gate which was tradition- ally called the portico. Inside was a completely enclosed quadrangle and it was virtually impossible to leave the school once the southern gates and the northern portico were closed.

There were four Houses all together. Houses One and Two occupied the ground floor of the administration block, and sandwiched between them was the classroom for Form One, which was also used as the school's assembly hall because it was the largest classroom. Houses Three and Four were on the northern perimeter of the quadrangle.

All the windows of the dormitories had stout iron bars in them to ensure that boys were securely barricaded in; and because of the iron bars the windows were never closed; indeed many of them had broken loose and were lost but since they served no functional purpose in the eyes of those who ran the school, they were never replaced. Thus, when there was a thunderstorm and it rained, some of the boys were drenched in bed. The roofs of the dormitories were of corrugated iron sheets that were tired, old and full of rust and scandalous holes. There was no ceiling. The floor of the dormitories looked like the surface of a colonial street in by-gone Accra. It was covered with hard tar with pinholes and potholes in it owing mainly to the regular, diligent and scrupulous sweeping with a hard broom it suffered every morning and afternoon and sometimes evening.

Each dormitory had about forty-eight beds. Each bed was two and a half feet wide and five and a half feet long. It stood about two feet from the ground on wooden cross-legs. It had no mattress. Boys had to bring their own blankets to school. Anybody who made the mistake of bringing a quilt or a light mattress along with him was doing nothing but displaying gross aristocratic pretensions which must be deflated and curbed forthwith by ruthless punishment and verbal humiliation. All boys must wallow in uniform hardship.

The dining hall was a detached building and did not form part of the taut monastic arrangement of the other buildings. It had only one door for entrance and exit. It was on the west of the administration block and faced one of the gates through which the headteacher passed for unannounced inspections.

The bathroom was about twenty yards away from Houses Three and Four and forty yards away from Houses One and Two. It had no roofing and was in all sincerity like a huge cattle kraal except that its walls were built of switch and thoughtfully covered with a thick, impenetrable coat of tar. It was not, like some kraals, partitioned; but as Mensa discovered later, each class obeying the hierarchical order of things, knew where to congregate to take their bath from buckets. The big bathroom had no running water.

The lavatory was so appalling that no amount of cleaning brought it to civilization.

There was an extensive playfield which was ringed in by a tall hedge of fine, sturdy evergreen plants. It was virtually impenetrable and of practical use for diverse purposes pleasurable or otherwise.

The general impression one had as soon as one was in

that school, then, was that it was old, tired, austere and yet flourishing. The quiet of the place, the old age even of the croton flowers and nim trees, the worn-out Bahama grass that served as turf in certain parts of the playfield, all these assured one that one was in a special world with its own laws for the correct moulding of the human body, mind and soul.

Soon after Mensa's arrival, his friend Torto arrived too, lanky, clean and barefoot, carrying his boxes on his head. It was not that Torto did not have shoes; he had them but it was a rule of the school which was served to parents that no boy should wear shoes; a boy could be allowed to wear shoes on the compound for reasons of health only and that must be stated and clearly signed by a gazetted medical doctor. It was also proper he carried his boxes on his head because that was a true sign of humility and poverty which would be amply rewarded in the life hereafter. Anyway, Torto had had a fresh hair-cut and was well-washed and groomed. Not long after his arrival, Antwi, Danso and Badu arrived. Mensa was in good company. All of them had their stories to tell and were visibly happy that they had succeeded in coming to the school which was both revered and reviled but which they still admired so greatly.

When they had been shown their dormitories and beds, the next thing they thought of was to settle down to a meal. Forewarned that the school had no kitchen or cooking facilities, they had each brought their own dinners. The school provided the refectory; what was eaten in it was no one's concern. For that reason a boy whose parents were not in Accra would have to arrange with a housewife to supply him with food, good, bad or indifferent for lunch and dinner. He paid a catering fee of ten shillings or so to the kind, sacrificial housewife at the end of each month the school was in session. As there were four classes, all of the same numerical strength, the arrangement was that junior boys in Forms One and Two fetched the food for senior boys in Forms Three and Four. A junior would go to the town and return carrying two enamel dish carriers, called canteen sets, one for himself and the other for the senior for whom he fagged. The time allowed for a junior to stay in the town on this business was thirty minutes no matter the distance and no matter whether he was held up by his cateress or the other cateress who had not finished the meal when he arrived. Boys were not supposed to have anything whatever to do with the town when they were interned for the term and any attempt to return late from this food mission was severely punished. It was common for a boy to do at least a mile and at most two and a half miles on this trip so that boys often had to run and trot, dash and walk fast when the bell went for the exercise. Despite all the good intentions and all efforts, very many boys were regularly late and they were regularly punished. For two years, a boy's heart would pound and break whenever it was time to go to the town to fetch food.

With their mission-school-training background, Mensa and his friends felt it would not be safe for them to take their meal where they could be easily seen. They looked round the compound and saw the tall hedge that ringed in the playfield and most of the school. The part of the hedge they chose was some fifty yards away from their new bathroom or bath-kraal and it looked very convenient for their purpose; for there, the hedge had grown some twelve feet high and could therefore swallow them up, especially as there was a convenient clearance within the walls of the hedge itself. They put their canteen sets down. They contained excellent food—the farewell food. There was the meat stew spiced with fine round onions; this was to be eaten with yam and had been brought by Antwi. Then there was the chicken stew and kenkey provided by the gentle Torto, and the vegetable stew, alias palaver sauce, to be taken with fried and boiled plantain, supplied by Mensa. Danso, Badu and Dua had brought theirs along with some sugary dessert.

They had started enjoying the meal, talking intimately, when they suddenly saw two people walking slowly in their direction. They looked hard and saw that one was a girl and the other a boy. The boy was lame in one leg, perhaps that was why they moved slowly. They could not recognize the girl though Danso swore she was the only daughter of the headteacher of their new school.

The possibility of an encounter with the lame boy sparked a discussion, mainly of a speculative nature. Danso said the lame boy was a senior in Form Four, he would probably threaten or punish them if he saw them there. He had been told that no one could be certain what a senior would do to a junior. It was better they looked forward to some kind of trouble.

Antwi was not impressed by what Danso said. He wanted to know what the boy and girl were coming to do there. Did their newly found hideout serve a special purpose for boys and girls? No one could give definite answers, but Antwi was secretly thrilled. He was sure he knew what they were coming to do there, and though he was scared, he thought he had won a moral battle already. Admittedly, young pupils, by a process of pooling ideas and sifting them can arrive at the truth more easily sometimes than by their know-all, over-confident teachers; but at that moment the boys had been so distracted by the unexpected approaching invasion that they could hardly think clearly. They resumed eating in silence.

They had barely taken three or four morsels each when the lame boy leading the girl, first burst in on them.

'Good heavens! Who are you?' he cried, having limped to get a good stand.

'We are new Form One boys, sir,' replied Danso submissively which was too bad; it encouraged the lame boy.

'Who showed you this place?' he asked authoritatively, as if the boys had made an unwarranted incursion into his own territory.

'Nobody,' Mensa replied. 'We thought we could have a quiet meal here.'

'A quiet meal?' said the lame boy with a sneer. 'You've already broken an important rule of this school and the punishment is going to be awful!'

'Which rule is that?' asked Torto, trembling. He was not used to rough life and had already taken fright.

'Eating between meals!' the lame boy announced.

'We aren't eating between meals. We are having our dinner,' Mensa protested.

'The usual trouble again this year!' said the lame boy with contempt. 'You boys come to this school raw and stupid to be trained to be sensible and law-abiding and yet you don't make any effort to stop talking like buffoons! Look, in this school what you've just said amounts to the commission of another offence. It comes under one of the most serious set of rules. It is altercating with a senior!'

But the boys did not understand the word so Danso asked: 'What do you mean by altercating with a senior?'

'Ha! Ha! Ha! Another silly question from a raw boy,' the lame boy sneered again, virtually dancing on his good leg in his glee. 'In this school, nobody seeks to know the meaning of words used in formulating rules for boys. Altercating is altercating; all I mean is that—and mind you, I'm really generous to explain myself at all—is that if any junior boy argues with a senior boy or says anything unpleasant to him, he's definitely altercating! I'll explain further so that you can enjoy your fine meal better. You must have kind parents. Once you're charged under this head, no teacher or parent or God himself will look into the offence. A senior is a senior and once he says you're altercating, it is enough. You've had it and the punishment follows as the night the day!'

The boys were dumbfounded. Perhaps the horrible stories they had heard about the school were true; or was it that the lame senior boy was bullying them? They had heard about the atrocities which senior boys subjected newly arrived Form One boys to, but they had not dreamt of how they were applied. Antwi was thinking hard, anyway. He felt the most important thing they had to do immediately was to talk their way out of possible trouble. He plugged a live line of action and said: 'Senior, we're not eating on the school compound and besides we haven't decided to report you to the headteacher for bringing his daughter here. You can join us if you like and have a good meal. We're friends, you know!'

'Hey! The Lord have mercy upon you and where you come from!' cried the lame senior, dancing on his good leg in malicious delight. 'It appears you don't really know or understand what trouble you boys are in. From the frying pan into the fire, it has always been said! First, I can easily report to the headteacher that you new boys who have not yet spent a day in the school, have already made a clearing in this hedge. This is a demarcating hedge carefully looked after by the school. What I'll tell him amounts to damaging school property which is punishable by caning and the carrying of gravel all day long. Besides, you boys should be extremely careful and watch how you talk, or you'll get sacked from this school in three hours. You want to suggest my bringing this girl here is an offence; but tell me, what kind of offence? You've dangerous ideas which two weeks in this school, if you're lucky to survive them, will ruthlessly suppress! The headteacher's daughter saw you boys coming here; ask her; she told me as the prefect on duty; ask her; that you were up to no good; ask her; and I asked her to come and show me where you are committing the offence; ask her! Now you want to imagine all sorts of obscene things which this school doesn't like at all. By the way, how can you even dare approach the headteacher with such a story?'

'By walking!' retorted Mensa, who was disgusted with the lame boy.

'Who said that!' cried the lame boy, having accompanied his words with action that messed him up a bit; for he was so definitely annoyed at the cheek that he did not take into account the fact that he always had to stabilize his bodily equilibrium. He bent forward violently to knock a plateful of food over on the ground. In doing so he plunged headlong in Torto's direction, who, finding the plunging head coming straight against his own, dodged it, allowing the lame boy's head no intermediary object to prevent a crash into one of the hedge plants. When the crash was accomplished, Mensa and his friends found that the lame senior's neck had been wedged in the fork of two branches and that his head was on the one side, his tongue sticking out, and the rest of his body was on the other, still, writhing and helpless. When the headteacher's daughter saw the crash, she vanished from the place. Mensa and his friends managed to extricate the neck of the lame senior from the fork of the two branches. His eyes were bloodshot and he breathed heavily. He was dying with anger and bitter disappointment.

When he had struggled to straighten his body and limped to get a good stand, he quickly wiped the dirt off his entire body. Then he decided to leave the place and spoke as if he was possessed. He jabbered strange things and the boys found it difficult to see what exactly he was talking about. But when he began to cool off as quickly as he had been excited, one thing became clear; he was promising them hell and torture. They would be superhuman to survive unscathed. He had seen boys cry like babies when they were given their Saturday punishment. They would appreciate his power and authority better when the whole school assembled for prayers in the evening. He had already decided to make each of them scrub ten dining-tables in the morning, afternoon and evening for two weeks. He laughed frenetically, grinding his teeth, the white froth showing at the corners of his mouth. As he was leaving them, they heard his last parting words in the distance: 'These boys look different. Either they'll give this school a pretty bad time or they will get badly hurt by this school!' And he hopped away.

'What does this mean?' asked Badu, who had been silent, trying desperately to grasp the significance of the incident.

'Well, I don't know,' Antwi shrugged and added: 'When we were staying in Mr Lomo's house, we thought life was too bad. Now here we are. We haven't spent a day yet and everything is getting wrong. Here's this sick boy who wants to make love to the headteacher's daughter; he sees us here and is disappointed. Instead of keeping his disappointment to himself and going away quietly, he turns on us. I think some of the things he says are true, though. For instance, how on earth can anyone of us approach the headteacher and tell him that the lame senior boy wanted to make love to his daughter? That we can use the phrase "make love" is in itself an unheard of crime. And to bring in his daughter and a senior pupil into the bargain will mean our being thrown out. Why is it that these teachers don't wish us to speak the truth?' he asked half-angry, half-puzzled.

'Well, the truth is what they want to hear!' said Badu with conviction. 'Can you believe,' he continued, 'that the headmistress of the girls' school was terribly upset because two dogs were mating? That was after school and those little boys and girls from the unrecognized primary school were laughing and giggling at what the dogs were doing. The headmistress said they were very, very bad children and saw to it that they were caned the following morning. But dogs and fowls are always mating. What's wrong in looking at them? Why don't they tell the dogs and fowls not to do that in public?'

'You don't quite understand the whole thing,' said Mensa, amused at Badu's complaint.

'What exactly don't I understand? Tell me,' Badu demanded.

'When you see animals mating,' said Mensa, with a grin to make Badu realize he ought not to be that simple, 'you pretend you haven't seen them at it and then you're a good boy. That's all!'

'Now I have my own idea,' said Danso gravely, speaking from past experience. 'I'm out of trouble so long as I don't do what teachers say I shouldn't, or what I've learnt they don't expect me to do. I don't like teachers; I'm very sure of that but I can't run away from them; I can't run away from school and walk about in the streets and be ridiculed by wretched foolish boys! All I have to do is to watch them, see what they like and dislike and please them.'

As soon as Danso finished, Antwi took over and said: 'Teachers are a wicked lot. That's all there is to it. Nobody can tell me they aren't. What didn't we do to please Mr Lomo? A boy must go to school and we have come to school, so we must be troubled, kicked, knocked around and made miserable. And here it has already started with this boy who is lame too. I can't eat any longer. We'd better pack the plates and leave!'

Their first week at the religious middle boarding-school passed without any extraordinary event. They had expected the lame boy to molest them and wreck their morale, but as it happened there were greater people in the school than the lame one. Moreover, there were so many things to do that they were ruled by a quick succession of events which they hardly had time to realize fully or even understand. They were however imperceptibly and unconsciously gathering their own impressions and these were obviously centred around the people who interested them most, their new teachers.

First, there was the particularly formidable headteacher, Mr Abossey, who was perhaps taller than Mr Lomo but definitely fatter. He had a huge paunch, a short thick neck, and, on the generous side, a rather handsome but positively cunning face, the cunning showing in the eyes. His skin was jet black like good tar and his hair was curly, beautiful and always carefully brushed. His buttocks were immense and appeared cumbrously mounted on his hindquarters. As he had deep bow legs the buttocks jerked up and down uncomfortably as he walked. If he walked fast, they bounced up and down. He appeared to be a man of huge appetite whether for food or for any other sensual thing. No pupil expected him ever to wear a pair of shorts because he would have to force his remarkable hindquarters into them thereby cutting a figure that would half-frighten or half-amuse the boys. He seemed to have sensed this, so he always wore a pair of long khaki trousers and long-sleeved shirts, no tie.

The teacher who came next In importance was also tall but not fat. He had a fair skin and a gentle smile. He seemed to be more interested in his teaching and music than anything else. Boys liked and respected him, and did their best to please him; but he seemed unaware of the love boys had for him and went about his duties without fuss and threats.

The third one was of medium height, stout, well-groomed and undemonstrative. He had a noble brow, fine big eyes, a brownish velvety skin and often wore well-polished, strong shoes. He looked surprised whenever he was told a boy had broken a rule.

The fourth and last teacher was a cadaverous-looking man who never smiled; he looked either angry or sour; but curiously when he smiled, he seemed perfectly human and innocent. That perhaps was due to the attractive dimples in his cheeks. He was notorious as the most impatient, irascible and efficient cane-wielding machine in the entire school. It was whispered that the kind of shorts he wore on Monday could indicate the kind of caning he would administer to boys throughout the week. He was a clever, hardworking but mechanical teacher who passionately believed that once a boy passed the entrance examination and was enrolled in his class, he was sufficiently talented to tackle all the diverse subjects with equal proficiency. If a boy balked at any subject, it was not that he lacked motivation or ability, it was because he was an unwitting prey of laziness and the only effective cure known to him was desperate beating. Some boys suspected that he enjoyed caning.

These, then, were their teachers and mentors and Mensa and his friends were carefully and thoroughly briefed on the character and habits of each one of them by the pupils in Form Two. Of the lot the headteacher was dreaded most because he was unpredictable and cunning, furtive and grasping, immoral and vicious, devious and entirely dangerous. The one who came next after him was not regarded as a soft man but as one who loved people and had human sympathy. He was good and kind and his teaching went down best. The third teacher, though respected, was in some ways considered funny and stingy. Funny, because he appeared surprised when a school crime was reported to him and stingy because according to boys he spent three-pence on his breakfast every morning. The fourth one was respected for his sincerity and zeal but was often dismissed as a thoughtless pain-inflicting robot.

Naturally, the one Mensa watched closely and very care-fully avoided was the headteacher; for unlike Mr Lomo he was so diverse in his crooked ways that it was absolute-ly impossible to escape him for long. For example, Mensa overheard some of the top senior boys saying that whenever he had a sleepless night he would get out of bed by five in the morning and wait for the bell to go. As soon as the bell went, he would break into the dormitory and whip, kick and slap boys. This, as Mensa soon realized, was a terri-ble thing indeed; for it was at this time that boys tended to sleep soundly to round off the night's uncomfortable sleep which was bedevilled by the hordes of bedbugs which relentlessly invaded them throughout the night and retired at day-break.

Whenever he entered a dormitory and began beating, boys bounced out of bed and ran helter-skelter oblivious to objects in their way. In the general confusion one boy would collide with another, his head hitting the other's mouth; another would run into a bed and gash his shin; another would run out of the dormitory stark naked as he was about to change when the surprise attack was launched. The climax was when the huge and terrible man would accompany the beating with shrill shouts which alone could make a boy lose his bearings completely. His language issued forth in short repetitive words, short phrases and staccato sentences.

If he attacked boys in this way at the beginning of a term, he was sure that the boys would not roll over in bed and go to sleep again for the next three weeks or so when the reveille bell was rung. Senior boys in Form Four did their best to reassure him in that belief; for, to demonstrate that they too had been properly trained to maintain discipline, they would whip boys out of bed and as soon as they routed them out of the dormitory, they would themselves go back to bed and sleep soundly for another hour.

The huge and terrible teacher had another impressive way of punishing boys. Every evening after eight-thirty, if he happened to be on the compound, he would be alert for action. It was the rule that no boy should utter an audible syllable when the curfew bell was rung. When the bell went, he would lurk behind a window of a dormitory, his head half-inclined, his ears cocked to detect the slightest sound of a human voice. If he heard a sound, he would not try to find out who had made it; he would yell at all those who slept in the area, that is, to about four or six boys, and ask them to come out and stand in the open quadrangle. He would then go to bed and snore off the rest of the night. By five in the morning if one of the boys had gone back to bed or had collapsed and slept on the gravel ground, he would be caned mercilessly.

Indeed, the way the huge and terrible headteacher performed his caning was so special as to be unforgettable. To indicate the way he wanted a boy to receive the lashes he would shout: 'Stoop! Stoop! Stoop!' Each shout of the word having been accompanied by a stroke of the cane in the back. His strokes were naturally heavy and once they were received on the back it was impossible to stoop to proffer the backside on which he insisted on striking. But a stroke on the back was not part of the formal beating; it was a signal that the boy should stoop before he was given the four formal strokes. No boy was ever able with the best will and determination throughout his career in that school to stoop promptly as soon as he was struck in the back. The natural and reflex action was to bend backwards, not forwards, to lessen the hurting effect of the cane. A boy would therefore receive, say, twelve extras before the formal ones.

Such caning was often done in the morning when boys lined up for their personal hygiene check-up. It was a thorough affair which appeared to be prompted more by a desire to punish than by any sound educational policy. For example, one rule was that nails should be cut short, if possible so short that blood would trickle from where the nail was firmly hinged on to the flesh. If a nail was so cut and was dirty, it was passed as correct. If a nail was not cut low but had been carefully cleaned without a dark spot inside or outside it, the wearer still qualified for caning. He would be whipped in the manner described above.

Mensa became aware of the fact that a day started in that fashion was too bad for his nerves. The beating, no matter whether he or anybody else suffered it, worried him a great deal. His nerves were either on edge or were frayed for the rest of the day. He could not understand why the other three teachers, human as they looked, would not, in the name of God, tell the headteacher that the way he beat the boys was like deliberate murder. He was so frightened of the teachers that he could not work his arithmetic sums correctly. He could not read without making mistakes. His fingers would be quivering if he wrote. He felt constant vague pains in the stomach. His heart thumped violently if he was called upon to read. During most of the morning session all life became blank and lived like a dream. His body was going to be destroyed and he had no idea when this would take place. He turned to activities of the mind, read any book other than a textbook hungrily. He spoke less to people and doubted the good intentions of all mankind; for it was not unusual for a boy to piss into his shorts at the prospect of caning which the teachers would laugh at very happily.

It was the headteacher who taught him in his last form, and no single day passed without some incident which affected him emotionally. He had his special method of conducting loud reading lessons. He would ask those sitting in front to read. Boys would do their best to read well. If a mistake was not made within fifteen minutes, he would rise and shout: 'The air is foul! The room smells! Some of you may not have washed this morning! Four lashes each! The whole class, come round! One after the other! Four lashes each!' The caning would start and he would be so happy that he yelled and laughed as he caned. Then half-way through the caning, having glutted the desire, he would stop suddenly and ask those who had not received the cane to go back and sit down. He would continue the following day, and it was their business to remind him if he happened to forget.

He had by now lost interest in the entire reading lesson and would be absorbed in thinking his own thoughts, biting his nails and humming some tunes to himself. Reading mistakes would be made but he would not hear them. Then suddenly he would remember that there was a lesson on and so he would turn to the class ready to administer some more caning and ask a boy in the back row to read. Any boy in the back row he called by name would jump because he was not expecting to read; he would be trembling and there would be no co-ordination between his brain and the vocal organs. There would be plenty of mistakes. But instead of walking over to the boy who was making the mistakes, he would rather cane a pupil who sat in front within an arm's reach. He would then shout at him while caning him: 'Why did that boy make a mistake, eh? Why did that boy make a mistake? Don't you think it's too bad, eh?' While whipping the innocent boy in this way, since he was not prepared to squeeze his bulk through the narrow gangway between the row of desks, he would be watching his face to see whether he would show any sign of having taken offence for being pointlessly punished. If he detected any resentful attitude, he would give the boy twelve formal lashes because it was the duty of a boy to show appreciation when being flogged by a teacher. A teacher by definition always had the welfare of boys at heart and a resentful attitude violated this definition and must be checked. What a boy had to do, then, in these circumstances, was to smile while being flogged and if possible thank the teacher in humility and in gratitude after he had borne the flogging on behalf of his classmate in the distant back row. Anybody therefore who sat in the front row was a likely victim of the man's caprices and spent the reading lesson praying to God to let the clock move faster; but God who knows about both order and disorder perhaps saw to it that the clock moved as it should and the whole forty minutes was always spent as usual.

Apart from caning in the classroom, however, no boy had to let his money, particularly a noisy coin, drop out of his pocket. A boy would want to wipe the tears off his face after he had been beaten; he would reach for the handkerchief in his pocket. If in doing so a coin or a paper money or a piece of candy fell down or caught the eye of the huge terrible one, he would confiscate it outright and never give it back to the boy. If it was some candy, he would eat it before the class and when he had finished eating it, he would smack his lips as a testimony to his having enjoyed it. While eating, he would ask boys to do private reading. If a boy waited in vain to have his money given back to him and finally had the impulse to go and ask politely for it he would be beaten out of the office.

It was also in his last form that Mensa noticed one more thing about the head of his school. It was that he was very fond of women especially widows of the local church and middle-aged women who for one reason or another were not living with their husbands. It happened that some of those women had their sons in the school and therefore got into contact with the man. He would invite one of them at a time to his office in the late afternoon after classes. He kept some wine in the office and would try to get the woman drunk. Then he would talk glibly and play tricks on her, interspersing his amorous antics with short silly laughs which sounded like the bleats of a he-goat to those outside.

But he probably never misbehaved sexually in the office. Antwi for one was quite sure of that because as soon as a woman went in and he felt it was safe, he and one or two of the boys would tip-toe to the door of the office and take it in turns peeping through the keyhole. Yes, it was in the evening that he executed his designs. But the details of execution were unknown to the boys.

There was a huge nim tree in front of the administration block. Under it was an abandoned steel pylon which was used by the boys as a garden seat. When it was dark, it was darker still under that tree and yet boys would strain their eyes from their dark dormitories facing the place to see what the huge, terrible man would be doing to the woman. Their imagination disturbed their sleep. The senior boys looked round for girls. They all fell in love with the very beautiful and neat daughter of the man. They knew she was not a loose girl and she knew they were not bad boys. But a flame burned in the boys and kindness flowed from the girl to the miserable and hungry boys. She became nice to one or two. It was said she was a nymphet which she was not. The lame boy was going to try his luck when his designs were fouled up by Antwi, Danso, Badu, Dua, Torto and Mensa.

Chapter Twelve

It was the practice for a boy of average intelligence to get a job in the administrative service of the country after finishing at this boarding-school. Mensa was no exception and was employed as a clerk first at the secretariat, then after a year was posted to the lands department and back to the secretariat again before he went through his probation period of three years.

He was hardworking, observant and diligent but a little impatient with those he considered dull or unimaginative. During these early years and some time after, up to the time of his marriage in particular, he had several memories of what happened in the boarding-school. One memory which made him think a great deal was a sermon preached on a Sunday by an ageing clergyman.

It was compulsory for all pupils to go to church on Sundays and most of them were simply bored and fed up with church services. Deep down in their hearts was the feeling that they were past the age when church services should be forced upon them. They loved their God but felt they should be free to worship Him when they felt they should. They dreamt of the day when they would finish with the boarding-school and never go to church until they were old and about to die; then they would return to the church not so much because the church would necessarily pave their way to heaven but because they would get a decent burial in a decent corner of a public cemetery that had been parcelled out to Christians, Moslems, pagans, foreigners, unidentified corpses, paupers and others.

The old clergyman had a habit of preaching long sermons. He would preach and preach and then suddenly lower his voice. Mensa would imagine he was going to finish and say amen. But he was wrong. The venerable man would raise his voice to full strength and shout at the quiet, well-behaved and tolerant congregation. While he did so the church elders, who had appropriated the last pew at the back, would be conversing in undertones amongst themselves and would also be eyeing the fashionably dressed young women who came to church late.

It was when he had raised his voice during one such long rambling sermon that Mensa heard: 'You young pupils of our beloved Church! It's a pleasure to see you here with us so politely and quietly seated listening to me. Very often you pretend you've heard and understood all that is told you from this pulpit; but you don't really. You don't! I repeat, you don't! And why do I say this? I mention this because when you go home on holiday, you don't go to bed at night. You don't go to bed! You lurk behind people's houses whistling girls' names! Whistling girls' names! And the result? You produce bastards for others to look after! Now I'll tell you what I as a minister of religion think of it. It is clearly this: God doesn't like it! It embarrasses Him! Besides, it is both embarrassing and inconvenient to everybody; to you, the girl, the parents of the girl and yours, the church, the child when he grows up and last, but not the least, to your conscience! Moreover and personally, I don't derive any satisfaction from baptizing bastards!'

He spoke on and on, the elderly male congregation very well satisfied that this time the wrath of the old minister was against the boys and definitely not against them. But some of them had and were still introducing illegitimate children into the world but held the comforting philosophy that they were already old and had erred and if there was any reincarnation after death they would know and do better. They upheld the excuse that while the boys were young they must be told in no uncertain terms that the practice was wrong. One thing they had forgotten, however, was that when they were young they were told often enough to eschew the practice. They were ruthlessly caned when they wrote love letters which happened to be captured in transit. Their girl friends' fathers had beaten them up in the dark under nim and coconut trees when they wanted to keep clandestine appointments with their daughters.

To Mensa, Antwi and the rest, the huge and terrible headteacher of the middle boarding-school was not only a scourge but a sexual model during those days. They had heard how their hero had fathered several bastards but, in each case, had denied completely that he sired them. The church authorities knew about it but did nothing openly because it was considered better to preserve the name of the church than to smear it with the lascivious aberrations of a single man. Nobody had the courage to question or reprimand him seriously about his sexual adventures or his involvement with bastardism. It was a scandal that must be hushed up and if possible forgotten.

One thing Mensa and another boy unwittingly succeeded in doing was to have his daughter as he had other women. They had groped their way blindly to it and had what they wanted but the girl fell pregnant. She was sure Mensa was to blame. Mensa was not sure whether he was, but felt strongly that it could have been him anyway. Yet nobody asked him any questions and after three months the girl was seriously ill, and when she recovered she no longer had to look forward to having a baby.

Though some time had passed since he left school, the affair was still bewildering to Mensa. The years that had gone by did not prevent it from dogging his mind. He could not fully understand it. What made him feel very guilty was the forcible destruction of the pregnancy. Antwi had told him about it, and they were both sure the huge and terrible headteacher must have arranged it. Mensa had been both happy and sorry about it, the usual ambivalence; for on the one hand, he was fortunately out of trouble; Mr Abossey had saved him and nobody would hear of it beyond this circle of his intimate friends who had also desired the girl. He was as free as anybody else. He consoled himself that he had after all done what he thought many others had done; he could not even be sure whether he was the potential father. If he had been claimed a father, what would his mother have said if she heard it; she who had struggled so hard to look after him while he was a pupil. What would his brother, Tete, think of him? It would make him more proud and self-righteous. It was very lucky it ended that way. It saved him the scandal, the worry and the sleepless nights.

On the other hand, he felt he was worried all the same; for the thing was on his mind and quite often when he worked at his desk in the office, the subject would occur to him and he would reconstruct it, formulate all the arguments for and against how it had ended and would get lost thinking about it until someone spoke to him. Then he would get a start and resume work. When he started working he thought it was all over and that his mind would never scoop it up again. Yet sooner or later, inexorably, it would. Then came the time when he became disgusted with his own mind for being so treacherous. 'My mind why wouldn't you stop thinking about it?' he would whisper to himself. His mind would assure him, 'I'll stop it one day. Never mind!' But it did not.

Mensa thought he was not like the other young men who worked in the office with him. There was something innocent about them. They never appeared to have anything on their minds or anything to hide. They spoke freely about girls and the indescribable things they would do to them when they married them. Mensa would listen to them and force a smile. He thought his colleagues, the young men, were merely dreaming; but he knew it was the dream that made them happy not sad or troubled.

One day an idea occurred to him; he would do well to marry. That could stop the harrowing thought. He thought first of marrying the headteacher's daughter to make up for anything wrong he may have done. But five reasons dissuaded him. First, he thought if he did so he would be the laughing-stock of his school-mates who would say, 'Here's this girl whom anybody and everybody has seduced before, and Mensa has married her! Mensa is a fool!' Second, he felt the headteacher was such a vicious and degenerate man that his grandchildren, at least one or two would inherit some of his bad traits and would be dangerous beyond control. Third, he was not sure whether he loved the girl or whether the girl loved him. Fourth, it appeared the girl loved sex just like the way people loved their food, and whether she really loved the man who satisfied her was a question he could not answer. Fifth, suppose, he thought, by coming forward the girl's father was able to conclude that he had impregnated her, what would the consequences be? He loved money as much as he loved women and if he had the slightest chance, he would institute customary proceedings against him and extort some hundred pounds from him.

Thus the sympathy he had for the girl and the desire to atone for any previous misconduct through marriage were outweighed by personal, social and financial considerations which made him wonder whether it was not wise to let sleeping dogs lie, however much the whole thing worried him.

He thought of consulting Torto who was working in another government department as a junior clerk. He rang him up and it was agreed they should meet in an obscure beer-drinking shop which was a mile away from their former school.

The keeper of this shop was a shrewd voluble man who no new story could upset because, by virtue of his profession, he must have been told a story of its kind before. He never made any attempt to eavesdrop, and nobody ever went to his shop having made up his mind beforehand to tell him stories. But as soon as he started selling the drinks and the buying was good, he became happy and looked as amiable, sociable and pleasant as he could. Naturally, the customer too after a few drinks would be geared to the correct temperature of amiability, sociability and pleasantness. So seller or barman, customer or drinker would now be on the proper footing, both apparently eager to exchange a few confidences.

But the shopkeeper always had an advantage because apart from the fact that he had no drink in him, he always had the propriety of never starting to tell secret stories. It was, however, his ingratiating smiles that would lure the customer to pour his now relaxed mind. As soon as the customer started, he knew how far he should let him go and then chime in with his own story sometimes identical or plausible, but never really true because, in view of the future, he hated being compromised in any way by a drinking customer. Yet since his fiction always rang true without a willing suspension of belief on the part of the customer, the customer was encouraged to say more with complete assurance. The more the customer told him something really new or interesting, personal or secret, scandalous or pornographic, the better. His eyes would be half-closed, steady and twinkling.

As the customer spoke, his mind would conjure up, say, a host of biographical case histories that could match what was being told him, let the customer have them to substantiate his points and, in short he would be in full control of the customer and elicit the whole truth and nothing but the truth from him. He and the customer would from then on become close friends. The customer having been satisfied that he had won a friend he could trust and consult in time of trouble and he, the barkeeper, would also be satisfied that he had won a customer whom he could rely upon to come to his shop every evening or quite often to buy from him and boost up the sales. There was therefore no need for him to expand his small shop. The sales were good and expansion superfluous. His business was successful and profitable and had thrived well.

At six o'clock in the evening, the two friends were in his shop. They were sitting on the high stools against the counter. Mensa called for two bottles of beer but Torto said he was not sure whether he would have beer; perhaps some Coca-Cola would do; yet before he could make a decision on what he would drink, the shopkeeper had already opened two bottles of beer and served two glasses. 'I'm terribly sorry,' he said, hiding his glee and also the contempt he had for Torto for not taking a more expensive or rather a better profit-yielding drink. Then after a second, with an enchanting smile he said, 'I didn't realize you'd ask for Coca-Cola. I've already poured the beer. You take it, sir, and then you can soften it later with Coca-Cola. Alternatively, I can give you Coca-Cola and Mensa can have the two bottles to himself. That will be a better arrangement, sir. The customer must have what he asks for!'

'I can't start with two bottles!' protested Mensa.

'Never mind, my dear,' he said charmingly. 'Beer always goes down well in this part of the world. It'll make you enjoy your dinner and, as you know, it refreshes as you drink it! And by the way, Mensa, what we're talking about reminds me of something I've decided to tell you. Antwi, your friend, was here the other day. He said he could never go beyond a bottle. I couldn't agree less with him because although I sell drinks, I entirely agree with the state that drunkards are a nuisance. Drink has sapped their strength and they're economically unproductive. But drunkards are few, sir; they're few. That's why the Bureau of Statistics doesn't supply figures as to how many drunkards we have in this country! Drunkards make a lot of noise in the neighbourhood but they're few, sir. Anyway, when Antwi had managed to drink the bottle of beer which I thought was negligible since he's got a fine constitution, he happened to see my niece who had returned from college. My wife had sent her to me with a message. He quickly ordered another bottle which I quickly supplied because if you don't try the next bottle you wouldn't know if you can take it! Antwi, by the way, pulled a wallet out from his hip pocket. Mensa, it was well loaded with banknotes! My niece was impressed, I was impressed too. I introduced Antwi to her as a matter of courtesy. Antwi was efficient that evening; he bought drinks for anybody in sight while keeping my niece's glass refilled. He bought drinks worth one pound ten shillings. Mind you, I didn't make much profit out of that! I didn't! The profit runs in pennies. It was his gallantry and charity which impressed me. I always hold that the charity which goes into buying drinks for others is the one best remembered!' He laughed uproariously and poured himself some iced water and filled Torto's half-empty glass with beer.

He went on: 'Although I'm drinking iced water right now, I know a lot more about the drinks I sell than many people, yes, than many people. I drink myself, you know, especially when I look forward to a good night's sleep.'

He laughed aloud again. In fact he guffawed and shouted jovially to an old customer who was coming in: 'Hello, Mr Doe, you're welcome! As I was telling you last night, when I was a private in the army I had a friend who was a recruit called Doe. He didn't like the Regimental Sergeant Major but loved his daughter! Ha! Ha! Haa! What will you drink, Mr Doe?'

His interest had now shifted somewhat entirely to the newcomer and Mensa seized the opportunity to broach the subject to Torto. Mensa made the effort to state the case for and against his marrying the daughter of the huge and terrible headteacher. He tried as much as possible to be fair to either alternative and asked Torto what he thought of it now that he had heard his detailed analysis of the subject. Torto who was not used to drinking beer beyond a glass but had now drunk a bottle spoke louder than was prudent considering the nature of the subject. It was also obvious that he felt strongly about it and was not prepared to mince his words. As far as he was concerned, the question of marrying the headteacher's daughter did not arise and he roundly condemned both father and daughter. As he spoke, it became clear that he was no longer able to control his indignation and Mensa was going to tell him to take it easy when to Mensa's alarm, he turned round and asked the shopkeeper who had one ear cocked in their direction all the time: 'Would you marry a girl everyone has seduced?'

'I'm married, so the question doesn't arise, Mr Torto,' he replied and laughed and added, 'But I can tell you one thing: a woman is seduced sooner or later; that isn't necessarily bad. What I don't like is adultery! If I caught my wife at it, I wouldn't cut her throat, I wouldn't drag her to court. I would pour gasoline on her and burn her alive so that she wouldn't do it to the next man!' He laughed again and asked, 'May I know who's in trouble? You don't have to say it if you don't want to. I insist on that!' He laughed again and appeared completely uninterested.

Mensa winked at Torto not to speak but Torto would not be controlled or signalled into caution. He cried: 'There's a slut and the daughter of a rogue whom Mensa wants to marry! The idea is preposterous! It's the last thing I can see Mensa do!'

'Mensa, do you love the girl?' asked the shopkeeper, taking Mensa's right hand into his hands and caressing it.

'I'm not sure I do,' Mensa had to say embarrassed, 'but I think, in a way, it's proper I marry her.'

'If you're not sure you love her, please don't marry her. That's my advice and it comes from a good friend. Your glasses are empty, any more beer?'

'Yes!' Torto replied gingerly.

The shopkeeper fetched another bottle of beer, opened it and served the two young men. As he did so he spoke: 'When I was going to start this shop, I asked myself: "Lartey, can you run a beer shop?" I answered myself and said "Yes." So I started and though business isn't as good as I could wish still I've faith in the future. By the way, your bill is fifteen shillings. You'd better make it a pound. You see, young men are better at settling bills than old men. You people are so young and strong. What about a tot of whisky for each of you? It'll clear the beer. I hear some Scotsmen do that! So, Mensa, don't marry that girl if you can take a humble advice from a good friend. Though I spend most of my time behind this counter, I know a lot more about human problems than the priests and ministers of religion! They talk from the books; I talk from experience. They advise, warn and ban people from the bread and wine; I advise, encourage and supply people with wine and spirit. People tell me everything because I've no hell to promise them; I tell them everything in any outrageous language and they like it. Mind you, I don't claim to be better than the priests and ministers of religion; everyone has his talents to exploit; but I've saved one or two couples from imminent matrimonial disaster and they have been very grateful indeed. It's only fair to them if I say they can be counted among my best customers, and I helped them free of charge, you know—no obligation whatever; and I always say man shall not live by money alone!' He laughed with a roar and then laughed heartily for a long time when he saw that Mensa and his friend appeared impressed, and suddenly mixing his laughter with speech he said; 'Gentlemen, may I serve the whisky to make the bill one pound?'

Chapter Thirteen

No doubt the whisky was served and the bill rose to one pound ten shillings before Mensa and Torto staggered out of the beershop, arm in arm, singing old school songs, each pledging he would soon marry the girl he loved.

Later on Mensa married the kind of girl he was looking for, and at this stage he was lucky. She was a good girl from a respectable family. Nobody would say his wife was perfect in every way, but everyone knew she was a good, and peaceful woman who was completely dedicated to him and shared in large measure his emotional and spiritual life. She was neither tall nor short, and had an attractive face and a glossy brownish skin. What stood out most about her was her grace and charm, but to some extent she was docile in her relationship with her husband. She was extremely hardworking and toiled at several odd jobs, the most lucrative being the baking and selling of bread and cake. She was therefore able to help Mensa save a large portion of his income. As the years rolled by, it became obvious they were not going to have many children. They had three in all, but one died soon after birth; thus they were blessed with Odole and Nee.

Mensa was devoted to the children. He used to wash and dress them when his wife was busy and he could afford the time. He always looked forward to returning from the office to them, to play with them and tell them stories and explain children's pictures to them. When it was seven or eight, depending upon when they slept, he would put them to bed and sometimes feel very sad afterwards because life in the office was becoming more intolerable each day, and he was determined to fight through, though he knew the sacrifice would be great; for, in his more than fifteen years in the Supreme Court offices, he had risen rapidly, having been promoted over others, and now it looked as if he would take the post from Mr Roberts, his only superior, and be the chief clerk. The prospects were fraught with hazards. Mr Roberts really hailed from a village near Saltpond but he told everybody except partially secret official documents that he came from Saltpond, a town which was neither dead nor alive but rich in historical associations and therefore, though somnolent, lingering on as an important town. He was fair-coloured, almost mulatto, and bragged repeatedly that his great-grandfather was an Englishman, by which he meant that his great-grandfather could have been Scots, Welsh, Irish or English, or a mixture of English and Irish or Scots and English or of three of the four stock, presumably. Nobody was sure who his father was except partially secret official documents and he never took the trouble to brag about him, except that he fancied the name Roberts thrown upon him marked him out from amongst the ordinary mortals in the Supreme Court offices.

Mr Roberts' face was round and his nose more European than African. He had a passion for clean white dress, food, drinks and women. He never read anything beyond the bible, the hymn book and the daily newspapers. All his serious conversations centred around the iniquities of imperialism and colonialism, both of which words he never really understood, except that had they not been embodied somewhere, his salary would have been seven hundred and twenty pounds a year instead of the two hundred and two pounds a year which he now earned.

He had worked for thirty years, but owned no house, or any enduring property. He had no savings and never went to Saltpond on leave because he had nowhere to sleep there; nor could he visit his mother's village near Saltpond, since he had no money to give to the poor old relations there, and the visit in itself would be a retrogressive step. Every week-end he fed on roast pig, or goat or turkey and drank either Haig Dimpled whisky or Gordon's gin laced with Rose's orange squash. As he grew older, his appetite for food and drink increased; but since he had eight legitimate children and six born outside wedlock, his financial resources were well siphoned to keep the fourteen children alive and in school. In this respect, he tried to deny himself, not by going teetotal, but by changing drinks during weekdays; the drink most favoured being illicit gin, a kind of unscientific vodka, but equally potent, particularly when the weather was hot. He became flabby, football-stomached, slightly hunchbacked, long, thin-necked, his head consequently jutting forward. This posture had slightly reduced his tallness, and made him look hollow-chested. He had forgotten all his English except officialese, models of which were a-plenty on the files. In the office he spoke a mixture of English and the vernacular and thus achieved greater linguistic efficiency than he would have either in pure English or in pure vernacular, and, in this linguistic hybrid, he was capable of displaying on occasion perverted insight or genuine lucidity of mind.

As chief clerk he had immediate control over the court interpreters: a mysterious batch of men who looked as if they had been born poor and were decided to look poor until they died. When a serious trial was on, they gave the impression of men who had been permanently vaccinated against human sympathy. These interpreters were technically multi-lingual, but they did not know any language well and unless challenged by a desperate advocate, their translations were the last word. Where there was no lawyer and the trial magistrate was an Englishman, unless the police charge was watertight, they could, as the sun rose and fell, decide the case by virtue of the fact that they were the interpreters. People got to know this, and Mr Roberts too discovered it. An agreement was made not on the basis of corruption, for they were convinced that every man is either corrupt or potentially corrupt, but strictly on the basis of their sense of poverty and a strong desire for vengeance. The money flowed in and men were either thrown into disastrous debt or got jailed though innocent.

What brought matters to a head was a simple case. A sanitary labourer, after a day's work and a good evening meal was resting in a home-made deck-chair in front of his single quarters. Another sanitary labourer for whom his wife had some liking went into his room and conversed in soft tones with her. When the man came out of the room, the husband followed him to the street and asked him to recount word for word the conversation he had had with his wife. The man refused to do so and said it was absurd and ridiculous. The husband therefore concluded that the man was trying to make love to his wife and challenged him to a fight. He got badly beaten because he was too excited to fight properly.

He felt that he had been cheated twice and that was absolutely intolerable, so he went to the police and complained. The police charged both of them with breach of the peace as they were sure of the fight but not so certain of the alleged love-making. The two men therefore had to appear in court.

Friends told them about the interpreters and Mr Roberts. Contacts shuffled through the darkness of the night, and each labourer found and gave away ten pounds so that they would not be sent to prison.

It was a Tuesday. The court was packed full. The wretchedly dressed and frightened labourers were called, and the first one climbed into the witness box, trembling, and was sworn in.

The English magistrate said to Mr Suka, the interpreter: 'Ask the first accused why they fought.'

'Yes, your honour,' Mr Suka replied and then said to the first accused: 'You wretched labourers shouldn't have fought. Do you know that?'

'Yes, sir, but I thought he was interfering with my wife. I'm sorry for what happened.'

'Your honour, the accused says it was due to a slight misunderstanding, and begs the court to deal leniently with him.' Then, turning to the idle crowd in the courtroom, Mr Suka, the interpreter said: 'Ladies and gentlemen, if I catch anyone making love to my wife, I'll stick a knife into his buttocks!'

There was an outburst of laughter in the courtroom, and the interpreter shouted: 'Silence! Order!'

The English magistrate asked, 'What are they laughing at?'

'Your honour, the accused says it's sad to go to prison.'

The English magistrate would have smiled openly, but he had once been told by a drunken Briton, an army sergeant, recruited from Stepney in London at the European Club: 'Never smile with a bloody native. They bloody well play up to you if you bloody well do that. If they bring a bloody native from a bloody gold-mine charged with hiding a bloody gold nugget in his dirty arse-hole, jail him. Jail the bastard, I says!' The magistrate, with Winchester, Oxford and Lincoln's Inn behind him, squirmed at the utterance but took the advice. So when the interpreter spoke about the labourer's theme on sadness and imprisonment, he bent over the evidence-recording book, pretended to be writing and laughed well secretly. He looked up with a stern face and said: 'Tell him to step down and swear in the second accused.'

'Yes, your honour,' the interpreter said with alacrity.

The second accused was sworn and then the interpreter asked: 'Have you washed this morning?'

The court laughed; the magistrate looked sterner, and the interpreter roared: 'Order! Silence!'

'Ask him why they fought, will you?'

'Yes, your honour,' and, turning to the second accused, Mr Suka said: 'You dirty rat, why on earth did you go to see his wife?'

'I wanted to ask her to find me a wife, sir.'

'Your honour, he says it was a brotherly misunderstanding.'

'It's strange these labourers call each other brothers and yet they fight frequently. Ask him whether they were drunk?'

'Look here, you've got to find a wife yourself, you understand?'

'Yes, sir.'

'They were not drunk, your honour.'

'All right. Tell them they have been cautioned, but if they appear before me again they will be fined. The next case, please.'

The two labourers, bowing deep with pleasure, chorused: 'Thank you, sir! Thank you, sir!' and hurried away to see their time-keeper.

But Mensa had heard of this bribe too, and felt it had gone too far now and had been done too often, so he braced himself and went to Mr Roberts, who was poring slowly over a file.

'Why did you take ten pounds each from those two labourers?'

Mr Roberts was so surprised that he jerked his head up pretty carelessly and the spectacles fell from his face.

'Who told you?'

'It doesn't matter who told me. Each time you do it with those two interpreters and the police inspector, I know.'

'Damn it! Do you know my salary, Mr Mensa?'

'Yes, two hundred and two a year.'

'Do you think eighteen mouths can live on that?'

'But that is not the point.'

'Answer me!'

'You know Mr Roberts that even if these labourers were found guilty, they would be fined ten shillings each. Why take twenty pounds from them?'

'I didn't take twenty pounds. I got five pounds from Mr Suka, he handled the case.'

'You shouldn't have taken anything from these poor labourers. They earn twenty-five shillings a month, and must have borrowed tis money with interest. How do you expect them to pay back the ten pounds each during the rest of their lives?'

'Oh, I see. You're now a champion of labourers, and no more of junior clerks, or are you a moralist?'

'I hate morality. I'm not interested in right and wrong. What you've done is downright wickedness. It's inhuman. Though these men will stay alive, you've already killed them. That's what bothers me.'

'Tell me where the law provides for what you're talking about? Do you think the law seeks the truth? Never. Do you think laws are passed to make man happy? Never. Do you think the government is interested in you and me? Never. They collect the taxes and I don't get a fair share. Who are the government but you and me? I collect the tax myself and make up. Have you ever heard of a wrong system producing good people?'

'You're the greatest stupid fool ever known in history. You should never have been born. You should never have been put in this post!'

'Aha-a! So it's my post you want, isn't it? You've climbed very rapidly, Mr Mensa. You're agitating for more pay, and now you want to be the chief clerk. We shall see!'

'Mr Roberts ...'

'No more! We shall see! As your chief clerk, I order you to go back to your work!'

So Mensa left Mr Roberts very disappointed. Mr Roberts laid his plan and went to the Court Registrar.

'Sir, I want to discuss an important matter with you.'

'What is it about?'

'It's about Mr Mensa, sir.'

'Ah yes, he's a first-class civil servant, Mr Roberts, is he not?'

'Maybe, sir.'

'What?'

'Maybe, sir.'

'Do you mean you're not satisfied with him?'

'General Orders, sir, and health.'

'What do you mean, Mr Roberts?'

'Well, Mr Mensa owns jointly with one Mr Torto, another civil servant, a motor transport and a corn-mill. He is organizing the junior clerks to ask for more pay. He is always rude to me and is suffering from hypertension, sir. Do you think he ought to remain in the service?'

'Thank you, Mr Roberts. Leave everything to me.'

'Thank you, sir.'

The Registrar thought over Mr Roberts' report for a whole week and then called Mensa.

'Is it true, Mr Mensa, that you own jointly with a Mr Torto, a civil servant, a motor transport and a corn-mill?'

'Yes, sir.'

'But that's against the G.O.s'

'We want to live in our own homes and we thought that was the best thing to do.'

'Is it true you've been asking for more pay?'

'Yes, sir. Here's the memorandum. If we get better pay we will work harder and honestly perhaps.'

'I see. Is the memorandum signed by all the staff?'

'Yes, sir; except Mr Roberts.'

'I see. What about your hypertension?'

'The doctor says I must control my temper, sir.'

'Very good, Mr Mensa. But why have you been rude to Mr Roberts?'

'I'm sorry, sir. I never meant to be rude to him, sir. I sometimes lose my temper easily and speak harshly, but I don't really wish to be insubordinate, sir.'

'Very well, Mr Mensa. I'll forward your memorandum and endorse your claim. You want the chief clerk to have two hundred and seventy-five pounds a year. I don't think that's too much. I'm going to ask Mr Roberts to be transferred from this office and recommend you take over his job. But with your hypertension, I advise you to retire at forty-five. I'll advise the chief justice to make you a commissioner for oaths and this plus your pension should keep you going when you retire.'

'Sir, I never wanted to take Mr Roberts' post if that is what you mean.'

'I know, Mr Mensa. If Mr Roberts can report you to me like this, he'll report me to the chief justice if I get in his way. Go back to your work, Mr Mensa.'

'Yes, sir.'

Some months later Mr Roberts received a letter transferring him to the Department of Agriculture. He was absolutely convinced Mensa must have engineered his transfer. It simply could not be otherwise; so he sought Mr Suka and when they met he said: 'Your life is in danger.'

'How Roberts?'

'Somebody has been spying on you.'

'Are you sure?'

'Very sure.'

'Who is it?'

'Mr Mensa.'

'I don't believe you.'

'Here, read this letter.'

Mr Suka read the letter of transfer with great difficulty, moving his lips as he did so, and when he finished he said: 'How is this connected with spying on me? You've been transferred, that's all. If I were you, I should try to make money there. See what I mean?'

'But Mensa caused my transfer.'

'How?'

'He approached me about the twenty pounds we took from those labourers, heaped insults on me and went and saw the Registrar and told him about it, you see. My punishment is this transfer. It's like death. I can hardly feed eighteen mouths on my present salary, and I'm not sure deals can be made at the "Agric" department.'

'Bad luck, old boy!'

'Mr Suka, you don't understand. You're going to be dismissed for inefficiency. I've seen the letter,' Mr Roberts lied, and Mr Suka instantly believed him.

'Did Mr Mensa ask I should be dismissed?'

'Of course, who else could? He's going to be the next chief clerk, and said either you go or he quits. So there you are!'

'Roberts, this man Mr Mensa has made a sad mistake. He will go first!'

'You'd better let him, or watch out!'

Three days afterwards there was a loud explosion at

midnight in the rented house where Mensa and his family lived. The explosion was so loud that the whole neighbourhood awoke in terror. The explosion ripped down a large chunk of wall facing Mensa's bedroom and the violent quake broke the window panes and cracked the walls. The police were called, investigations were made, but no one was arrested.

Mensa was frightened because he knew whoever did it wanted him dead. One midnight while he lay awake thinking over who might have done it, it occurred to him suddenly that it could be nobody but Mr Roberts or Mr Suka. Then it flashed upon his mind that it was definitely Mr Suka, for the explosive used was a gelignite. Mr Suka was Hausa. He had relatives in the stone-quarry business. He must have used one of those men to help him blow up the house because of what he had said to Mr Roberts. It was the same thing Antwi, his school and domestic mate in Mr Lomo's house, had done to him.

Antwi had visited him and said he had heard he and Torto had a lorry and a corn-mill. Mensa should help him to buy a corn-mill with a loan of fifty pounds. Mensa denied having a lorry and a corn-mill because he did not trust Antwi. He also said he had no money to help him with. Antwi told him it was a lie because he had been reliably informed that he did own the transport and the corn-mill and had even lent a hundred and twelve pounds to a Nigerian petty-trader. If Mensa could help a Nigerian, why not him, Antwi? Mensa again denied having helped a Nigerian. Antwi thought Mensa did not want to see him prosper, so he went to Mr Roberts and disclosed the ownership of the lorry and corn-mill to him.

Mensa turned in his bed in agony. He felt he was being sought by people who would not come out into the open. He could not sleep.

Three days after, he received an eviction notice from his landlord. It was like throwing him on the streets; he went and saw the landlord about an extension of the time limit.

'Well, Mr Mensa, I received an anonymous letter saying that if I didn't throw you out of my house, my house would be blown up. I thought it was a joke, but you know what has happened, don't you? I never thought you could have such dangerous enemies, Mr Mensa. I'm sorry for you, but I've got to save my house.'

'Mr Akrofi,' Mensa replied, 'if you don't mind, I'll repair the damage. I'm getting my own house and in a few years I'll quit the civil service. Can you give me nine months?'

'I can, provided you sign an agreement that if the house is dynamited again, you will pay for the damage. Is that all right?'

'Thank you, Mr Akrofi. I trust all will be well.'

Mensa had eight hundred pounds in the bank. He borrowed four hundred pounds from the same bank, and his superb house was finished a year after the explosion. He moved into it. He was now ahead of most of his schoolmates and before the house could become his undisputed property, it had become obvious in the neighbourhood and elsewhere that he was now a force. But he himself was looking forward to retiring fairly soon from the civil service as a commissioner for oaths, and living in peace; but would he?

Chapter Fourteen

Mensa was determined to lead his own life and have less to do with or say to others. What else could a man wish, he had thought to himself. He had his own house, had thought his children were receiving the best education; for what he had tried to make sure of was that his children should not get the same kind of schooling he had endured. He was very fond of Odole, and had made it his habit whenever she returned from school to ask her how her teacher or other teachers had treated her. His plan was that his children should start with the local religious school and after the first eight or nine years, they would go to any of the good secondary schools in the country.

It was fashionable while Odole was attending school for the female teachers who taught her to teach housecraft in an interesting and practical way. To ensure that girls learnt how to wash clothes very satisfactorily, the headmistress in particular would order some of the girls to go to her house every Saturday morning to do the laundry of her household. Other female teachers shared this view, but in practice their inferior status limited them to an occasional deployment of school girls in that manner. Officially, this was not allowed but the headmistress had nothing to fear. She and her colleagues argued and appealed to tradition that when they were going to school, they did the same thing. When it was first thrust upon them, they thought it was wrong and horrible but later when they were married they discovered to their shame that it contributed tremendously to making them successful housewives. Why then should they not train the younger generation by the same method which had stood the test of time? If it had made them successful, why should it not make others successful? That kind of ratiocination, however, obviously led people into seeing only part of the picture. Indeed, the real and immediate consideration of those female teachers and the headmistress was that by asking the girls to go and do their laundry for them, they themselves were saved the trouble, they would not have to pay a laundry bill, they would not have to employ a housemaid, in short, they would have the chore done for nothing.

One Monday evening Odole returned from school full of tears and her father asked her why she wept. She in reply asked her father to examine her legs and hands. There were bad cuts on them inflicted by the cane. Mensa was very angry. He realized that time had not eliminated the cane and common sense was pegged. He asked his daughter why it was that she was so savagely beaten. She told him that she was to have gone to the house of her headmistress on the previous Saturday morning to help with the laundry but, as she was helping her mother to bake the cake that would be sold to the spectators of a football match that was to take place in the afternoon at the sports stadium, she could not go. On Monday morning, the headmistress asked her why she did not turn up and she told her. Her excuse made the headmistress angry and she poured insults on her.

Mensa asked her what exactly the headmistress had said and Odole replied that the headmistress told her she should not think because her father owned a beautiful house, she was superior to any of the girls in the school. She would like to know how her father made the money and would be glad to learn also whether her father had led a flawless life. She said when the headmistress spoke the last sentence, she started weeping because it was before the whole school and some of the girls were giggling at the humiliation of her father. When the headmistress saw her weeping, she became unaccountably excited and said many things she could neither hear clearly nor understand. Then the headmistress suddenly came to where she stood and caned her.

That was the story and it was enough to stir that deeply entrenched hatred Mensa had for religious educational schools and their hypocritical, cynical and malicious teachers. He had done the normal thing to send his daughter to have the necessary elementary education; he was only waiting patiently, his fingers crossed, for her to finish there so that he could transfer her to a good secondary school, say, Achimota College. And now this had happened; that which he feared and dreaded most, but hoped time had reduced. It was an intolerable thing, he thought. He was as good a full church member as the headmistress. Very soon he would be a church elder since he helped the church a lot with his services and money. Why should his daughter be so tactlessly and shabbily treated. He must do something positive, ugly and unheard of to help kill the undying practice.

'I'm going to beat her up!' he cried, grabbing his walking stick.

'But you can't do that!' protested his wife.

'Which do you mean? That I can't beat her up or that she shouldn't be beaten up?'

'What I mean is that nobody ever does that! It will bring shame on all of us! It will in the long run hurt your daughter most!'

'There you are! You're hopelessly bound hand, foot and mind by tradition. I'm not. If you're a coward, I'm not. Church or no church, police or no police, tradition or no tradition, I'll whip this woman and damn the consequences!'

'If you trust in God, don't!'

'I've trusted in God long enough. I'm sure He's aware of how brutally my daughter has been treated!'

'Please, don't forget what Jesus said: if you get a slap on one cheek, turn the other. You're being rash like always and you know this kind of excitement and anger is no good for your health!'

'I see! But let me tell you this: you're merely referring to one section of the Bible. The same God approved of an eye for an eye and a tooth for a tooth before He allowed His Son to introduce an amendment. So far as He's in Heaven, He'll judge each case on its merits! The woman shall be whipped!'

He left the house while his wife wept. He went straight to the house of the headmistress and picked up a rough quarrel with her. Both had short tempers and they noisily and explosively handled the quarrel, arms and walking stick swinging wildly and menacingly in the air. Mensa was firmly warmed up now and he was at the point of executing the beating when the woman's husband arrived home from business.

He was a quiet man who had great respect for Mensa not only because of his disinterested social service to unfortunate people in the area, but more importantly because he had been able, despite the fact that he was a civil servant, to own his own house at a fairly early age. He had never dreamt that it could be possible for Mensa to come to his house and pick a noisy row with his wife, no matter the cause; for he had known Mensa to be a frank person who spoke a great deal of sound sense whenever he was consulted on problems which some members of the church had. In fact, he could not even believe his eyes.

True, it had become the established practice that when people in the neighbourhood had their differences, it was to Mensa they appealed for an amicable settlement of them. For his wisdom, tact and patience, they called him Old Mensa though he was not yet advanced in age. Old Mensa always hated violence, cheating and malice; he was an original thinker and said things, not because he was supposed to say them, but because he thought they were right by his own estimation of them.

Now, in a matter of this nature, there were many established and satisfactory courses open to Old Mensa, thought the headmistress' husband. He could have gone to the school and talked over the matter with his wife in a peaceful manner, and his wife in the privacy of her school office would easily have apologized to him; he could have reported the incident to him, the husband, and he would be very glad to tell his wife where she was wrong if he thought her guilty;

he could have informed the minister of their local church who was also the manager of the school and it could have been settled there as a minor misunderstanding between two members of his flock; he could even have asked two or three elderly people in their community to hold an arbitration on any complaint he had against his headmistress wife. Why Old Mensa ignored all these processes and cantankerously assaulted his wife in his house was what the man could not understand.

He was startled when Mensa said: 'I decided to give your wife a little humiliating whipping because it's the only thing that can give the signal. I never whip my children; I had enough of it myself and it's never my wish to inflict physical pain on others. But what I've decided to do to your wife is an instrument of a mission; it's meant to be an instrument of liberation. It should be symbolic and it should also work like the vaccine. Mind you, she's so fat that a little caning won't hurt her. But her mischievous profession will be hurt. Which sensible man will ever think of whipping a woman as a punitive exercise? Anyone who does that is a savage. I, Mensa, tell you that he's a savage. But once in a hundred years one man may have to do the wrong thing to set a senseless practice right. Do you think if this matter is settled verbally, your wife will stop this savage beating of children? It's a pity there are people today who believe the only way to make people do things properly is to inflict thoughtless bodily pain on them. In this there's no difference between the illiterate and the educated, the savage and the civilized. The whole thing makes me angry! It worries me day and night. The root cause is laziness and thoughtlessness. Sheer laziness and thoughtlessness! You take a priest, a minister of religion and a teacher; they are all in charge of men and children, and yet far too many of them in this country lack the self-discipline of their office and hide behind the spurious façade of an excuse that what they say or teach is what is important, but their personal lives are their own business. And yet it's their personal lives that others, being lazy and thoughtless too, are really interested in. To check the result of this interest, brute force or treachery is used and the loose personal life persists in the life of the one who punishes or is treacherous. Your wife belongs to this class of abject, thoughtless and lazy characters who wreck human life and are paid to do so! The sight of her makes me sick!'

Old Mensa would have said more but he felt his heart pounding heavily; he realized that his frenzied outburst could lead him to say things that might do irreparable damage as people had gathered round to listen to the quarrel. In addition, the woman's husband looked so pathetic—his lips apart, his eyes kicking out of their sockets—under the weight of his words that he thought he was giving him pain which he did not directly deserve.

As for the headmistress, she thought Old Mensa was, for that moment at least, a wild raging bull. By training and intellectual capacity she could never understand him; for what was more sacrosanct than the limitless right of a teacher to bring up a child to fulfil his responsibilities to the full when he has grown up? Old Mensa was a radical parent bent on toppling what had taken ages to establish. If he disapproved of whipping, why did he come to whip her? If there was darkness, Old Mensa himself was also groping in it. She was unable to accept Old Mensa's reasons for employing that method. She could not accept the argument that one adult should whip another adult to get him reformed; that what he wanted was to shock everybody by doing what nobody did to stop the tradition; that his whipping her would act like a vaccine to prevent the spread of an entrenched disease; and that if his preventive was not the best one, at least it was a step forward. She thought such words were nothing more than the cant of a humbug.

Old Mensa's next move was to withdraw his daughter from that religious school. He had her enrolled at a Government Girls School in Accra where there was less religion, false or misinterpreted vision and hypocrisy. Odole did well there and three years later she passed an entrance examination which enabled her to go to Achimota College.

The next thing he did was to send Odole's younger brother, Nee, to the Accra Broadway School which, though at the time was less well known, was probably more liberal than most of his countrymen realized. It was a school that had no expatriate staff and was free from religious bigotry. Lack of academic qualifications among the teaching staff was compensated by sheer zeal and hard work. Though textbooks did most of the pedagogic work, pupils knew they had to learn hard and fast to earn a pass.

It was a day release secondary school sited in one of the worst slums of Accra where civilization had to contend with backwardness, where an experiment was being made in education which was not copied wholesale from any alien country, but where indigenous genius was evolving its own methods to produce indigenous people who could have, if nothing else, the self-reliance and the development of those creative capabilities that could make them survive triumphantly in their crippling environment and transform it into a flowering, comfortable and happy spot. Whoever founded that school, Old Mensa was led to believe, must have been inspired.

During his first two years in that school, Nee was fond of telling his father a great deal about the school. Sometimes Old Mensa could hardly believe what his son told him. In the first place the student population was over five hundred and was holed up in two overcrowded two-storey buildings. All manner of boys were in that school; ageing teenager thieves and rascals, cigarette-smoking boys, occasional drunks, apprentice magicians, boxers and ridiculous playboys. Yet nobody cursed those diverse elements and damned them to an everlasting inferno. Their vices were allowed to peter out by themselves and that was helped in no small measure by the sterling qualities of the headmaster who directed the day-to-day life of the school.

The habitation of fishermen surrounded the school premises and foul language was hurled about as a matter of course. Sometimes, during a serious lesson a well-fed fisherman would release a lusty obscene abuse at his friends. Boys would enjoy the abuse, forget about the teacher who would be shouting at the top of his voice, and start drumming on their desks, while one or two in the back row would be exchanging the same filthy abuse to the merriment of those who sat in front who would like to hurl it back but desisted because they had the respect for the poor master who was shouting at the top of his voice.

Some of the masters were either so amusing, or, for some reason, so popular that it was impossible for them to conduct the daily morning religious service without some tumult. A master who belonged to either class undoubtedly had his pet nickname and since the assembly hall was so small that many pupils stood outside, as soon as one such master entered the hall looking very solemn to conduct the morning service, a tiny urchin hiding among the tall big boys would shout his nickname. For five minutes hell would break loose. Boys would yell, roar, whistle, cry, shriek and shout the nickname. A handbell would be rung solicitously to make pupils keep quiet. If the master was one of the really amusing ones, the ringing of the handbell was taken as a signal for more noise. Then suddenly all organs of speech or of noise would be temporarily unemployed and dead silence would reign and pupils would be ready heart and soul for the morning's worship. And once the worship started, God, being accommodating, should have been pleased. The organ which was competently played would melodiously set the pace and pupils would sing loudly, cheerfully, loftily and refreshingly. A spirited short sermon would be given especially on Monday mornings and pupils would find it spiritually uplifting and gracefully let it sink into their minds.

Old Mensa realized that Nee appeared superficially casual and in many ways unorthodox; he could discern however that underneath he was a very serious young man who worked hard at his books; for according to his son, boys did not look serious when teaching was going on but they did that merely to deceive and worry the master. They were listening intently and believed in keen competition among themselves particularly during examinations. Indeed, the idea that a master must work hard to inspire a pupil was non-existent and no pupil tried to shift responsibility for his failures or incompetence onto a member of staff. If his mates discovered he wanted to do that they would mock him into shame and humiliation. Every pupil took the school life as a grim proposition and grappled with it grimly in his own personal style not much aided by anybody.

Old Mensa noticed another thing. It was the way secondary education was moulding his two children into widely different types. He thought Odole of Achimota College was mannered, gentle, charming but supercilious. He felt she thought highly of herself and was above everybody in the neighbourhood. That attitude, Old Mensa thought, put her in a class that existed neither in Heaven nor on earth. Nee was somewhat crude, earthy but socially better adjusted. He got on well with everybody, particularly with the illiterate folk in the area and yet in some ways he was different from them. Thus, though Old Mensa would wish Nee to be a little more refined still, he had faith in him and was confident his future would not disappoint anybody. He therefore hardly interfered with him.

He was not so sure of Odole. Her culture seemed to him to be a veneer that would peel off when subjected to the slightest rough treatment. Besides, she carried it uncomfortably and this made her an embarrassing nuisance to him sometimes. For example, she was too eager to make him feel he was boorish and rough-hewn. He needed her civilizing influence and her high modern standards. She was very sure

he would feel uncomfortable if he had the slightest inter-
course with her select schoolmates who were the vanguard
of civilization in a backward society. Old Mensa, on the
other hand, was persuaded that Odole did not belong and
that she was far more vulnerable than she realized. He was
fond of her and knew she needed his protection though he
could not make that clear to her without her resisting it.

One day, Old Mensa was visited by his brother Tete. They
had a lot to say both about themselves and their children.
When Old Mensa told his brother his son Nee was a pupil
of Accra Broadway School, his brother burst out laughing
in mockery of the arrangement. He said: 'Why, in the name
of progress, should you let Nee go to that school? Don't you
see there are no expatriates on the staff? All the delinquent
crimes committed in Accra are perpetrated by boys of that
school! The pupils in that school are no pupils at all; they are
fathers who have littered Accra with bastards! I would like
to know what kind of education they can get. Can you take
a school seriously when its playground is three miles away
from the home of any of its pupils? Can you take a school
seriously when its headmaster has no car? Answer me! A
slum is a dunghill! Any school founded in a slum is nothing
but a festering of that slum! I hear the Latin master of that
school is a boxer. Your son will come home one day with
a broken jaw and you'll understand what I mean exactly!'

'I hope I will!' Old Mensa said sarcastically.

'I'm sure you will!' his brother said, and went on: 'There
are three good secondary schools in this country. One is
at Achimota and two are in Cape Coast. They're all God-
fearing schools but Accra Broadway School is not attached

to any religious denomination and if it had its way it would be pagan! Anyone in this country who wants his child to be distinguished in future must have him go through one of the three schools I've mentioned. Why not withdraw your son and let him have a sound education in one of them?' He laughed and slapped his thighs, very satisfied with the points he had made. He took a long shot of the whisky he had been served and waited to see what Old Mensa would say.

Old Mensa did not expect that kind of denunciation from his brother and was frankly startled by some of the revelations made. He was quite rightly convinced however that Nee was not being badly educated, and, in any case, would like to have a few points clarified by his over-confident brother.

He asked: 'What's wrong about a magician teaching boys if he does his teaching well?'

'Magic and Christianity are opposed, so a school which has a magician on its staff is wilfully training boys for hell!'

'What do you mean by "training"? Are you suggesting he teaches boys magic instead of art? Suppose he teaches magic, what's wrong about it?'

'Don't be ridiculous. I hear a mathematics master in that school is a bandleader who sings filthy lewd songs when he gets carried away by drink! I learn he's also a good dancer and therefore must be a seducer of women! When a man holds a woman so close in a dance, what do you think will be the inevitable result? I know this is a good question. Answer it! I'm always sure of the questions I ask. They make people tongue-tied!'

But Old Mensa was not going to be tongue-tied; he had his ideas and so he said: 'My daughter has been learning how to dance at Achimota. Whether the authorities there know about it or not I can't tell. What she's fond of is European not African dance. I don't know of any dance of this country in which the man has to embrace the woman firmly and closely to his body. If it comes to seduction, then according to your argument, it's these very recently European-dominated schools which you rate so highly which have been spreading the evil. This teacher you're condemning doesn't teach dancing in the school; he teaches mathematics. But in the schools you consider great, it's possible you have dancing clubs run by boys and girls. Dancing and seduction are two separate things entirely; they need not be connected. I know ministers and teachers of our church aren't supposed to frequent dancing and cinema halls, nor are they encouraged to put on Kente to public meetings. Have you ever seen any of our ministers in Kente cloth at a public gathering? Don't you think the prohibition of simple pleasures and common-sense undertakings can make people hypocrites and secret evil doers? Did you not, with all your good Christian education, seduce your wife as a school girl when she was in Form Four, but you were lucky she was in that last form so you married her as soon as she finished school and was expecting a baby? Did the church expose you or expel you from its membership? In fact nobody ever asked you any questions and you're now an organist. Why do you turn round to damn and condemn others, Tete?'

'Now! Now! Now! Now!' protested Tete. 'The trouble with you, Mensa, is that you talk any how and too much!

You don't know the difference between an argument and a secret. It's good only the two of us are here otherwise what you've said could revive a scandal which is dead and buried. Right now, I lead a clean life and that's what matters! The teachers in our time led clean lives and that was what mattered. I'm not too sure of the morals of the masters at Accra Broadway School!'

'It's good you've said you're not sure. So, please, don't parade your opinions and prejudices as facts when you can't sensibly prove them. You know our father hated it and warned us against it.'

'Ah, but our father was not realistic. He saw the world in terms of absolutes and not in terms of adaptations. He wanted to be different and I've always been sorry he did that,' Tete said looking sad.

'I'm not sorry he recreated life in his own way. It must have been both a source of pain and happiness to him. I think it was the happiness that won in the end. But I've one thing to tell you, Tete. You know in your kind of business there's the temptation to steal. I've been told you've been playing tricks with the cash you get out of your daily sales. Be careful or you'll be in a mess one day. Very few shopkeepers in this country end up their days in happiness!'

'Nonsense! Trade is trade. If you don't cheat you don't survive. The companies cheat; what's wrong in cheating them? In fact, it shouldn't be called cheating, it should be known as making money or business. You either win the money or lose it, no more! Right now you're doing your best to make life comfortable and to give your children the best education possible. I'm making more money and in four or five years' time my children will be going overseas. You will have to depend on government aid and that's no good. Your children will be bound by bonds. My family can easily be a leading one. Surely, I've a greater opportunity in this than you have! You have to encourage me. I must strike while the iron is red-hot. If you need money come and see me! I can only spare you a few hundred pounds, though. We're brothers, aren't we? Our mother will be pleased if she hears I can help you!'

'Tete, you know I'm not the kind of man who stands in the way of others,' Old Mensa said, quietly and thoughtfully. 'I'm glad you've been honest with me as I've been to you. It's something in our make-up. But you can't be thoughtlessly straightforward in the wrong direction. Please, don't go too fast. No one can be in the way of fortune, I guess; but still don't try to push things too far. They may get out of control and break you!'

'Mensa, you're being foolish. I've never been defeated and I'm not going to be defeated now. By the way, are you going to withdraw Nee from that Broadway school?'

'I don't think I will. I hate the idea of children migrating from one school to another. It's not very good for them. I'll let him finish there and see what can be done next.'

Chapter Fifteen

As the years went by, Old Mensa became more and more prominent in his neighbourhood. People came to him with their private problems to be sorted out for them. But the business of helping people, especially when they came as complainant and defendant for their differences to be settled for them, had a two-way effect. Though Old Mensa tried as much as he could to judge cases impartially, he sometimes wound up having pleased one party and disappointed the other. The emotional reaction of those who felt he had not handled the case as they had expected could be intense and quite often they spared no effort to make him see clearly that he had incurred their displeasure. And yet these very people would come to him again when they got involved.

At first, Old Mensa was disturbed to find that what he considered to be an honest and impartial arbitration was ill-received and so he became in effect an object of hatred and sometimes contempt. He would therefore spend several sleepless nights going over previous cases again to see where his judgements went wrong. Later he stopped worrying and when he was satisfied that he was right, he would in turn react by showing disregard and contempt for those who thought he had not treated their cases as he should. One way in which he did this was to use unhappy words against the young school children of those people when they either eyed or attempted to steal the fruit on his trees. Instead of insulting them directly, he would use their parents' mistakes to tell them what he thought of their entire families.

He also discovered that whenever women hawkers came to sell things to his wife they added more money to the price. If they sold three smoked herrings at sixpence to everybody in the neighbourhood, they would, when they came to his house, double the price because they thought he was rich.

Old Mensa decided to stop the racket once and for all. From one of the windows of his living-room, one morning, he saw a smoked herrings hawker selling. She entered a house nearby so Old Mensa went out and stealthily stood behind the wall of that house to listen to the bargain. He distinctly heard the woman sell the fish at two for threepence. Before the woman could leave that house, Old Mensa had quietly dashed back unseen to his house and went and hid indoors making sure he stood where he could hear what took place in the yard of his house.

The fish hawker arrived and when Old Mensa's wife asked her how she sold the fish, she said two sold for sixpence. Old Mensa rushed out and shouted: 'You filthy woman, didn't you sell the same fish at two for threepence in that house? You've lost one of your eyes and whenever I see your scarified face, you make me think you're a descendant of a stupid slave!'

But fishmongers and fish sellers of Accra were not the type of people to be insulted without their fighting back especially if it would create fun for them; and so it was not unexpected when the woman replied: 'Old Mensa, the chronic trouble with you is that you're far too cantankerous. What have the transactions of women got to do with men? Not only my face is scarified, other unmentionable parts of my body too are scarified, you foolish troublesome man!'

'I see! Like your face they will be pretty nasty if they are! I'm the head of this house; the money that is going to be wasted in buying your fish is mine. I've every right to intervene. I'm not surprised you stole your husband's money so he had to throw you out.'

The hawker started weeping. Old Mensa's wife was alarmed; for the occasion did not call for the revelation he made. She was also disturbed because the consequences of his last statement could be serious. Before the woman left the house, she said: 'What you have said is a clear case of defamation of character. I'm going to take court action against you so that one of us is cleared.'

The woman did institute court action against Old Mensa but she chose an interesting court. It was a court which dealt with private and civil cases which were settled by customary practice and usage. It should not be said that the court had the full backing of the state, nor could it be categorically stated that its existence hurt the essential legal set-up of the country, since most of its cases were perhaps simple and its main purpose was to redress grievances that affected personal relations. No fees were charged and its decisions were only morally obligatory. Its survival depended on the willingness of people to appear before it. It was not clear whether the court had judges and for this reason it could be regarded as an arbitration caucus that was not backed by any statutory authorization.

There were seven members on the panel of the court, all of them old government pensioners who thought they knew more law than trained lawyers. One thing was common to all of them: they could talk. In addition, most of them by natural disposition were litigious. They were a formidable group of quite serious men who knew about everybody's past which enabled them to judge cases penetratingly and sometimes disconcertingly. Whenever people appeared before them they could tell who those people's great-grand-fathers were, the kind of life they led and whether they were respected during their life-time. They could also tell the crimes the grandfathers and grandmothers, fathers and mothers and uncles and aunts of those people commit-ted before they died or grew old. And since they believed absolutely in persistent immanence, the unalterable law of heredity, they could be sure before the case was heard who was likely to win. Once in a while they would find a man they considered too ambitious or too successful guilty just for the pleasure of it or perhaps to bring him down to earth.

Naturally, Old Mensa had little respect for that kind of court because he thought he could handle cases better himself. He was also aware that not all the members on the panel were qualified to judge others. He particularly despised the most senior man on the panel who often acted as chief judge.

When a young man was sent to summon him to appear before the court to hear and defend the charge against him, he lost his temper completely and told the young man that the members of the panel were rogues and fraudulent ras-cals and that he held all of them in absolute contempt. He asked the young man to tell them what he had told him about them and he could, if he liked, come and hear the proceedings and observe how he would handle the usually respected judges.

Old Mensa spent the whole night before the day of trial thinking carefully over the words he would use. The more he thought about the whole affair the angrier he became. He believed that that kind of court or arbitration committee ought not to exist. He thought it did more harm than good because it never contributed in any way to making men better, that is, in encouraging harmony, love and trust between man and man. It was poverty and ignorance, he believed, that forced many people to help perpetuate the life of the court.

Before he left home for the trial, his wife warned him to control his tongue during the hearing of the case otherwise he would merely make things worse for himself. Old Mensa said he would make his wife less apprehensive, because she was too prone to worry over his conduct and sometimes Old Mensa felt she was fed up with his unconventional ways. Old Mensa's wife was happy about her husband's assurance: yet little did she know that her husband had in fact taken two neat shots of whisky to boost his courage, if not his morale.

The court was in session and ready in the house of its most senior member, the chief judge. As soon as the members of the panel saw Old Mensa enter the room where they were, they coughed and hemmed and shifted in their chairs. They knew Old Mensa was an intelligent man who had nothing to hide. He was a dangerous upstart who wanted to run their community in his own way. They would blow up his pretensions once and for ever.

When Old Mensa had gone a few paces beyond the door-step, he paused to look round the room and to size up the situation. In doing so, he was unable to say good morning quickly enough to the self-respecting old men who were going to try him. For that reason, one of their number virtually cried out at him: 'Look here, Mensa, you aren't any older than any of us here! The ordinary rules of etiquette require you to say good morning to us, you understand?'

But that was not the kind of shaft that could hurt or disturb Old Mensa. He had a lot to say and he did not want to be hurried. 'I'm sorry,' he said politely. 'It wasn't my intention to be rude to any of you here. Excuse me, I had entirely forgotten myself.'

'Although your apology is not very satisfactory,' said the chief judge in measured tones, 'we intend to ignore it because you don't in any way matter to us! What matters to us, we shall soon let you know.'

A squat, half-blind old man, also on the panel, was so pleased with what was told Old Mensa that he cleared his throat violently and carelessly. The physiological repercussions as usual were also violent and disorderly so the throat clearing developed into a series of coughs which shook him so painfully that the tears ran down his cheeks. As he wiped them nervously, Old Mensa smiled.

The squat, half-blind old man darkly saw the smile and understood it or thought he did understand it. 'Mensa,' he cried in a hoarse voice, 'Do you laugh at a man in pain? Do you know your mother does not belong to any clan in this town? Do you have any respectable background? And you laugh at me! The cheek of it!'

Old Mensa kept quiet. He was not prepared to be drawn in yet. It was now very clear to him that those old gentlemen were determined to wipe the floor with him; they were not really anxious to try the case. Either he won or they did or they all got nowhere. The smoked herrings hawker was a mere pawn.

The chief judge began the trial and said: 'Mensa we are prepared to ignore your pretensions and insolence. The complaint of this poor woman before us is simple and straightforward. A week ago she was selling smoked her-rings as she had always done. Despite the fact that you think you're the lord of this area dispensing charity and sitting in judgement on people's private quarrels, you enjoy her fish though your naughty children especially your proud daugh-ter, we learn, say her fish is unhygienic. Still, you being as ordinary as any of us here, and as a decorated donkey is yet an ass, it must be emphasized that her fish has always been bought by your wife to be consumed by proud you and your household!'

'I don't like the language you're using,' Old Mensa said quietly in protest.

'Who? Me?' asked the chief judge hurriedly, and then he exploded: 'Look, Mensa, I'm seventy-two, you're fifty-five. We are all retired civil servants. The only thing you can do to me is to drag me to a state court. As far as I am con-cerned the outcome of any contest between us will depend on money. Money can decide the case. And so long as it's you against me, I'm prepared to go the whole financial hog.

I don't care if I get ruined! But I need not waste the time of this gathering.'

Old Mensa said nothing; he was biding his time.

The chief judge continued flushed with hatred: 'Your children are proud and they think because you've been helped by your wife to own a house you and they are better than anybody in the whole world! They are just like you, and so we are not surprised to learn that when this poor woman came to sell fish to your wife, you went out of your way to defame her in three particulars. First, you said she was a descendant of a slave. Historically this may be true but you said it maliciously to discriminate against her. This is an attitude which is almost dead in our society today but which you would want to keep alive. And if it must be kept alive, I can ask you about the background of your own mother! Second, you said she had an ugly scarification on her face. This is clearly out of order because the scarification is on her face and not on yours! You had no right to refer to it unless the intention was either to provoke her or hurt her feelings. Thirdly, you said she stole her husband's money so he threw her out. This may be correct but who told you and why did you say it? One thing emerges. You think you're so very superior that you don't care what language you use against others. Now you've over-reached yourself and before we pronounce judgement, it's our painful duty to ask you to say whatever you have to in defence!'

Old Mensa was happy the time had arrived. The panel members were also happy but for a different reason which was that they had at last got their man by issuing a carefully worded and co-ordinated indictment against him.

Old Mensa said: 'I'd like to explain myself by telling a story.'

'Very good! An Ananse story, probably. It's been told before; you can tell it again. We are anxious to enjoy it! Make sure you embellish it for my relish!' jibed the chief judge.

'Once upon a time,' Old Mensa coolly began.

'Hear! Hear!' cried the squat, half-blind old man in outright mockery.

'Once upon a time,' Old Mensa said again, 'there was a quarrel between a man and his loose callous wife. The quarrel unfortunately developed into an ugly violent fight and to harm her husband in many ways, the wicked woman used her young baby as a club in hitting her husband. The baby was not only injured but lost consciousness and the man had to stop the fight to see what he could do to make the baby regain consciousness.

'As a result of this unpleasant incident, the marriage broke up but there was no formal divorce. The woman took to the streets and the man too went after all sorts of women. Both led that kind of life for a long time.

'One day, the woman was picked up in the streets by a man who was about twenty-six years old. The young man was in his own car and the negotiations were not difficult to be accomplished. So man and woman were satisfied that they were going to have a good night. To impress the woman and also to ensure an enjoyable night or perhaps to make sure he could prop up both his strength and courage, the young man stopped his car in front of a drinks shop, got out, went in and returned with a pint of whisky which he had bought on credit. The woman eyed the whisky with satisfaction and the young man put it down in the shopping tray of the car with high hopes. I may add that the young man was married, but his wife had gone away to visit her parents in the Volta Region. He therefore felt free to have that kind of fun before his wife returned.

'Well, the young man drove the woman straight to his empty house. He asked the woman to sit and relax in an armchair in the living-room. He went into his bedroom and changed into his sleeping cloth. Naturally he also removed his shoes and wore his fine Ghanaian sandals. He returned to the living-room where the woman was patiently waiting for him.

'But before he could open the bottle of whisky, two hefty men suddenly landed in his room and without saying a word to him, started beating up the woman. At first, the man was, as one would expect, paralysed into inactivity by shock; but when he recovered he felt he must do something about the bad situation. But then he was in his Ghanaian cloth and wore no under-dress. He could therefore not engage in a scuffle with those hefty men without ending up naked. He decided prudently to go back to his bedroom and change into shirt and shorts. The two men saw the move and what did they do? They got hold of his cloth and pulled it off him. They made practical the very nudity he had planned to avoid. Then they dragged the woman out of the room and took into their possession not only the cloth they had already pulled off him but the unopened bottle of whisky as well. Then one of them told the young man: "This woman is my wife. I've caught you about to misbehave with her. I'm going to take action against you and I'll use this bottle of whisky and your cloth as exhibits."

'The man was shaking with anger and frustration but before he could rush to his bedroom to put on some clothes and return, the men had vanished with the woman and the exhibits into the darkness. Do you wish me to continue with the story?' asked Old Mensa politely, displaying no emotion whatever.

'Go on! What you've said so far is grossly irrelevant but we've got to hear you somehow. Wind up and let's see the intelligence those gullible people say you have,' said the squat half-blind old man. As for the chief judge, he seemed to be studying a diary he had pulled out of his pocket.

'Thank you, I will,' said Old Mensa, who went on: 'Two weeks later that young man received a summons note asking him to appear before a lay magistrate's court to answer a charge of seduction. He didn't like it at all because his wife had returned from her visit to her parents and if she heard of the scandal, anything could happen to their hitherto peaceful married life. He thought the best thing he could do was to prevent the case from being heard in a lay magistrate's court since that kind of court was often crowded with people from all sections of the community. The affair could be the flash news of the town and since his countrymen had the genius for altering the details of any news, the consequences with regard to his social standing could be shattering.

'What was he to do? He decided to corrupt the lay magistrate who would sit on the case. He had heard he was not strictly above corruption. He tapped and made use of all the usual devious processes and finally got access to that magistrate. He bribed him with fifty pounds, twenty-five of which he had raised from an unlicenced moneylender at fifty per cent compound interest. He had wanted the magistrate to strike off the case from the books altogether but the magistrate said the case had reached a stage where that would be impossible. He should therefore appear in court and he knew what to do so that the case would not in reality be heard. He would so frame his words as to hide the true nature of events and quickly declare it a frivolous one that should be dealt with out of court. He assured the young man that he would instruct the local council police to drive people away from the courtroom when his case would be heard. That would ensure that nobody heard it.

'The young man was relieved of his anxiety and felt confident that all would be well. The day for the mock hearing came and he went to the court as a matter of formality. But to his horror, the courtroom was fully packed. Not only that. To his mortification, every detail of the case was heard and he was found guilty of gross seduction which, in fact, never took place. In addition to that he was fined seventy-five pounds, fifty pounds of which would go to the aggrieved and supposedly cuckolded husband. The cloth that was taken off him was never used as an exhibit nor was the whisky.

'He went home and his health broke down. Of the fifty pounds given to the husband, fifteen pounds was given to the lay magistrate for seeing the case through in the husband's favour. He accepted it.

'A year later, the young man heard that the very magistrate who sat on the case and had found him guilty after accepting the bribe, had fathered twin babies by the same woman. The very woman who had made him suffer so much ill-health and degradation! And who was that lay magistrate? It is the same man sitting right in front of me now whom you rogues, deceivers of men, wreckers of human happiness and devils-let-loose have chosen as chief judge over me in this case! I, Mensa, condemn him! I spit upon him! And I invoke the wrath of God, if ever God does hear man, upon him!'

While Old Mensa was uttering the last sentence, the chief judge was gasping for words and then suddenly fainted clean away.

There was confusion confounded by unco-ordinated instructions and different immediate actions. For some of the members of the panel shouted for cold water to be splashed on the face of the unconscious chief judge. Others cried that an ambulance should be phoned for, while one of them had actually dashed out to do just that on his own initiative and, meanwhile, during the hustle and bustle, the squat, half-blind old man sat motionless helplessly moaning that the end of the universe was at hand.

An ambulance arrived and the chief judge was loaded into it. It was naturally impossible to continue with the case, so the court was adjourned *sine die*, everybody having forgotten the poor woman who had been abused and had sought redress.

A few days later, Old Mensa sent for her. She refused to go and see him, so the next day, at dawn, he went to her house, apologised to her and asked for forgiveness. The woman felt Old Mensa was being honest in asking to be pardoned so she softened and the two were reconciled.

Chapter Sixteen

One good thing which Old Mensa and his brother did was to recondition their father's house at the village where they had spent their memorable childhood days. They were very fond of the place, particularly Old Mensa. At Christmas time every year he would remember how when he was a little boy there he would look forward eagerly to the slaughter of a goat, the meat of which was used by his mother for cooking excellent soup and stew. His mother's cooking was always the best and though his wife was undoubtedly a better cook, at that time of the year, it was his mother's food he longed for.

His mother was now quite old; she was over eighty, and was given to counting her days to make her exit from a world she had faced with sorrow and happiness. She looked upon one thing as her greatest achievement: that she was able by sheer determination and harrowing hard work and faith to educate her children as their father had wished. Her daughter was happily married, her domestic life equally tranquil. Now she was spending her last days in a more comfortable house; some of her grandchildren, especially her daughter's, often visited her and, while they romped about the house thrilled and happy with life, she enjoyed

And as it happened that most if not all of their boy-friends sang either bass or tenor, the liquor having stimulated them as it should, there arose a desperate competition between bass and tenor, the frail treble and alto having been successfully and completely drowned.

In addition, the perpetually drunken and also unemployed man of the village who usually provided fun on such solemn occasions was in full session. He was thoroughly drunk and all he could do now was to lean his poor mortal frame precariously against the organ, singing in his own special way. His singing had no timing and when all had finished a song, he would carry on with the last bar, his voice dropping from tenor to bass and then rising unpredictably to falsetto; his lips would be half-twisted like those of a person in a paralytic fit; his arms swinging feebly in the air to signify that he was his own conductor and also the conductor of those who would care to look in the direction where he stood.

After some time, it became apparent that many of the people who had gone to the place to condole were now no longer aware that someone had died and her body lay in state. They were aware that not much unnecessary condolence should be displayed on an occasion when a woman who had been fortunate enough to live for eighty-five years had died as she should sooner or later.

Indeed, some youths in the choir and singing band had forgotten completely about the death, mourning and the funeral. They were in love and, excited by the drinks, were waiting impatiently for the wake to be over, say, by one or two in the small hours of the morning so that they could have the girls to themselves. The parents of the girls could have no legitimate cause for complaint that their daughters had returned home late since no wake-keeping was ever run on any precise time schedule. Moreover, girls always needed the protection of men on such occasions since just after midnight it would be naturally dark and a close physical protection given could never be seriously questioned, at least in principle. But there were, surely, other opportunities and those were what the young men were spoiling for.

And now Old Mensa was getting worried. He felt the funeral gathering had lost its solemnity and had become transformed by drinks into a drunken jamboree. He complained to his brother that he did not like the prevailing levity and that no more drinks should be served. But his brother was not impressed by that kind of talk. What he wanted to do was to display his wealth. He was also drunk and was more interested in hearing the flattering words the villagers showered on him than in stopping the ill-timed conviviality. The villagers too were quick to discover that they could make small fortunes by flattering him, so they followed and praised him all over the place. The more he was praised, the more he grinned with satisfaction and pulled out pound notes and ten shilling notes and tossed them around.

He was therefore disinclined to give the order that no more drinks should be served. But Old Mensa pressed on and managed to get the minister to use his influence on his brother. Of course, the minister too had taken just enough strong drinks to stimulate his faculties but not to overpower them. He was therefore quite ready to use his good offices tactfully. He called Tete aside, spoke to him and asked him to tell the girls to stop serving the drinks. He finally explained to him that even the singing had degenerated into cacophonous utterances and as things stood, no respect was being shown on the occasion of the death of his mother.

After hearing the minister, Tete was still determined to have things his own way. He went and stood in full view of everybody and cried: 'Stop talking and singing, every one of you!' As he gave the order, he banged a table that stood near him with his fist. People were surprised because that kind of thing was never done at a funeral, but they thought perhaps he was drunk and did not know what he was doing. They therefore started talking and singing again.

Old Mensa had now realized that it was possible his brother would misbehave so he drew near to him to ask him to come away with him for a discussion of the arrangements for the next day. But his brother had sensed his intention so he hurried up and shouted again at the gathering and banged the table: 'I say stop singing and talking you dogs!'

The village folk were dumbfounded and dismayed. But one elderly farmer who was careful not to get befuddled by drink saw at once that Tete wanted to insult and humiliate them. He got up and shouted back: 'Tell us who those dogs are!'

'The whole damned lot of you!' cried Tete, reeling back and forth completely drunk.

Old Mensa and the minister were shocked and disarmed and before long another farmer shouted from behind the gathering: 'Tete, you're a vain swine!'

'Yes, I'm a vain swine,' yelled Tete, his eyes half-closed,

his face displaying every sign of the contempt he had for the poor villagers, 'but I can feed the whole stupid lot of you!'

'Tell us, you thoughtless ass, is it for tonight or for ever?' demanded a young farmer very annoyed.

'For all time, you penniless rats!' Tete cried back.

The young farmer now maddened cried: 'If you're not a boastful idiot, you won't say this. Feed virtually a whole village for all time? This is a thing God himself hasn't succeeded in doing otherwise there shouldn't be starvation and famine, even water shortage! You're a hopeless imbecile!'

Meantime, the minister had had another shock and he whisked round and told Old Mensa: 'Somebody is blaspheming there, I think. Mr Mensa, this kind of language is most outrageous. It cannot but be a joke in bad taste. Tell them to keep God out of this quarrel!'

'I will, sir,' Old Mensa assured the minister and shook his head in disappointment and disbelief; for he had never dreamt that that kind of situation in which he was, was ever possible.

'Old Mensa,' somebody cried at him from the gathering, 'drag away that dirty brother of yours! He's a disgrace to your family! This isn't what a sane man should do when his mother is dead and not yet buried!'

'Fools!' Old Mensa's brother exploded again for another savage denunciation of the villagers. 'You've lived in this village for your whole lifetime and yet you're still miserably poor! I'm rich; and yet I started life like any one of you here, you worthless rats!'

The minister helped Old Mensa to drag his brother away. The funeral gathering had been destroyed. What started as a solemn coming-together had now broken up. To Old Mensa, what his brother had done amounted to an extermination of their family or clan in the village. Those villagers as a rule had no special regard for the rich; their earthly philosophy was not based on ruthless acquisition of wealth. Their faith in the bible was generally so strong that they counted more on their wealth in Heaven than on any material well-being on earth. A man could not be any different from them because of his riches. They regarded his wealth as his own business and though they would gladly accept gifts from him, they would not envy him his wealth. They respected a man who had made a success of his life and would like to congratulate him generously, sometimes fatuously. In return, they expected him to respect them, since theirs was a difficult job out of which they got little, but on which depended the survival of city and urban dwellers whom they often regarded as thoughtless and heartless people. Old Mensa knew that his brother's conduct would also deepen the prejudice which was already well-entrenched.

On the following day at nine o'clock in the morning, the body of Old Mensa's mother was conveyed to the church for the funeral service. Almost all the villagers attended not so much because of Tete and Old Mensa but because of their dead mother for what she had done when she lived. They had nothing against Old Mensa, they thought; for they were convinced that he did not share his brother's sentiments and besides they had not heard of him as a hopelessly vain and boastful man. One other reason which was a secret one why they had flocked to the church was to see what Tete would look like in the church after his disgraceful behaviour the night before. They were disappointed; Tete was nowhere to be found in the church.

The various songs were sung with that fine gusto that one could only find in a good Christian village. The Accra minister delivered the sermon and in concluding it said: 'The deceased lived a full and useful life. She was dedicated both to her husband and to her children. She never went to funerals to drink and blaspheme against Almighty God. She walked in the ways of humility, and in humility she brought up her God-fearing children whose useful and productive lives should be an example to all of you here. I have the right to let you know that we do not reckon a man's life by his occasional failing and lapses, otherwise all of us will stand condemned before God, but his total achievement. For that reason, we should be grateful to the Lord that a family has existed in this village, the offspring of which is a pride not only to this village but also to the entire country. We pray God to accept the soul of the deceased. We pray God to succour her children who have already improved upon and are still improving upon the achievements of their departed parents.'

The congregation was clearly not satisfied with the sermon, particularly the last section of it, but did not complain openly; that had never been done before. But they wondered what else a minister brought down by Tete would say.

Chapter Seventeen

Odole had finished her sixth form course successfully and was going through the ritual for a scholarship award to fly to Europe to do medicine. Nee had also done so well in the West African School Certificate Examination that a mining company had generously given him a scholarship to do mining engineering in West Germany.

Odole had become rude to everybody in the house particularly to her father and mother. Old Mensa found it extremely distressing but felt he should not indulge in giving her long speeches on the subject. Speeches, especially moralizing ones, never appealed to him. He had had too many of them when young and was tired of them when old. A friend had told him that as soon as young girls become rude and overbearing in the house, their parents had to suspect young men lurking behind the scenes. Still, though he was worried by his daughter's behaviour, he had too liberal a mind to be suspicious.

Odole would leave the house and come back late and bang on the main gate rudely to be let in. Her father gave her a duplicate key to the gate so that she would not have to disturb his sleep when she returned from her nocturnal engagements, but she would forget to take the key away with her and would come back home and bang on the gate. If her mother complained, she would also complain that she was being old-fashioned and should get adjusted to the times. She would, during the argument that ensued, reel off her school notes on psychology and use terms which overawed her mother linguistically but, alas, left her unimpressed in terms of the practical. What was wrong in going to the cinema with a boy-friend, she would ask. What was wrong in dancing far into the night, she would demand. Both mother and daughter were agreed that she should have some fun but her mother was unable to state clearly the basic proposition, namely, that with her scholarship award in view, motherhood on her part was not expected. That, of course, Odole herself never thought of nor was her mother able to put it across to her in unmistakable terms.

One day Old Mensa's wife told her husband that they ought to take a closer look at Odole. She was likely to be expecting a baby. Old Mensa dismissed the idea as silly; his daughter was old and sensible enough to look after herself. What if they asked her and it was not true? They would simply appear ridiculous. A young woman who was going to have a medical scholarship should not be disturbed with inquisitive questions.

It was something different, however, that alarmed Old Mensa. The daughter of the huge and terrible headteacher of the middle boarding-school Old Mensa attended, married a Nigerian sand and stone contractor. Before the huge and terrible headteacher, Mr Abossey, died, they had had six children. The first of those children, a boy, had grown up and had not only become infamous but was also greatly feared by many parents in that part of the city where Old Mensa and his family lived.

He was in his twenties and was apparently rich but how he made the money, nobody could tell for certain but many people thought he was a crook. Nonetheless, he was visibly rich and rode in a new fashionable car every year.

One morning, his car pulled up in front of the main gate of Old Mensa's house where Old Mensa was leaning against the gate waiting for his daughter. Old Mensa saw him and his heart sank. The young man drove off without saying good morning to him. Old Mensa turned to his daughter when both of them had entered the house and asked: 'Odole, who asked you to accept a drive in that crook's car?'

'He's not a crook. He's a decent man!'

'How do you know?'

'Of course, I've eyes to see!'

'Do you know the history of his family?'

'I don't judge people by others or by their family background. I judge them by what they are. That's the realistic approach!'

'But he's a lout!'

'And why is he not in jail?'

'He's been there twice!'

'*You* say so but the police haven't told me. Nobody has told me. Look, Dad, be your age. The man is nothing to me. I can't marry him. He has a wife with two children and I'm better educated than he is. He asked whether he could give me a drive and I accepted the offer. Why fly into tantrums over this?'

'Only harlots go in his car!'

'And I'm the exception that will uphold his good name!'

'Look, child, the facts of life are not always enshrined in sophisticated reasoning or in verbal manoeuvres! In matters of this nature, either you're wrong or you aren't. I've fought life at various fronts but if I'm to engage at a front of this nature, I don't think I can fight hard again. There's always the last blow, however light, that can knock a man down! My dear, the conspiracy of the past and the betrayal of the present can be a terrible blow, you know.'

'I like your fine turn of phrase, Dad! It's a pity in your time there was no university in this country. You would have made a fine scholar and a writer.'

'You've a way of catching me on the raw, my daughter. That's all right if all were not so bad!' Old Mensa said and then lowered his voice and said with controlled passion: 'My dear, there are things I know which you don't. There are things I did which I had to regret later. There are things you must be warned against in time because it's possible you can see things darkly while others don't. I wish you well, my dear! Promise never to have anything to do with that man again.'

'My promise should be as good as anything I do in future. If that is what you want, you can depend on it!'

Odole's promise had only a palliative effect on Old Mensa. His apprehension had so shaken him that he broke down completely. He was a man of deep faith and hope and his life now hanged on these.

A week later, he received a letter from Nee. He opened the envelope with pleasure for Nee always had something interesting and reassuring to tell him. The letter ran:

Dear Father,

I know you'll be surprised this letter is not really about me. I know you'll be upset by the time you've finished reading it. I know my mother will be angry with me for writing to you a letter which I know can upset you.

When I was at home, she always told Odole and myself especially that she was tired of and worried about how you took life so seriously for that had been gravely interfering with your health. It was this which prevented me from telling you what you should have known about.

Still, it is a matter that transcends secrecy and, more importantly, which has been worrying me ever since I came here. I can no longer keep it to myself because I know I'll feel guilty one day if I don't do anything about it. And though I don't like quoting worn-out phrases, I sometimes think they come in useful; therefore I'll say prevention is better than cure. So this letter is meant to make you act to prevent something that can bring disgrace on the family.

You'll also be surprised, I think, to learn that when I was leaving for this country I was not on speaking terms with my sister. Both of us tried as much as possible not to make you see it because we knew it was the kind of thing you detested.

There is a young man at home in our area who has been flirting with Odole. The whole affair started one day when Odole and myself were going to see the pictures. I suppose the young man may have had his designs well-planned out beforehand, because his car was parked in our way. We tried to ignore him but he was determined not to be ignored, so he asked us if he could give us a drive. We didn't reject the offer because strictly speaking, there was nothing wrong in a man giving us a drive as an act of kindness just as I still think there is nothing wrong about going to the pictures or to dances fairly often—a point you've always disputed and which I still maintain is right!

During the drive, the man started flattering our family by saying that many people respected you for your integrity and the way you helped people in distress. I tried to stop that kind of talk by suggesting that there were, on the other hand, people who didn't like you because you were embarrassingly outspoken.

He laughed and said that people who were publicly condemned for being outspoken were privately respected for saying the right things which cowards feared to utter. He went on to say that you were giving us the right kind of education and that it was a good thing we did not disappoint you by failing to use our brains.

Though I'm young, I'm deeply suspicious of people who either praise or commend me in gratuitous circumstances. I may be wrong but I don't intend to do anything about it; it's already part of me. I therefore disliked the man immediately he took the trouble to sing our praises so easily.

Soon my suspicions were confirmed because instead of taking us to the cinema, he drove us to the Ambassador Hotel. I decided to quit but Odole would not hear of it because to her, it would be an act of discourtesy. I thought perhaps women were more patient and forbearing in situations of that nature and that I may have been harsh in making that decision. Odole also said that since that was the first time we had come across him we shouldn't have any preconceptions but rather relax and have some fun and a change for once.

At the bar of the Ambassador Hotel, the man took a wad

of five-pound notes out of his pocket. I think it was some two hundred pounds all together and he pulled out a note. It struck me he must be a vain man whose intentions were suspect. I rose to leave when he excused himself while we were drinking but Odole gave me such a bad look that I thought she was once again thinking that I was going to behave crudely which she had always accused me of.

Fortunately, the man entertained us for only thirty minutes, drove us to the cinema hall and bought the tickets for us saying decent boys and girls must always be rewarded. He did not go in to see the pictures himself and I never saw him again for some time. Only his odd name, Frankadua, as he told us, lingered on my mind.

He confronted us once again when we had gone to a dance. He was alone and forced his company on us. I need not go into detail as to what he did or what he said but, to put it briefly, I didn't like both his person and his pretensions.

The day after the dance, I told Odole that we should give him a cold shoulder if he tried to force his company on us again. Odole told me my idea was wrong and I should learn to be a good mixer. I therefore told her I was not prepared to go out in her company again if she insisted on entertaining the man. She told me I could please myself and that she was old enough to look after herself. She therefore, as you know, started going out alone.

Later, my boy friends started telling me stories. I didn't like them, Father. They said Odole was now the topic of our neighbourhood's gossip and they were surprised that after her pride and superciliousness, she had chosen a smuggling crook as her boy-friend. On top of that, they said, she was going to break up a home as the man had a wife and children with whom he shared the same house.

I told Odole what I had heard and warned her but she would not listen to me. I would therefore ask you to use as much tact as possible and put an end to the whole scandalous affair.

Well, Father, this is about all this airmail letter-card can take. Do write to me soon.

Best wishes to mother, Odole and yourself.

Your loving son,
Nee.

This letter had a devasting effect on Old Mensa. It was as if a poisoned dart had been shot through his heart. For two days he would not and could not eat well. He stayed in his bedroom having told his wife he had a fever. He would not receive visitors for he neither had the strength nor was he in the mood to welcome them.

In his pyjamas, he seemed a tall man now though he was neither tall nor short. His face was lined but his eyes retained their quick sparkle, and his forehead looked noble and intelligent. His hair was short, not wholly grey or black. It was soft, stretched and firmly brushed back. With his spare body he would have passed for a dedicated monk who had committed a sin before, but was now doing penance for human ills.

The news got round that he was sick. Those who loved him prayed for his recovery. Those who did not like him appealed to God to take him out of this world. Children were happy because they could steal the fruit in his garden.

Chapter Eighteen

Outside the compound wall of Old Mensa's house Joe Fio said to Jimmy Boi who was smaller and perhaps a year younger: 'Old Mensa is a sick man. He's not in the house. What about stealing his mangoes while we have the chance?'

'But his dog is there,' said Jimmy Boi, who could still cry easily if menaced by a dog.

'Never mind his dog,' Joe Fio answered with confidence. 'As soon as it starts giving trouble we'll dash off to the Nigerian shopkeeper's place and quickly get mixed up with his children. You know, that Nigerian doesn't like dogs to worry his children. He's been having noisy quarrels with dog-owners.'

'Shall we call the other boys?' asked Jimmy Boi.

'Don't be silly,' Joe Fio said. 'We want the mangoes for ourselves, don't we?'

'Yes, but can't we get the Nigerian children to steal some bars of chocolate from their father's shop for us? You see, one chocolate for one mango. I know they'd like it.'

Joe Fio thought Jimmy Boi's suggestion was very good for a small boy. He had found before that Jimmy Boi often had bright ideas and that was why he let him in on enterprises of this kind.

'All right, Boi. It's going to be like this: one hard green mango for a shilling bar of chocolate. They will agree. I won't give them a ripe mango, though, not me!'

The boughs of the mango and guava trees slightly overhung the wall of Old Mensa's compound and they were well within reach because they were always laden with fruit, most of which was ripe. The boys stalked up and down, short stout sticks in hand, under the branches, trying to find which plump red mango they could knock down most easily. They were sure a powerful throw, well directed, could get them not only the ripe, red mango that would be hit but also one or two other not-so-ripe but equally welcome mangoes.

A good throw by Joe Fio hit, and broke loose three mangoes, one of which was deflected by a twig, and fell inside the compound with a plump thud. Hope yelped and shot straight into Odole's room to report but was hustled outside, asked to behave and told to go and lie in front of the door to Odole's room and to stop making a noise.

When the dog yelped, Jimmy Boi promptly concluded they had been seen, so he leapt backwards and landed in the uncovered street drain. He lay there badly stunned but, as he had not broken any bones, despite a cut on his lower lip and a tooth knocked a bit loose, he decided to make a getaway with the two mangoes before anyone came chasing out of the house after them. Joe Fio, who was physically stronger and not as easily scared as Jimmy Boi recovered his stick and threw it straight and hard, knocking down five more perfect mangoes.

Joe, with Jimmy in tow, bruised and rather tear-stained, but recovering fast, passed in front of the Nigerian man's shop, half-displaying the mangoes and quite sure they would attract the Nigerian's children. Predictably, the three Nigerian children—two boys and their sister—were attracted. The shop was being looked after by them and their mother's brother who had come to Ghana to join the Nigerian diamond diggers in the Bonsa field in the Western Region. He had arrived penniless but his sister had received him well and fed him generously. If he made good she would benefit. To demonstrate his gratitude, he was attentive and helpful with her children and did whatever he could to please them.

When the children, who could speak the local language fluently and so could sell and bargain with customers better than he could, vanished from the shop, he gave up any hope of calling them back and just hoped that nobody who didn't know some English would turn up whilst they were away.

Joe Fio and Jimmy Boi made for the nearest corner, stopped and waited confidently for the Nigerian children to arrive.

'Give us some of your mangoes,' said the eldest of the three.

'Why don't you say, "Will you please give us some of your mangoes"?' Joe Fio asked, imitating the voice of his school teacher. 'You go to school for nothing. You must learn to ask politely.'

The Nigerian boy was hardly impressed; he thought manners were an impediment in life, so Joe Fio had to buckle down straight away to the business in hand: 'Here we are, Ikoku; we got these from Old Mensa's place. I know your father doesn't like dogs and you're scared stiff of them. So there's not much chance of you going and getting any. Look at these, aren't they nice? We've eaten lots and lots of them. They're very sweet and juicy. What will you give me for one?'

'What do you want?' Ikoku asked enthusiastically.

'I'll tell you,' Joe Fio exclaimed. 'Go to your shop, all of you. One of you start talking to your uncle. Tell him about the film we saw at school the other day. He'll like that. Is it true Nigerians like boxing?'

'Yes,' Ikoku replied.

'Tell him about the boxing, and while you're at it your brother can take a bar of chocolate from the big jar and run off with it. You'll get one big mango for one bar of chocolate. Look at this one! I'd like it myself!'

The Nigerian children dashed off fully armed with the stratagem. They got the bar of chocolate easily enough, as their uncle was no match for them and was easily distracted by Ikoku's chatter while the younger boy fished a bar out of the glass container. When they returned triumphantly to Joe and Jimmy, a lot of time was lost in arguing over which mango was big enough for the chocolate. Joe Fio thought any mango would do, particularly a green one; but the Nigerian children demanded a fat, red one and just as they had come to terms and Ikoku was about to exchange loot with Joe Fio, a hand grabbed him by the scruff of the neck and he heard his father's voice saying: 'Why did you steal the chocolate?'

Ikoku squealed as if he had received a death-blow and then managed to say, 'It was Ademola who stole it!'

'It was Joe Fio who asked me to take it from the chocolate jar,' explained Ademola. 'He said he would give us one mango for a shilling bar of chocolate.'

'One mango for a shilling's worth of chocolate?' the children's father exclaimed. As a shrewd trader he thought it was simply bad business quite apart from the theft involved. He would have spanked his own children there and then, but he was not given to punishing them easily. Then an idea struck him.

'Where did you get the mangoes?' he asked. Joe Fio and Jimmy Boi were suddenly immobile and tongue-tied. It had been a sudden and unexpected shock and they were caught off-guard. Normally they were experienced enough to make ground fast in a situation like this, but now they were both struck dumb and their legs felt weak.

It was Ademola who answered, hoping what he would say would lessen his father's anger: 'They stole them from Old Mensa's garden.'

'From Old Mensa's garden? This is a horrible thing to do. Very horrible! Well, both of you will have to come along with me to your parents. Your foolish parents think we Nigerians are here just to make money, and think of nothing else but money. They say we starve ourselves for money, eat the same food for four days on end to save money, sleep in the same filthy smelly shop to save money, that we don't buy from Ghanaian petty traders but from our own people so that we keep the money to ourselves; day and night we think of nothing but money. They talk as much nonsense as you boys are thieves. Do you understand me? Thieves! I'll take you to them and tell them to their face how their dirty children can corrupt my children. I don't understand! Do you boys mean you would bribe my children with a worthless mango for a large shilling bar of chocolate? What sort of parents have you got, you wretched little brats! Come along, quick!'

He grabbed Joe Fio and the trembling Jimmy Boi by the arm and roared at his own children to double back home, adding 'You'll catch it when I return! You'll be sorry you got up to this!'

As he marched the boys along he became less angry and more upset by the whole affair. As usual his thoughts revolved in a well-worn groove. 'Why should these people think they are better than those of us here?' he asked himself. 'We work harder than they do. We know what business is. We don't credit things to relatives and friends who never pay so that we go broke and think of quitting business altogether! It's envy, plain envy. They start a shop, make a little profit and think they are terribly rich, right on top of the world. They talk big, dress big, drink freely, chase women and go bankrupt. Instead of blaming themselves, they blame others whose mischief and malice they say must have ruined them; then they start talking maliciously about other people and try to ruin them. They are bad but they never talk of their own faults; they delight in talking about ours. We Nigerians never hide our faults; we are courageous. We can tell a man to his face what we think of him. They can't. They always want to appear good. Who is good in this world, anyway? Of course, they are tolerant and easy-going, in a way, otherwise we wouldn't flourish here, but they have their faults and we have ours. Why do they call us names then? Now they're teaching my children to steal and if they get along like this they'll have no future. Why do these boys want something for nothing? They're just like their people: big desires that must be swiftly satisfied and then endless boastful talk and self-congratulations. Why? Why? Why?

'I know Old Mensa is a different type. He once told me my shop was filthy and I was angry, and yet he lent me one hundred and twelve pounds without interest to buy the fridge for the soft drinks. He told me to keep the fridge clean, and when he buys from me he pays. He tells me what he thinks and if he doesn't like my ways, he likes me as a man. That makes the difference. I know that makes the difference. But some of his people appear to get on well; they look impressive; but there's always something wrong somewhere. They're never themselves. They're confused and unhappy.

'Am I happy? I think I am. At least I'm not afraid. I'm discreet. My children must be free like me. They must not be corrupted. I'm not going to force a quarrel with their parents, otherwise they'll stop buying from me and call me and my children names. It's peace I want. I'll tell them to tell their children to keep clear of my children. That's all.'

He held the boys mechanically but firmly, until they reached the twin houses which were the homes of Joe Fio and Jimmy Boi. They were twin in the sense that the families that lived in them were closely related and more or less shared a common life. Neither was particularly modern but they were both clean and neat inside. The Nigerian noticed how things were neatly arranged and orderly.

Though the women he found there had not had much education, they looked well-fed, neat and very attractive. He had always secretly wanted one of them, but knew that would complicate matters economically for him and had had to abandon any actual skirmish but all the time, carefully and surreptitiously, he feasted his eyes on her. It was this woman who first saw them and asked him in a slightly taunting, mocking voice: 'Papa Lagos, what have the boys done to you?'

'They're bad!' he cried.

'And what has that got to do with you?'

'It would have nothing to do with me if they had not caused trouble.'

'I see! Are you a policeman? I don't know of any Lagosian policeman in Ghana. Why? Who will sell the charcoal and the pepper and the ginger and the wrist-watches and the bicycle spare parts or even the gari? By the way, are you tall enough to be a policeman?'

The Nigerian saw at once that if he did not take his time, the situation could easily get out of hand. The two boys too had sensed such a possibility and hoped that if the adults got involved in a noisy quarrel, they could slip away unnoticed.

But the Nigerian said: 'Well, I didn't mean any offence. It's these two boys who have caused the trouble, and I wouldn't be here if they had not led my children into it. You see, when Fio and Boi saw that Old Mensa had been taken to Korle Bu Hospital, they went and stole his mangoes. To my thinking, this is simply wicked. It's—'

'Please, get on with your story and leave the judgement to us,' the woman said impatiently, possibly to embarrass him again.

'The plain fact is,' said the man unsubdued, 'it's both unwise and ungrateful! Old Mensa is a good man, at least, to me. Your boys didn't stop there, but came to my shop, lured my children out, and tricked them into stealing a shilling bar of chocolate so that they would give them one worthless mango. One worthless mango, you understand! My foolish children went and stole the chocolate and were about to give it to them when I pounced on them. Now what do you have to say?'

'To whom?' asked the woman.

'To my mother!' cried the man, completely overcome with anger.

'Then go to Lagos and tell her. And while you're there, I'm sure your family will be eating the same gari and sticky vegetable stew for four days!'

'Is this all I'm going to get from you?' cried the man, anger mingled with disappointment. 'Nothing but deliberate insults? Aren't you going to take the matter seriously?'

Joe Fio and Jimmy Boi laughed openly when reference was made to gari and stew. It was a threadbare, overworked abuse they had heard often enough before, but in their present plight it sounded fresh and witty. Besides, it looked as though they might get away with it.

In his country the Nigerian would not have let things rest there, but he was somewhere else rightly or wrongly, and to trade successfully one must be prepared to stomach petty insults. He knew they were often meant as a joke, but this time he felt they were completely out of place. He was very disappointed but his trade being more important he concealed his disappointment.

'All right, all right,' he said casually, 'just do one thing for me. Tell your boys not to interfere with my children again. Good-bye.'

As soon as he left their house, Joe Fio and Jimmy Boi eyed each other. They thought it was all over. They had neither lost nor suffered anything, and they still had their mangoes to enjoy. In the light of their experience they had not committed a serious crime by stealing those mangoes. They had done worse things before. There was the time they had written an anonymous letter in bad English to their headteacher telling him that their class teacher was in love with one of the girls in the class. The girl had been hostile to Joe Fio and so he and Jimmy Boi got together and wrote the letter with their left hands; one wrote one line and the other wrote the next. The letter misfired. The headteacher took no action. Angry, they decided to take action themselves and wrote dirty things about the teacher and the girls on the walls of the school lavatory. The teacher was furious and whipped any pupil in the school after that for the slightest mistake. But they were never caught. The Nigerian was merely fussing, they thought.

Later when Jimmy Boi had left for the other house, and Joe Fio had finished his meal, he was about to leave the house when one of the women called him.

'Don't go out yet, Joe Fio,' she said.

'Anything you want me to do for you?'

'Why did you steal those mangoes?'

'I thought you said they were nice.'

'Yes, I did. But you haven't answered my question. Why on earth did you steal those mangoes?'

'Because we wanted to eat them.'

'Weren't you fed this morning?'

'I was but I thought they were nice and we could have them.'

'But it was a dreadful thing to do,' said the woman, looking very serious now.

'Why, I thought you didn't really think it mattered. You didn't scold us. You didn't say anything to us while Papa Lagos was here. I don't understand.'

'Joe Fio,' the woman persisted, 'you know there's no question of scolding you because you're thick-skinned. You know there's no question of beating you because you can easily run away. What has shocked me is how it could possibly occur to you to go and steal Old Mensa's mangoes. He's such a good man. No one should rob him. Why should you of all people try to rob him?'

'But I don't understand,' protested Joe Fio again.

'I know you don't understand and you'll never understand. That's the real trouble with you. It's a pity I've wasted my breath on you so often. Look at the shame on your face!'

Joe Fio was now beginning to feel uncomfortable. He knew from experience that this aunt of his had a caustic tongue. Not that he ever took her words to heart; no, the trouble was that once she started talking there was no end to it and the thought of what she said now could haunt him later. He thought it was plain hell listening to her; a lot of the women in the neighbourhood were like her, and many boys like him would sometimes prefer any other punishment to this one.

'When your grandmother was dying in this house, do you know who brought in the doctor?'

'I was in bed?'

'You were, and very much asleep too. Your grandmother was dying whilst you slept and dreamt and the doctor was brought in. It was Old Mensa who hired a taxi to go and fetch the doctor at dead of night. The doctor didn't want to come, but Old Mensa persuaded him to. Think of the inconvenience. Yet he did it gladly to save your own grand-mother who was fond of you.'

She paused to watch the effect. The veins showed on Joe Fio's forehead. His heart was sinking. He could not understand all that was being said, but he felt deeply the bereavement all over again. The woman now looked at him with cold, hard eyes and said: 'Do you know that when your mother was very ill it was Old Mensa who brought in the doctor? You were not asleep that time because you were very upset. You wouldn't eat and were crying. You saw Old Mensa count the money to pay the doctor. It was his own money. Tell me, where was your own father? And this is the man you've chosen to rob at a time like this! The very man who did so much for your mother and grandmother. Tell me, are you taught at school to return wickedness for kindness? Tell me! Please tell me!'

Joe Fio was weeping by now. He thought his aunt was being cruel in reminding him of his dead mother and grandmother: they had been kind to him and up to now he was not sure how and why they died. He had missed them; they had always mattered to him.

Old Mensa was probably a kind man but how could he know or appreciate it? Old Mensa quite often insulted boys in pretty damaging language, whenever they passed by and eyed his fruit trees. Most of them he had called bastards, the rest he said were idle paupers; but generally they were all hopelessly underfed criminals. How could such a man be called kind or good? None of the boys ever reasoned whether Old Mensa was kind or good. They only knew him as a fierce old man who stood between them and the fruit they wanted. Sometimes his insults were so near the mark and they hurt so much that Joe Fio could never believe Old Mensa had any goodness or kindness in him.

'Aunt,' he sobbed, 'I know it's wrong to steal mangoes, but I didn't know Old Mensa was so kind. If I had known I wouldn't have gone after his mangoes.'

'I knew that is what you'd tell me, you wicked boy!' the woman shrieked.

Joe Fio hesitated and then came out with something Old Mensa had told him before.

'If Old Mensa is so good,' he asked, 'why did he say my mother never had a decent husband, that I would grow up a criminal, that I came from a house waiting to be fed, that I would grow up to make things worse for the state and that I should watch my step? He said all this simply because I had looked at his mangoes on the way home from school with my friends and he was leaning against his gate-post looking at passers-by. My friends laughed at me.'

'What you've said is not true. Old Mensa never told you that. You boys nowadays are so clever that you're successful at anything but books. I shudder to think of what will happen to this country in future. The whole world is in a mess these days! You're simply an impossible boy!' she said finally, tired and breathless and drained of ideas. And suddenly she added in a despairing voice, 'Old Mensa is very ill. Anything can happen, and who will be the losers?'

Chapter Nineteen

On the third day of Old Mensa's illness, Odole too became ill, bleeding to death. She was now a fairly tall, graceful girl with well-shaped legs, good hips and an attractive bosom. Her face normally wore a natural soothing smile which some observers thought proud and disdainful while the more perceptive realized that the disdain was consciously assumed. Yet her face inspired everybody with a lasting impression of a beauty that was at once civilized and serene. She had long, usually well-kept hair which was tousled now and added to her attractiveness although it was obvious she was in great pain.

Her mother was weeping and told Old Mensa that their daughter was in terrible pain.

'But why should she be so ill suddenly?' Old Mensa asked feebly.

'It must be a case of miscarriage or something. I told you and you wouldn't hear of it. Anything can happen to her in her present state. If people get to know of it she may lose her scholarship award.'

'Let the worst come. She's dug her own grave. I've done the best I can for her. She's twenty-two and must carry her own misfortunes.'

'You just can't talk like that. You've always helped people

in trouble and cheered many in distress, why can't you save your own blood? That's not the way things are done!'

'But I'm no doctor!'

'And that's why you have to send for one.'

'Suppose it's a case of abortion? The law doesn't allow it. Think of the disgrace it'll bring on us. Death ends all human misery!'

Old Mensa's wife said nothing in reply and left her husband's bedroom to go and phone the doctor. As soon as she was leaving, Old Mensa had a severe heart attack. The ambulance was called and he was taken to Korle Bu Hospital. His wife had to stay behind to nurse Odole and wait for the doctor. She was herself near exhaustion, her nerves completely upset and was not sure whether she was alive or dead.

The telephone rang just when the doctor was doing all he could to save Odole's life. She listened calmly for there was no other way left to her in which she could have listened. She had been hit suddenly by three disasters of which one was now clearly beyond earthly redemption. The telephone call brought news of the death of Tete, her husband's brother, at the age of fifty-six, from a cerebral haemorrhage.

Tete's death had been sudden and unexpected. Though he had suffered a stroke three months before his death which left his right arm and leg paralysed and had made him partially bed-ridden, no one, as always, thought he would pass away at the time he did. Mrs Mensa felt rather vaguely that Tete's death was only the beginning of other deaths. Which next, she did not know. She was only beginning to appreciate the final nothingness and the futility of it all.

About the Author

AMU DJOLETO, also known as Soloman Alexander Amu Djoleto, is an author, poet, and educator born in Manya Krobo, Ghana, in 1929. He was educated at Accra Academy and St. Augustine's College before earning his English BA at the University of Ghana.

Djoleto is a prominent figure in Ghanaian literature, having published over a dozen novels, children's books, poem collections, and works of non-fiction. His most well-known novels include *The Strange Man* (1967) and *Money Galore* (1986). He also worked to promote and revitalise Ghana's literary culture as the executive director of the Ghana Book Development Council.